MY WORK

Also by Olga Ravn

FROM NEW DIRECTIONS

The Employees

Olga Ravn

MY WORK

*translated from the Danish
by Sophia Hersi Smith & Jennifer Russell*

A NEW DIRECTIONS
PAPERBOOK ORIGINAL

Originally published in Danish as *Mit arbejde*.
Published by agreement with Gyldendal Group Agency.

The text by Margaret Atwood is from *Dancing Girls & Other Stories*,
copyright © 1977, 1982 by O. W. Toad Ltd. Reprinted with
the permission of Simon & Schuster, Inc. All rights reserved.

First published by New Directions in 2023 as NDP1571
Manufactured in the United States of America
Design by Erik Rieselbach

Library of Congress Cataloging-in-Publication Data
Names: Ravn, Olga, author. | Smith, Sophia Hersi, translator. |
Russell, Jennifer, translator.
Title: My work / by Olga Ravn ;
translated by Sophia Hersi Smith and Jennifer Russell.
Other titles: Mit arbejde. English
Description: First edition. | New York : New Directions Publishing
Corporation, [2023] | "A New Directions book"
Identifiers: LCCN 2023016471 | ISBN 9780811234719 (paperback) |
ISBN 9780811234726 (ebook)
Subjects: LCGFT: Domestic fiction. | Novels.
Classification: LCC PT8177.28.A87 M5813 2023 |
DDC 839.813/8—dc23/eng/20230407
LC record available at https://lccn.loc.gov/2023016471

2 4 6 8 10 9 7 5 3 1

New Directions Books are published for James Laughlin
by New Directions Publishing Corporation
80 Eighth Avenue, New York 10011

MY WORK

First Beginning

Who wrote this book?

I did, of course.

Although I'd like to convince you otherwise.

Let's agree right now that someone else has written it. Another woman, entirely unlike me. Let's call her Anna. Let's say Anna has given me all the pages that follow this preface. And let's say that with these pages, Anna has given me the task of arranging them. Let's say that some nights, after reading these many, many pages Anna has left me, I'm gripped by greed and hysteria. I don't want anyone but me to read Anna's texts. I don't want anyone but me to know her.

For many months I tried to come to grips with Anna's papers, and during this work I was again and again overcome by something I cannot describe as anything but an animal impulse, a deep instinct that made me jump up from my desk, propelled by a single thought: Anna's papers should be read only by pregnant people and parents with small children.

And each time, I had to sit back down at the desk, breathless and baffled by my own foolishness. But I admit I was seized by this microscopic rapture often.

Perhaps I thought that such a select readership would protect Anna by keeping her experience a secret. These pages she left in my custody—reading them has felt like carrying confidential information.

My biggest challenge has been understanding Anna's relationship with time. She doesn't seem to adhere to any chronology, and I cannot pretend to grasp the timelines of her writing. The pages were piled haphazardly when she gave them to me. In the notebooks, one event might follow another that took place years before, as if she suddenly gained access to a different layer of time in the text and carved out space for it.

Meanwhile, like all new mothers, she seems obsessed with the passage of time relative to the child's development. She often notes the age of the child, sometimes down to the number of days, at the top of a text, even if what follows is not about the child.

Her seemingly inscrutable approach to time was recently underlined by a strange coincidence.

I found a journal from Anna's pregnancy. I can't quite explain why, but some vague impulse prompted me to insert the notebook later on in the sequence rather than placing it as the opening act, which would have been logical.

Perhaps it was a way of mimicking my own experience. This notebook was the last part I found when, preparing for the eldest child's fourth birthday, we moved the black dresser away from the wall and a blue notebook fell down. It had been pinched between the wall and the dresser on top of which Anna's papers lay piled before and while I read them. (Later, I sealed up the papers in three boxes and stored them at the office. Only when the last notebook turned up did I, in a sudden fit of common sense, find the strength to begin organizing the pages with the hope that others might read them.)

The pregnancy journal must have fallen behind the dresser one of the times I retrieved pages from the stack, and I therefore cannot say whether Anna left this notebook on top or, as I suspect, in the middle of all these points in time.

4

Placing the pregnancy at the midpoint of the composition was my own first breach of chronology, and the rest followed easily. Or more easily, at any rate.

Second Beginning

This book began when the child was six days old and I found myself in a darkness.

I have tried to arrange the various parts based on what I surmise to be the order in which I wrote them.

I have no recollection of having written any of it.

Over the past few years, I have found more and more pages of writing.

If it weren't for my handwriting, I might have assumed it was all written by a stranger.

These handwritten pages, as well as a large number of documents on my computer, emails sent to me from my own email address, and notes on my phone together constitute such a vast amount of material (which, again, I have no recollection of writing) that I, after typing it all up and seeing the staggering total number of pages, was filled with a feeling I can only call horror.

The section titled "the pregnancy journal," a blue notebook with tattered corners, was the last to appear—two weeks ago when Aksel and I moved a chest of drawers to make room for a game of musical chairs at the child's birthday party.

Collecting and arranging these papers and documents has ultimately been an attempt to re-create the three years of my life that have disappeared from my memory, and which, just as the reader, I can only access here.

Something tells me that the reason I have now finally been

able to complete my work with these pages is that I am pregnant again.

I feel I have returned, like a time traveler, to the state of pregnancy, as though I could travel up and down through the layers of time.

In one week, I will reach the last day of the first trimester.

I fear it's merely an illusion, but it appears to me that the impending birth of my second child has given me the strength to both step away from and step into the psychological crisis that accompanied the arrival of the first.

Of all the parts in this book, however, it is those in which someone (myself?) writes about a woman with my own name that disturb me the most. As though there were in those years another power at work, mercilessly scrutinizing me and keeping record of my every move. Someone who considered me a she, hysterical. And when I read it, I sometimes get the feeling that a hand is gripping my neck and forcing my head down. That someone else stepped out of my closet at night to write these texts.

Third Beginning

Time:	Last half of the 2010s / The time of pregnancy
Location:	Copenhagen and Stockholm / The darkness of breastfeeding

CHARACTERS

Anna:	A pregnant woman, 28 years of age. Author, since mother. Danish.
Aksel:	A man, 30 years of age. Father of the child. Playwright. Swedish.
The child:	Whose name we keep secret for the child's sake. Born 2016.

Furthermore:	A large number of healthcare workers (nurses, midwives, doctors, psychologists, therapists, etc.). The child's grandmothers in the distance. Psychiatric patients, people in general in public spaces and in hospitals, and, of course, the narrator.

Fourth Beginning

When she thought about it, all her problems could be traced back to that bitch at the childbirth class.

All around the table sat pregnant women with their husbands. There were only couples, most of them a little older than Anna and Aksel. It was the most heterosexual space she had ever been in.

The midwife wore a bright-blue shirtdress and a long gold chain around her neck. Contractions accompanied the anxiety.

"Are you okay?" the midwife asked.

"It's just Braxton Hicks," said Anna, sweating.

"I could tell. Would you like to lie down for a bit?"

The midwife gestured toward a bench under a chart illustrating pelvic expansion.

The muscles of Anna's stomach tightened. With each contraction, it hardened. She felt dizzy and hot and nauseated, her lower back and neck hurt. She didn't know where the Braxton Hicks ended and the anxiety began. Maybe they were the same thing?

The midwife continued her lecture, something about breathing. Aksel sat on his own at the table and paid close attention. Anna saw that he was taking notes.

All the couples appeared to be in their thirties and have their lives and finances in order, they had steady jobs and many had cars and investment pieces in their homes, they bought the latest design and had spent several years prepping for Project Baby, and then Anna noticed that all the couples in the room were rubbing their faces with their banknotes, they rubbed and rubbed them all over, and they bought all the plant-dyed 100% organic cotton cloth diapers their hearts desired, and they bought slings and natural rubber pacifiers and lambskin rugs. And they bought handmade mobiles with felt clouds to hang over the child's crib, and they bought aromatic oils to prevent stretch marks and to soften the perineum for childbirth, and they bought lanolin wool nursing pads, and they bought the highest-rated car seats, and they bought big, enormous, atrocious coffin-shaped monstrosities: baby carriages.

Suddenly, Anna understood her mother better than ever before. The midwife said: "You men shouldn't expect to have food on the table as usual when you come home from work once the baby is born. It's hard work taking care of a newborn. How much time do you think women spend breastfeeding per day? Take a guess!"

"An hour?" ventured one of the men with an unsure smile.

"No!" the midwife practically shrieked in triumph. "What do you think?" She had turned toward Aksel.

"Eight hours?"

"Yes, that's correct," she said, disappointed he knew the answer. "That's a whole workday."

"Do you have children yourself?" asked one of the pregnant women.

"No," the midwife replied, with a click conjuring a Power-Point slide on the wall behind her with the alarming title *Sex after birth*.

"Sex after birth!" she screamed. "Don't worry if you don't have sex again until six to eight months after giving birth." Next slide, WordArt. Anna gulped.

A drawing of a red-bearded man in a Fred Flintstone costume on a desert island. Next to him, a crab with eyes on stalks and a big smile on its face (a crabby smile? A crabby face?). On the opposite side of the slide, another island on which stood a woman with a black bob and a pink heart in her arms, so big it nearly eclipsed her. She had been drawn with a sheepish, apologetic grin. Between them was pasted a picture of the Golden Gate Bridge. The man and the woman. Two islands— connected by a bridge in San Francisco.

The midwife said: "It's important that you women listen to yourselves and your bodies. Don't do anything you don't feel ready for. As for the men, all I'll say is that you've got to arm yourselves with patience. The mother often has her physical needs satisfied by being with the baby. But you can always try knocking on other doors."

The room was quiet for a moment.

"The neighbor's?" asked a confused pregnant woman.

"No, no, no," the midwife shook her head.

"Do you mean ... anal sex?" whispered a small, girlish woman on the verge of disappearing behind her giant belly just like the character holding the heart on the slide.

"More often than not, the rectum is just as afflicted as the front," replied the midwife. "What I'm saying is that there are many other forms of intimacy."

An awkward silence descended over them as the thought *blow job* flashed through everyone's mind.

"Next slide!" bellowed the midwife. "It's okay not to love your child! Men, don't worry if you don't love the child right from the get-go. It can easily take up to six months for you to feel anything since you haven't been part of bearing or birthing the child in the same way."

The best part about being pregnant was that when something completely normal happened, it could, with the proper staging—since no one really talked about their pregnancies—seem extraordinarily horrible to people who knew nothing about pregnant women.

Pelvic pain and sciatica, short-term hospitalizations and gestational diabetes, gingivitis. It would make them shudder and shower the pregnant Anna with extra care and compassion, even if only in the time it took to relay her misfortunes. The physical pain was brutal, and pregnant women were discouraged from taking any kind of painkillers, but the additional compassion made up for it. Anna loved being cared for, always wanted more compassion, more caresses. She was always in want of pity. She lived for pity. Give it to me, Anna thought as she told her colleagues about her awful pains, I want to drink their pity like semen, her mind screamed.

About three months into her pregnancy, Anna stopped sleeping. Not because she had to pee at night or because lying down was uncomfortable, but because when she went to bed she could not stop thinking. Had you asked Anna what she was thinking about, she wouldn't have been able to say. All she knew was that the way her thoughts moved kept her awake.

"Have you considered acupuncture?" her midwife asked and gave her the name of a midwife who had been an on-site acupuncturist at the hospital before the recent layoffs.

"She has a clinic in Christianshavn."

It was Friday the 13th when Anna went to the acupuncturist. She hadn't given the date much thought, but the acupuncturist had. The door was locked.

"I don't dare leave it unlocked on a day like today," she said as she let Anna in. "Mille Sille," she introduced herself, shaking Anna's hand. She had big, crimped gray hair and wore dangly silver earrings.

"Anna," said Anna. "I'm 17 weeks and 4 days along."

Mille Sille nodded.

The clinic was on the ground floor of an old, half-timbered house by a grassy embankment at the end of one of the canals. There were tubs with withered plants, wind chimes, and a chipped garden gnome in front. Inside, the room was stuffed with bookshelves, potted plants, Buddhas, and anatomical models with shiny plastic body parts. Two bulky sofas were covered in Indian rugs and above the counter hung a massive poster of the Crown Prince and Princess. There was a weird smell.

"Come on in," said Mille Sille, leading Anna into a small adjoining room. Anna sat down on the treatment table.

"So, what brings you here today?"

"I can't sleep. I feel anxious," said Anna. "My midwife recommended you."

"Who do you have?"

"Marianne, at Rigshospitalet."

Mille Sille nodded. "She's good."

"Yeah."

"Let's start off with an exam. Have you tried acupuncture before?"

"No," said Anna. "But I'm trying to be open to everything."

Mille Sille lifted Anna's wrist with two fingers. "Hm," she said, furrowing her brows.

"Do you have an old stress injury?"

Immediately, Anna was gripped by terror.

"Um, yes?"

The strange smell from the stuffy examination room forced its way up Anna's nose and filled her.

"You have too much fire in you," said Mille Sille. "That's also why you've got those red spots on your cheeks." Anna involuntarily touched her fingertips to her burning cheeks.

"It means you have an excess of yang. You lack water," said Mille Sille. "You've blocked the flow of yin. I suggest we start with cupping."

"May I go pee first?"

"It's the second door on the left."

In the bathroom, Anna stared at a piece of crumpled paper glued to the door: *Nina and Martin's birth plan.*

—*No medical pain relief*

—*Follow Nina's rhythm*

—*Let the birth take as long as it takes*

—*Preferably in water*

—*Rebozo massage*

So she was also a practicing midwife, thought Anna.

"Let's start with a few cups to try and open you up to the yin."

Anna lay on her stomach, naked from the waist up, while Mille Sille placed plastic cups on Anna's back that attached to her skin by suction. It hurt a lot. Anna lay very still.

"How long have you been like this?"

"What do you mean—pregnant?"

"No, anxious."

"Since I was a child, I think."

"I'm sorry to hear that."

Anna felt ridiculous and terrified, doll-like. Am I completely mad? Am I insane, she thought. Who is Anna? Was she in fact hopeless, beyond saving?

"Now try to let the water flow. Imagine large bodies of water just running through you," said Mille Sille. She had removed the cups, asked Anna to turn over and was now inserting the needles. One needle in particular gave her trouble. She took it out of Anna's hand and put it back in, again and again. Be open, Anna told herself, paying close attention to where the needles were inserted, in her face and her hands and ankles.

"Normally I would put one here," said Mille Sille, pressing a finger behind Anna's ear. "But not when you're pregnant."

"Okay," said Anna.

"Now I'll put on some relaxing music with water sounds."

"Okay," said Anna, lying still, her needles quivering.

"I'll be right outside, but there's a bell by your hand you can ring when you're ready. Take your time, it's different for everyone. It's a bit like going to the toilet; when you're done, you're done."

"Okay," said Anna, staring up at the ceiling while the sound of crashing waves rose from Mille Sille's stereo.

At first it was pleasant, a tingling sensation. Anna felt a little drunk, which she hadn't been since finding out she was pregnant—as though she had downed an ice-cold beer. The needle in one of her hands hurt. Gently, Anna tilted her chin toward her chest so she could see it. A thin line of dried blood led to the guilty needle. Then things started to feel scary. Anna couldn't move. She didn't dare ring the bell, she didn't know how long was normal to lie there. She could hear Mille Sille welcoming another client. Anna had no sense of how much time had passed. The water roared from the stereo in an endless loop. She wanted to get up and shake off the needles, the words "stress injury." She felt weak, as if she hadn't eaten all day, her throat swelled with nausea, Anna wanted to scream. Now she could hear Mille Sille saying goodbye to another woman, so there was at least one other room in which a woman had been lying with needles in her body all this time. How long were you meant to lie there? Anna didn't dare ring the bell for fear of disrespecting the process.

Finally, Mille Sille opened the door. "You're still here?" she asked.

"Yes," said Anna.

Mille Sille removed the needles.

"How'd it go?"

"Great," said Anna, smiling. She rubbed her hand. "What time is it?"

"Quarter to two." She had been lying there for an hour.

"Do you take debit cards?"

"Yes, no problem," said Mille Sille. "Let me get the door for you. It's Friday the 13th, you know, I don't dare leave it unlocked."

Anna fumbled with her bag.

"Besides, I just got back from New York," Mille Sille said. "I'm probably a little jet-lagged."

Was that an apology? Did Mille Sille know that the treatment hadn't worked as it was supposed to? Could she tell just by looking at Anna? That it had been terrible for her? That she hadn't been able to stay open-minded, that she had too much fire in her and too little water? Or could she not tell at all and was merely making small talk? Why didn't acupuncture work for Anna, what was wrong with her?

"So how many treatments do people usually need?" Anna asked while Mille Sille held the door open.

"It depends," she said. "Let's see how it goes, whether this has helped or if you need more."

"Okay," said Anna. The door slammed behind her, ringing the wind chime.

She walked along the canal and crossed to the other side. She had forgotten her scarf and soon her neck was cold; she couldn't close her jacket all the way because of her belly. She sat down on a bench with her back to Mille Sille's clinic and called Aksel.

"Hi, it's me," said Anna. "I'm done now."

"How did it go?" Aksel asked.

"Um, I don't really know."

"I'm sure it was fine."

"It was pricey."

"How much did it cost?"

"800 kroner."

Aksel whistled.

"I feel a bit weird," Anna said.

"It'll be okay."

"I'm just calling to say I love you."

"I love you too."

"Sometimes I'm afraid of being left out, you know, being left out of the family, and now you're my family, or we're making one, and what if I'm left out of our family too?"

"Darling, you're not going to be left out."

"Alright."

"See you at home? Then you can tell me all about your acupuncture adventure."

"Okay," said Anna. "See you soon."

"Bye," said Aksel.

"Bye," said Anna.

She let the hand holding the phone drop to her lap, then looked up at the crooked half-timbered houses, at the cars parked on the narrow street, at the cobblestones. It was an expensive neighborhood. Anna wept.

Fifth Beginning

P0, 41+2

Contacts ward due to increasing contractions starting today, 07:30, regular and strong from 10:00, duration 45 sec.

12:00
Heart rate monitored after contraction 11-12-11.
Transferred to labor ward.
Cervix 7 cm dilated, head engaged.

Requests to be put in tub, with some effect.
Heart rate monitored after contraction 12-12-13.

Handles contractions very well.

12:50
Passes urine on toilet.
Following vaginal examination, spontaneous rupture of membranes, light-green amniotic fluid, initially identified as clear, initiation of external CTG monitoring.
4 contractions in 10 min.

Anna is in a lot of pain.
Sedated with Entonox 30% (N_2O) with mild effect.
Breathes through contractions, with some use of mouthpiece.

13:15
Anna requests epidural. Anesthetist is summoned.
IV is inserted. Larger amounts of light-green amniotic fluid, FSE applied, shows reactive heartbeat.
4 contractions in 10 min. of 45 sec. duration.

13:35
Anesthetist is summoned again.

13:45
Anesthesia in labor room, epidural is attempted a second time without complications, positive effect.

14:15
Epidural is effective.
Anna is shaking, is given socks and a heating lamp.
Complains of tightness in throat, difficulty swallowing, efficacy of epidural is assessed with alcohol swab, blockade found successful.

Anna says it could be her anxiety as she often has a reaction to intense episodes and it was very intense to be in so much pain.
Consultation with anesthetist regarding effect of epidural.
Px reduce infusion rate from 5.0 to 3.0.

14:45
Eats some toast.
In good spirits, talks about next steps, but also about difficulty of setting a time limit.

1,000 ml NaCl administered, this is relayed to night shift on account of bladder.

Midwife: Amanda Andersen
Relieved by Midwife Agnes Aaby

Handover of care to Matron or colleague. Progress, condition
of mother and child, any new risk factors reviewed.

15:15
Anna in left-lateral tilt position.

15:40
Anna can't move her right leg and is offered bedpan or IC.
Void on bedpan unsuccessful after first attempt.
Bladder emptied of 200 ml of clear urine with IC.

15:50
Lateral position.
Increased pain and increased pressure in vagina.

16:05
Feels increased pressure.
CTG normal.

16:20
Increasing pains and urge to push.

Vaginal examination: cervix hardly effaced, thin edge on
mother's right side.

Square fontanelle no longer perceptible, a smooth suture felt
in an oblique diameter between 11–13, vertex between pelvic
entrance and spines, clear amniotic fluid + spotting. Epidural
infusion increased to 5.0.

16:45
Pain breakthrough.
½ bolus, 2 ml Marcain + 2 ml NaCl administered.
BP: 123/66 P: 91.
Increased urge to push.

18:00
Increasing urge to push, check performed during contraction, head 2 fingers above pelvis.
A lot of green amniotic fluid leaking.

Anna is somewhat discouraged, complains of constant pain. Entonox of 40% is adm. for the pain, with good effect. Active pushing technique is orally instructed, pushing during contractions relieves pain. Small pushes at peak of contractions.

Contractions slightly reduced in intensity and interval 3–4/10 min.

19:15
Contractions further reduced in intensity, are short and ineffective.
Consultation with Matron Annette regarding introduction of IV with Syntocinon to strengthen contractions.
Anna is offered Syntocinon to improve contractions. Agrees and consents.

19:20
Syntocinon drip set up due to lack of progress.
Patient is informed of effects of Syntocinon drip and consents.
Number of contractions / 10 min.: 3–4.

19:25
Is put in dorsal position: pushes slightly at peak of contraction.
Contractions now at 1.5 min. intervals and lasting 30–45 sec.

19:30
Now 6 contractions in 10 min. Duration 30 sec.

19:45
Syntocinon drip is increased to 40 ml/h.

20:05
Syntocinon drip is increased to 60 ml/h.

20:15
Head crowns during pushing contraction.
Great progress.
Actively pushes in semirecumbent position.

20:43
Head emerges during contraction, shoulders delivered during pause in contractions.
Live birth of male, regular posterior head presentation and back toward mother's left side (LOA), umbilical cord wrapped twice around the neck.
Baby is handed to mother, dried, umbilical cord is cut.

Midwife present at the birth: Agnes Aaby + Matron Annette Amtoft

20:53
Placenta is delivered spontaneously, three vessels counted in umbilical cord, weight: 532 g.

On inspection of placenta, three coin-sized infarcts identified. Uterine involution observed, permissible bleeding. Total bleeding: 200 ml.

21:15
On inspection, lacerations identified.
Labia:
Vagina: x
Perineum: x
Rectal fascia deemed exposed on mother's left side. Matron summoned for examination of laceration.
Junior Doctor Arne subsequently summoned for examination. Grade 3A laceration identified, sutured by Arne. See note on suturing of laceration.
Corresponding to
Grade 1: (labia laceration is also grade 1)
Grade 2: Palpation of sphincter ani
Assessed as intact yes: no:
Grade 3/4 ?: 3A
Doctor summoned for assessment and documents suturing.

22:43
General condition: Tired but well
Uterine involution: yes
Permissible amount of bleeding: yes
Patient urinary output: yes, minimal
Patient can walk:
Skin-to-skin contact for at least one hour within the first two hours: yes
The baby is positioned for B/F: yes, but not latching with correct technique.
EWS to be determined later as the patient will remain in the ward: yes

23:30
Midwife Afsaneh Aliakbari and Midwifery Student Anni Andersson relieve Midwife Agnes Aaby.

Anna attempts to breastfeed from lateral position.
Baby latches onto nipple but does not suck effectively.
Breastfeeding position and mother's latch-on technique appear to be correct.
Syntocinon infusion complete. Uterus well-contracted.
Normal amount of bleeding, Syntocinon drip discontinued.

23:45
Anna goes to bathroom, passes urine.
She then becomes very upset and expresses feelings of anxiety and is afraid of whether she will feel enough attachment toward her son.
Discuss with Anna that this can also be due to fatigue after a long labor that can affect her mental state.
Couple requests moment of privacy.

Referred to postnatal ward 4021 Perinatal Mental Health Clinic.
Midwife from 4021 comes and collects the family.

N.B. — sphincter regimen, laceration: grade 3A.

Midwife Afsaneh Aliakbari and Midwifery Student Anni Andersson

Sixth Beginning

Days 1–14 after the birth

*
the atrium
at the hospital
with squares of green and brown
a child playing in the sun
in white in ecstasy she
does cartwheels
four figures in lab coats
sit on chairs and smoke
half-hidden behind a hedge

breastfeeding
a black shiny needle
floating in the dark
it releases its
iron and a forest wet with night
heavy metal

at night
7-Eleven's lights
from the ground floor
the red lamps
above the cafeteria tables
like gas cylinders transparent under water

the atrium in the window

like a painting
I want to step into

is there a child

who gave birth

in the washing machine's drawer
not separate compartments for detergent
but two swollen labia
gray and covered in
meat juice

breastfeeding releases
its black syringe
the black earth
it wishes me neither
ill nor well

I'm drowning

I'm not breathing

it's the middle of May
everything blooms

is there a hospital

is there a child
there is a child

*

I wake up and anxiety is there

in bed I fall backward

the Earth's surface disappears

there is soil and water and metal
blood's recipe

the nurse takes the child away

for a long time his cries carry down the hall

my hands miss him like skin

what has the child cost
what has the child cost me

I wake up and I'm about to die

*

to love the newborn child
it brings me no joy

to breastfeed

I am the white rose hip's white
blossoming fragrant

in the landscaped park landscaped so it
looks wild a wilderness

I smell of milk into the night

he wakes up quiet quiet

in the park blossom the night's white flowers

through the window I see the bushes

*
love for the child
is animal

not love

but hunger

all these
preliminary motions

with the child too
my heart's mistrust

my heart's mistrust

he wakes quietly

the night is light

I call him sweetheart

*
I understand
the child through things

the child through his objects

the onesie
the blanket
the hat
their patterns

what money can buy

buying
has become a way
of knowing

the child's eyes

I have bought the child
with my body

is it worth the cost

is the child worth the cost

*

have I forgotten writing
as the place
I can redeem myself

I went blue like a baby
while giving birth freezing
from the shock

who gave birth

now the hawthorn has bloomed

who gave birth

did I forget
that writing could
make me live again

*
in the maternity ward
the various
midwives and
nurses
who came
into the room
with each their
face
the one
with filler in her lips
her crisp
scent of perfume
the young one
who billowed
in and filled the room
when she stopped by
at 11 p.m.
ready for a night out
wearing a black dress
and smilingly asked
whether the milk
had come in
who said of
me of the few
butter-yellow beads

of colostrum
that strained
from my nipples
that I that they
were a success
the stern head nurse
and her remarks on
my mother's visit
the redheaded one
who came the night
after the birth
and helped him latch
the one who
we later learned
was named
Helene
who you called kinky
because of her
sheer tights
and purple lacquer clogs
you've always been
so vanilla
I live with that
now we must live
together forever
the poem
must be
simple
in my hand
before he wakes
they all had
their own opinion

about breastfeeding
the pumping
the success rate
the milk
my body
the child's cries
the long hall
at night
in the beehive
inside the lamp of flesh
the sweet stench of blood
I'm surrounded by
recent labor
I bleed
when I get up
the scent rises like a
hot breath from
the disposable
mesh underwear
all these midwives
nurses
women
who stand
on wax
the poem changes
in the night
by the child's side

*
but if this is breastfeeding
then it's the same darkness
that makes rock move
across the forest floor
over thousands of years

*
I know the milk
      is somewhere in there
            and that the milk is not me

but as it
shoots from
the breast
in thin almost invisible jets
I come to doubt
      whether I exist

*

it's as if night is injected into the brain

it's as if a night
from before there were humans on Earth
is injected into the brain

*

his whimpers reach me in the dark
his whimpers push into me like a
speculum of steel

*
Bodil
I read your poems
a book given to me
in the ward
for some mothers
breastfeeding is difficult
we name him
we call him by different names

what you wrote
blooms
with such fervor
you want to be
no one
to dissolve
you're exalted
almost manic
your voice on the verge
of becoming
nonhuman
this is what you long for

the hospital is brutalist
the hospital is black

in your poems the night is light
white ecstasy
the elder in bloom

the night is light
is the night light
Bodil
did you have a child

I don't want to know
only the poems

no biography
just a child

a child
in the May night

who wakes
quietly
quietly

*
if the woman
is no longer
a muse
in your poetry
Bodil
but extends
out of herself
with all her might
against God
and modernism
Bodil
what then is the poem
in the hand that breastfeeds
who then is the woman
who writes it
who by
the power of breastfeeding
is pulled out of herself
and toward a
precivilized darkness
where I don't know
whether
poetry exists
whether poetry
can exist

*
here
the birthing pool
fills with a gurgling
in the golden light
of a setting sun

*
what is it that happens
to the poem
inside breastfeeding
according to the scientist
on the radio
the first colors
a civilization
learns
to articulate
and hence to see
are red and black
only later
as the very last
the color blue

I live
in the red
the black
the red darkness
where breastfeeding
becomes

*

I love conventional
expressions
the fatigue
the sun
upon every leaf
soccer on TV
a new onesie
the child has grown into

every time
I breastfeed
my heart breaks

giving birth
left me
dead and buried

*

breastfeeding
goes through me
like a heavy metal
I nurse the child
I breathe
I hold him
I tense my arm
soil swells up in me
a drowsiness
rooms in the body
where no one goes
the child has no language
not even body language
we bond like two animals
without purpose
without personality
it makes me suspect
that love
is man-made
since the child and I
don't love each other
but live in
infinite mutual
dependence

*

about a minute
before the milk
comes in
I am struck
by a deep despair
without cause

then
a burning sting
in each nipple

after which
the milk forms
in gray watery
drops and
fatty white ones

they surge
unstoppable
like blood at
the mouth of a cut

with the patience
only possessed by
what is not human

*

this writing must
adapt to
the child's time

it's here
to keep me alive

this writing will
grant me

a nonhuman
patience

this writing will
turn me into
iron

will turn me into
soil

into the one who can
receive
all seeds

into the one who can
offer the breast
every time

*

each time I strode through summer
these youngest leaves that cried

iron rubble on the forest floor

metal-written shadows
where breastfeeding turns
like a mirror

*

I see the delivery room
its two examination tables
the birthing pool
slowly filling
with water
outside the three big
windows facing
the park
the sun sets
in the trees
and the room fills
with a reddish
a copper-colored light

the room is empty

only this pool
quietly filling itself
with water and golden light
from the evening sun
where there is no time

this room
has emerged in me

the heavy scent
from inside the body
which comes with the child

this room
has emerged in me
after the birth

in the hours after
the door to the room
slides shut

this room
I carry with me
from now on

and to which I
can never return

in the darkness
that surrounds the room
my voice
as if from
another woman
screaming
the midwife's name
as a plea
Amanda!

Seventh Beginning

2 years and 5 months after the birth

This endless manuscript overwhelms me. It's bringing me to my knees. I do not want it, this destruction. Take it away from me. I write from a brain-dead place. Without aim. Without connection. Without recognition. There's madness here, and exposed flesh. This is why no one wants to read the books of mothers. No one wants to know her. To see her become real. But if we don't look, we live stunted half lives, each isolated in loneliness, shamefully pushing strollers down the boulevards and suburban streets, between the apartment blocks and through the cemeteries among the dead.

Eighth Beginning

When they placed the child on Anna's breast after the birth, she felt nothing.

"Congratulations," said a mouth. Hands washed themselves. The child looked up at her with big eyes.

A white noise enveloped her like a wool mitten.

Even though she was lying with the child on her chest, she now saw him back in the arms of the midwife, who quickly began unwrapping the umbilical cord from around his neck.

"Why isn't he crying?" Anna asked, and the placenta was delivered, another doctor summoned, and then another doctor, and another, all concentrating on her injuries.

"Why isn't he crying?" she asked from within the white noise. The midwife unwrapped the umbilical cord. Finally he cried.

Anna lifted a hand, black with mucus, and regarded it.

"Meconium has passed."

"Is that shit?" said Anna.

They took him away and moved her onto a bed in the corner. The whooshing grew louder. Far away, the infant was examined.

"Aksel, what are they doing? Tell me what they're doing."

"They're counting his fingers and toes," said Aksel reassuringly. "There are ten of each."

The doctors finished and disappeared.

Aksel took off his shirt and lifted the newborn child up to his bare chest. They lay down on the bed where Anna had given birth, all signs of the labor already washed away. A fresh paper sheet rustled beneath them.

It was at the sight of the child against the man's stomach, the love that seemed to exist between them already, the pride in Aksel's face as he gazed down at the boy, the happiness she saw but did not share, that the whooshing sound went from encasing Anna to penetrating her.

Aksel stood up gingerly with the child in his arms and went out into the hallway. Anna was lying by the window. She couldn't move. She assumed she had been forgotten.

A new midwife came in and placed the child at Anna's breast, but he wouldn't latch.

"I need to talk to a psychologist," Anna rasped.

"There's a priest," said the midwife. Her face was so big and close to Anna's, then it was gone.

They were transferred to a different room. Aksel carried the child while Anna was supported by the midwife and a nurse. She was told not to sit down for the next six weeks due to the tearing. All Anna could think of was the white noise. She could not speak.

That the child had left her body and now existed outside the deafening whoosh that was Anna caused an afterpain to course through her. She wanted to ask if she could hold him, but the words didn't come.

That night they tried many times to get the child to latch, he had swallowed amniotic fluid and couldn't suck.

As soon as the midwife concluded that the latest lactation attempt had failed, Aksel would take the child. Anna was so weak she could hardly lift the boy. She only had the chance to hold him for a few minutes at a time.

Then a pump was rolled in on a stand with wheels, and Anna

sat through the pumping every three hours. All the darkness was sucked out through a tube, and yet there was always more.

At two o'clock in the morning, the midwife on duty ordered Aksel to get some sleep, and they rolled in a bed for him. Anna couldn't sleep. The child began to cry. She couldn't get out of bed. A new midwife came in.

"Why don't I give him some formula?" she asked.

"No," said Anna, remembering her mother's warning that the bottle could ruin breastfeeding altogether.

"Has the milk come in?" the midwife asked, nodding at Anna's breasts.

"Not yet."

The scene repeated itself throughout the night. The midwife returned and said, "You need to get some sleep. Have you slept since giving birth?"

"No," said Anna. The child cried, Aksel slept, she rocked the cradle from her bed.

"Can't I give him some formula?" said the midwife.

"No," said Anna.

"Has the milk come in?"

"Not yet," said Anna.

The night and the child's cries intertwined into a rope that tore through her, pulling tiny parts of her with it and carrying them away. Yet there was always more. The door opened.

"Aren't you asleep yet?"

"No."

The child cried.

"May I give him some formula?"

Anna said nothing.

Carefully, the midwife approached the cradle. She looked over at Anna. Their eyes met. She gently carried the child away. Anna could hear him crying further down the hall. Then he stopped. She stared out into the dark. The room was dimly lit by the lights in the windows of the hospital's opposite wing. Anna pulled the cord by her bed and heard a buzzer go off downstairs at the nurses' station. It took a long time for someone to come.

"I can't sleep," said Anna when a nurse tiptoed in.

"Have you still not slept since giving birth?" asked the nurse.

"No," said Anna, "could I get a sedative?"

"Are you sure?"

"Yes," said Anna.

The nurse left. It took a long time for someone to come.

They think I'll fall asleep on my own, she thought. They didn't know her. The night was very long.

After a while, the midwife wheeled the sleeping child into the room in a plexiglass crib.

"Could I get a sedative, please?" asked Anna.

"Have you still not slept since giving birth?" asked the midwife.

"No," said Anna, "I can't sleep."

The midwife left. After what felt like an eternity she returned with a little white pill.

"I took these when I was pregnant," said Anna, "they're not strong enough, I need two."

"Just start with one for now," said the midwife. The child was sleeping. Aksel was sleeping. Anna took the pill. The hospital was quiet. Occasionally, the sound of a buzzer from one of the other rooms where someone was calling for help.

Aksel stirred in his bed, it was early morning. Anna pulled the cord again.

"Could I get another sedative?" she asked. "One pill isn't enough."

"Have you still not slept since giving birth?" asked a new woman who had just begun her shift.

"She needs two pills," said Aksel, who had woken up and was lifting the child out of the crib.

The woman left the room and came back with one more pill. The round, white shape of the pill in the woman's hand sank into Anna like something from a dream.

The woman gave the pill to Aksel, who handed it to Anna. He placed a glass of water on the chair by her bed. She looked at the child in his arms. Red and wrinkly. She took the pill and swallowed. As the room brightened and the awakening patients murmured in the hall, Anna let herself fall deep down into the ground, to sleep.

Ninth Beginning

Dear

Nothing reminds me more of writing than doing laundry. My thoughts come together in a similar way. I do it while the others are sleeping. It's a pleasant loneliness. I think of all the women who have stood here before me, carrying out these same movements. Each time I lift the clothes from the basket and up to the line, I feel these women throughout hundreds of years passing on their stories through me. Time flows through me. I feel their temperaments. This inner place to which work takes you, and where no one can follow. And I feel how, here, by the clothesline, I become invisible to the world but clear to myself.

Everyone has their own system, order, and pattern, rules for how each item is to be hung and folded. Once the clothes are dry, I always take down the child's first, then my husband's, and finally my own. I always have to fold everything right away, I can't stand things getting wrinkled. That's one of the reasons I try to keep my husband from doing the laundry. It always turns out wrong, and he leaves the clothes inside out when returning them to the laundry basket.

I'm leaving you my papers in the hopes that you will find order where I could not.

Yours
ANNA

Tenth Beginning

The night Anna and Aksel came home from the hospital, they put the boy to sleep in a little wicker bassinet, an heirloom they would soon replace with a hanging cradle.

The child slept, and maybe Anna had just nursed him, or she was awake like always, or maybe she had woken up with a start in the middle of the night. Whatever the case, Anna lay awake in the night, convinced that if she did not actively remember to inhale and exhale, she would stop breathing and die.

She woke up Aksel. He saw her shaking. Aksel seemed to be outside the dome of reality in which she was confined to breathing air in and blowing it out so that she would not die. He was faceless in the dark. Where was the boy? There was a narrow built-in cupboard above the radiator. The cupboard came toward her. Inside the cupboard the child's clothes lay in neat stacks. There was orange yarn and a bib with mint-green four-leaf clovers. There was a wire basket she planned to use for socks, and in this basket lay a little ziplock bag with two pills. Two round, white pills with a groove down the middle so they could be broken in half, white pills, eyes, the doctor's hand giving them to her. In case you feel anxious at home, he said. It's important that you get your sleep. They repeated this to Aksel several times. Later, years later, Anna believed Aksel had forgotten what the doctors had told him: For Anna, sleep was not the same as for other people. That if Anna did not sleep, it could kill her. The two pills were sedatives. Why didn't Aksel remember what the doctors had told him? Should

Anna remind him? It was shameful to ask. Still, she reminded him over and over. She hated him for forgetting. She started to suspect that he did remember the doctor's counsel, but that his love for Anna had faded over the years, and so too his concern for her sleep. Other times, it was as though he couldn't bear the worry. That Anna's sleeplessness was too hard, and he was angry at her because of it. That he saw it as a problem he had to solve. If only she would exercise more, eat more healthily, go to bed earlier. But no habits could change Anna. That was what Aksel didn't understand. The parts of her he didn't want to see grew bigger the less he wanted to look at them.

At night, the two pills in the cupboard; the cupboard that at this moment transferred its soul to Anna and rebuilt itself inside her, with the baby clothes and the darkness, the wire basket with the pills at the bottom. As I write this, several years later, the cupboard that entered Anna that night is still inside her, and she loves the cupboard as if it were a child. That other child who slid out of her in the delivery room, the child she had loved while it was inside her belly, a whole other child than the one who came out of her. That child was now a cupboard, and the cupboard lived inside Anna.

"Should I take a pill?" Anna asked Aksel in the roar of the darkness no one could hear but that rose and fell inside her.

"Yes, good idea."

She got up and took out the wire basket from the cupboard.

"You put them there?" Aksel asked.

Anna stared at the pill in her hand. The whole room turned into a funnel with the pill at the bottom, pulling her toward it. She swallowed it and climbed back into bed. The responsibility she had to take for herself, for life being insufferable in that moment, it was almost too much to bear. Aksel, who was turned toward the child, patted her on the shoulder and fell asleep. Night was there.

Eleventh Beginning

2 years and 5 months after the birth

I asked myself why I no longer dreamed. Then I realized it was because the child's crying woke me so often throughout the night I could never recall the dreaming part of sleep.

He was two and a half and still didn't sleep through the night. Perhaps due to our inadequacy as parents. Perhaps merely a coincidence, an inalterable circumstance, like the weather.

In any case, I no longer dreamed. I suffered from a dream deficiency. When the child was born (or perhaps it happened stealthily during the pregnancy, like a brewing storm), life was divided into separate entities that had to fight among themselves for the right to exist. The child, the mother, the partner, the father, the woman, the family, the couple, the individual, the writing, the housekeeping, the work.

It was unclear to me what my task was. I was charged with a duty of the utmost importance, but when I rolled up my sleeves and got to work, my hands plunged into an enormous shadow and I could no longer see them.

How to live in such a divide? Cut off from oneself and from love. How to connect these murky worlds?

Twelfth Beginning

I want to write a normal book, wrote Anna. Did this longing for normalcy come with giving birth to the child? This longing to be readily accessible like a breast filled with milk.

When I got pregnant, wrote Anna, I became obsessed with averageness. I wanted to give birth to an average child. Of an average height and weight. With an average number of fingers and toes. This was how I would protect the child against death.

I wanted an average pregnancy, with an average weight gain, the average circumference around my belly, the norm, a normal body. The child's viability and strength.

This is my book, wrote Anna. When I had given birth and breastfeeding had been established, I became obsessed with the thought of writing a normal book.

It's very difficult to put together a whole, wrote Anna, to figure out what wholeness is and what it looks like. What is a whole Anna? What is the sum of her parts? These parts of me, separate yet linked, to connect them, to gather them in one place; that is my work.

After giving birth, Anna dressed and undressed the child for the first time. Carefully she coaxed the hospital onesie over the boy's head. He began to cry and flail his arms and legs about.

"Childbirth is hardest on the child," she had read in a book on parenting her aunt had given her. In another book she had read that Marguerite Duras had said that birth was an assassination of the child. Gently she lifted his soft arm and pulled his clenched fist through the sleeve.

While she slept, Aksel had asked a nurse to show him how to change a diaper, and Anna laughed when he told her.

She dressed and undressed the child with a confidence that reassured them both.

She didn't think it was innate, but indoctrinated since childhood.

Throughout the years, thousands of dolls had been dressed and undressed in Anna's hands, and now, in the maternity ward, Anna felt as though all this doll play had existed solely to prepare her for this moment, for this child. She raised and bent the boy's arm to pull it through the sleeve. She carefully lifted him toward her and pulled the leggings up around his belly while his feet rested on the changing pad. Nothing had prepared her for his eyes and for the horror.

Many years later, it occurred to Anna that the reason people didn't tell mothers-to-be about the terror was that they themselves wished to forget it. When the child was older, Anna too had almost forgotten, and it was only in reading these documents she was reminded that it had existed, that it still existed in her, and even then, when faced with these pages, Anna felt a deep ambivalence, tempted to destroy them, delete all signs of this terror that lived deep in the heart of becoming a mother. There was no room for it in society. There was no room for it in Anna. The terror took up far too much space so there was hardly any room for love. To love was a mother's foremost task, her most important work. How to love when there is terror? How to live with terror instead of a heart? It would have to be Anna's secret, she would carry on like everyone else, with a smile and a heart, a mother's heart, a mother's offering.

She washed the child's clothes with the utmost care.

She separated the little items into whites, darks, and reds and washed them at 40 degrees. Cloth diapers and bedding at 60 degrees. Sweaters and wool and silk, delicates, thin summer knitwear at 30 degrees.

She hung the clothes on the drying rack on the balcony while he slept. She smoothed them out and folded them meticulously.

Before giving birth, she washed and ironed all the baby clothes she had collected, then folded and packed them in a box she stowed at the bottom of the closet, along with a gray plush penguin. Her favorite item was a bright-red onesie made of wool with a zipper in the front edged with white trimming. A Christmas onesie.

If clothes or diapers were still yellow from feces after washing, she would lay them out on the kitchen windowsill for the sun to bleach the stains away.

The objects were a means of approach. She understood the child through the objects that belonged to the child's world. She understood that the child was growing through the increasing size of his onesies.

When Aksel did the laundry, he couldn't tell the difference between wool and cotton, to Anna's endless amusement, so she showed him two sweaters, one of cotton and one of wool.

"See, you can feel the difference," she said, rubbing the fabric between her fingers. But he couldn't, no matter how hard he tried. He didn't have the same affinity for textiles as Anna, although he too enjoyed nice clothes.

He didn't have it in him, this eye for it, the ability to zero in on the weave, the length of the threads, the fine raveling, the very fibers that made up various textiles. He hadn't conversed with sales assistants in artificially lit department stores about the correct way to wash chiffon. Most likely, the majority of his garments had been designed to be washed in a good old 40-degree cycle without any fuss. Sadly, most men did not wear lace.

Anna, meanwhile, lived in the world of textiles. She had long dreams about moving through swaths of wet and dyed fabrics. And often she would dream about sorting through piles of clothing someone had left behind in the attic, or about packing endless heaps of clothes into bigger and bigger bags.

Anna realized her relationship not only to textiles but to all the objects of the home was different from Aksel's. Objects settled deep inside her; she *knew* them.

The herbs on the windowsill, the various glasses and jars of flour and beans, the linens in the closet, several of which were monogrammed with her grandmother's initials, and also the scent in between these folded sheets when you lifted out a clean duvet cover, the dough rising in its bowl, the wool sweaters on the highest shelf, the soap. Anna suspected this deep union with the objects of the house was the result of her upbringing. Had Anna been taught not only to be a housewife, but to be one with the house itself, to be an object among objects? Had the work of the home given her a particular sense of the life of objects?

Anna had always preferred to read and write in secret, and she would tell people that books and writing offered a refuge, a secret life.

But was the real reason not that writing brought Anna closer to all the objects in the world? And that in this way she became less human, that in her writing she could seek to become an object? Here, happily objectified by writing, she felt more like Anna, more alive than otherwise. Was Anna not human?

It was not through housekeeping but through writing that she wished to approach all the objects of the world. Was writing in that case a form of housekeeping? A way of bringing things into order? When Adam named everything in the Garden of Eden, was he in fact doing the work of a housewife?

Anna wanted to live and did live close to the textiles, the minerals, the food, to the plants and the dust and the smells and to the elements and the small animals. And in Anna's eyes, everything was knickknacks, everything was miniature, it all belonged to the world of objects and animals. The toys and the children's clothes. The organs in their bodies. The child's liver and heart.

When the boy was born, Anna was afraid he would be an ugly child. Or rather, she wasn't afraid of him being ugly, but of not being able to tell whether or not he was beautiful. That visitors would walk over to his crib and say "what a beautiful child," but would be lying to Anna out of politeness.

Anna was afraid of being trapped in the lie without knowing it. Sequestered from everyone else in another reality from which she could not escape. How could you truly see your child?

"I'm afraid he'll be ugly," she said to Aksel, who got angry and said: "Of course he won't be."

It tormented her to live inside the lie of the beautiful child.

It tormented her to have to wonder whether the child was beautiful or ugly. It tormented her to have such thoughts about her own child. *The child was her flesh and blood*, literally. *He had been formed inside her and expelled from her body a few days ago, uncorded, examined, washed, alive.* He was her and he was not her. She could not see herself.

When Anna was pregnant, she and Aksel, who was Swedish, agreed to move to Stockholm for a while after the child was born. Everything had been planned before the birth, they believed they had the next twelve months all worked out. With the help of his mother, Aksel had found an apartment for them in Hammarbyhöjden—a charming suburb, Anna gathered, close to the woods and a lake, as well as to public transport. He had also managed to arrange it so that the play he was working on would premiere in Uppsala in December, while they were in Sweden. He was proud of having landed it, was keen to show he had connections in Sweden. They would wait to move until the child was five months old, that fit with the timing of their parental leave; there would be an overlap where they would be at home together once Aksel had finished a play in Malmö. The plan was that Anna would gradually start writing again, perhaps return to Denmark with a manuscript for a book when the child was one, or they could stay in Sweden, perhaps she could get a job, they knew someone who taught a group of young Scandinavian students, a literature class, where Anna had been offered the chance to run a week-long seminar later in the year. It was still a long way off. It was September. They packed up and sublet their apartment, held a small goodbye dinner, Anna pushed the stroller out of the yellow shed in the courtyard and looked up at the windows of the apartment that had been the child's first home. She felt a chill at the thought of what was to come. She was extremely tired and very, very awake.

Thirteenth Beginning

2 years, 9 months, and 2 days after the birth

The child soon three, impossible, he cries day in and day out and has done so for two months. He still doesn't sleep through the night, and we let him watch too much TV. But he's outgoing, he eats well, he climbs and rolls around and jumps and runs. I love his little voice and his obvious sense of humor. I love the way he smells and the drool around his mouth and his pointy little milk teeth.

Yet there are days, particularly Sundays, when I feel like closing the door to his room and covering my ears. And days when I feel like taking revenge, when I want to shake and slap him to make him be quiet.

We're talking more and more about having a second child.

First Continuation

There are different degrees of sedation.

The first is just to hold the knife in your thoughts.

She has been forbidden to drink. She has been advised against taking sedatives.

The second is to stand in front of the drawer of knives in the kitchen.

She can look at the drawer. She can pull the drawer out. She can place her hand in the drawer and stay that way for a long time. She can pick up a knife and hold it in her hand.

Every three or four hours, she nurses the child. Between eight in the evening and one in the morning, there is an interval of five hours in which the child skips a meal and doesn't need her.

She can draw the knife across her skin without applying pressure. She can apply various degrees of pressure. She can draw the knife across her skin lightly so it doesn't break the surface, but leaves a red line that's gone the next day.

It snows almost every day. It's November in Stockholm. They moved here a month ago. The child is five months old. At night she gets up and looks at the tree outside the kitchen window. It's a plane. The snow lands on the speckled branches.

A whole day can be survived if she holds the drawer of knives in her mind. There is power here.

The child grows. With each knife it becomes clearer to her, takes shape inside her with a cool calmness: the thought that she can kill herself.

They live in a small apartment, 41 square meters. It consists of one large room that they have divided with a curtain into a living room and bedroom. A kitchen and a bathroom. The building is in the Swedish functionalist ABC style and has four stories with identical units. On all sides grow big trees that billow and blow, casting their shadows on the building's yellow walls.

When did Anna start believing that Aksel no longer loved her as a human being but as a dog?

He asks her to leave the apartment. Reluctantly she sets off toward town and wanders around the shops. She dislikes being there. One day Anna finds a little café opposite the metro station. Every morning at ten o'clock when Aksel kicks her out, she walks across the open field. At the halfway mark, the path leads up and over a rocky hill. After thirty minutes, she arrives at another yellow multistory building, almost indistinguishable from theirs. On the ground floor is a little café beneath a looping pastel-green neon sign spelling *Santa Fé*.

Does she have them in her? The parts that make her a mother?

She sits and writes for three hours while she drinks coffee and eats cake. *Anna, my name is Anna*, she writes. When she sees the words on the page, they appear to be the truest thing she has ever said. At the same time, the words appear very far away, as though written in another world. Does she need glasses? Then she walks home to nurse the child before it's time for his nap, and then she folds yesterday's laundry. In the evening she streams series Aksel doesn't want to watch. He goes to bed two hours earlier than her. She takes the child at night, he still wakes up frequently. At five in the morning Aksel takes over and she sleeps for another two hours. This is the structure of Anna's life.

Let's look at her. Anna. There's a light snow. It falls on the field in front of her. Anna is standing on the hill, higher up in the snow, as if in another time. The sun sets across her face.

In her mind, an image at the bottom of a long funnel: She's at the hospital, one or two days after giving birth. She's drowsy from the sleeping pill, the room smells of flesh and liquid hand soap, the light is yellow. Aksel lifts the child to his chest, he has a thin tube taped to his finger, in the tube is colostrum from Anna's breast. Gently Aksel guides his finger into the child's mouth so he can suck the scarce fluid. The scene doesn't end but repeats endlessly until it is worn down to a dry crackle.

On the hill, Anna sees this image of the man with the child as a round dial hanging between the spruces, the snow doesn't touch it.

I will have to write it for her: she thinks something went definitively wrong and it can be traced back to this moment. The gratitude she initially felt has since turned into the belief that she cannot manage on her own. That there is a fundamental flaw in her that Aksel had to make up for, and she has started to fear being alone with the child.

She suspects that in the first days of its life the child needed to form an essential bond with Anna but something went wrong between them. Or even worse, that Anna didn't bond properly with the child, and now it was too late. That the child bonded more strongly with its father because it too, in its infancy, sensed this flaw in her.

"Weren't you going to go out? Explore the city, meet some new people?" said Aksel.

"I have to nurse," said Anna.

"You could pump."

"I don't like pumping."

"Besides, don't you think it's time for you to cut down on nursing? We need to start feeding him baby food."

"He's much too little for baby food."

"He just needs to get used to it."

"The Danish Health Authority recommends exclusive breastfeeding for the first six months."

"The Swedish National Food Agency writes on their website that you can actually feed the child solid foods starting at four months."

"Just give him to me."

"No, he needs to eat some food first."

"But he wants to nurse, I can hear it."

"What do you mean you can hear it?"

"From his crying. May I please nurse him?"

"Fine. But then you have to go out afterward."

"I will."

"Are you crying? Anna, I'm the one on parental leave right now."

"I don't have a job here anyway."

"Weren't you going to write?"

"I'm not ready to be away from him."

"Please go."

"You can't just take him!"

"I'm perfectly capable of burping him, Anna. You're going to have to let go if we're going to do this together, you know."

"You don't know what it was like when he was little."

"Well, I could just as well have taken him."

"No, you couldn't."

"What do you mean? Of course I could."

"But I had to nurse!"

"I could have given him a bottle."

"You couldn't have given him a bottle. That's not how it works."

"Sure it does, Anna. I could have bottle-fed him."

"No. Give him to me!"

"Anna, you need to go now. That was the deal."

When a mother gives birth to her child, something radical happens to her. The child who was once part of her body isn't anymore, but remains part of her consciousness. *When she is with the child, she is not herself,* but something else. She feels a restless longing to return to herself, to remove herself from the child. *But when she is without the child,* it's as though parts of her are missing. *She is not herself.* She is neither herself nor not herself. From this position, she will *struggle.*

When Anna realized this, that she could be neither with nor without the child and also be Anna, she stopped telling Aksel about herself.

The temperature in Stockholm fell to -10 degrees Celsius. In the morning, they wrapped the boy in a wool bodysuit, wool overalls, a sweater and a neck warmer, an organic alpaca wool onesie, thick knit socks and the big, yellow pom-pom hat that slipped over his eyes when they put him in the bunting bag in the stroller. The hat made him sleep. Then Anna pushed him through the towering snow. Down to the station, over the rocky hill, across the field, past Santa Fé and back home. After an hour her feet and hands were frozen and dead despite the many layers, and Aksel came down from the apartment and took over. Then Anna went upstairs and warmed up with a shower. When the boy and Aksel returned from their walk, she breastfed the child as agreed, kissed Aksel and went back out again, the same route, down to the station, over the rocky hill, across the field. It had started to snow again. As she stepped into Santa Fé, the cold swept through the open door and the few guests shivered in the corners, all of them with their coats still on; the room couldn't heat up when the door opened so often. She ordered a *liten latte* and sat at her favorite table by the window facing the field. The air was still, the snow fell in fat flakes. She liked Stockholm for its snow. In Copenhagen it rarely snowed. She heaped sugar into her coffee, drank the sweet, lukewarm drink. It was half past noon, she lifted her black leather bag onto the table and pulled out a number of identical A4 folders, piling them in front of her. She watched the café's clientele. An old man in a hat, a grandmother helping her grandchild onto a chair. The young girl who worked there was leaning against a table, checking her phone.

Anna had no education. She had attended a creative writing school for a few years and taken some classes at university without ever finishing.

Instead she had worked since she was very young. Anna thought about what she would do now, and how she would earn money. She thought about her previous jobs in order to glean what skills she had accumulated, and which principles she had been taught.

Not having any profession apart from motherhood made Anna consider what sorts of qualities defined her.

She was not a member of any union, and she had never held a permanent position. She joined an unemployment insurance fund for journalists when she realized she was pregnant so she could get maternity benefits.

Anna wasn't poor. Her income fluctuated. Some years were fat years, others lean. Because she didn't have a fixed salary but freelanced and wrote books and worked six-month gigs, it was hard for her to gauge her own finances.

There were periods of six or nine months when Anna would be quite well off, wealthy even, but then the curve dropped and she would have no income at all.

During the fat months, Anna couldn't resist spending a lot of money, but at the back of her mind she feared she was living beyond her means and would soon be punished for it with a pile of bills she couldn't pay.

But these unpayable bills had not yet managed to catch up to Anna, which led her to believe she was perhaps very rich and in fact lying to herself and everyone else about it.

In Sweden they lived off Aksel's parental benefits and a grant Anna had received while she was pregnant. They had enough money to tide them over until sometime next year when they would move back to Denmark.

The first thing they did when they moved to the city was buy new clothes. It became their obsession. Everyone in Stockholm was well-dressed, and their clothes were always new. There was none of the shabby Berlin style they knew from Copenhagen. Here, you needed elegant garments made from understated, luxurious materials. A long, dark coat, black dress pants from Hope, a heavy, blue velvet jacket with pearly buttons from Our Legacy, crisp white shirts and platform shoes, matte lipstick and a stylish haircut, which was one of the most important status symbols in Stockholm. All Stockholmers were always slightly overaccessorized, Anna thought; the addition of a hat tipped the scales. It was ridiculous, but Anna and Aksel couldn't help themselves; they spent all their money on new clothes at Brunogallerian on Götgatan and (on sale) at NK, the upscale department store on Hamngatan. Anna couldn't think of anything to do besides shopping. Loneliness drove her to massive sprees. It became her language and preferred mode of expression. Shopping became an art form. The juxtaposition of materials in the shopping bag, orange corduroy paired with green-and-white beaded earrings, a fuzzy black angora sweater over a pair of blue slinky pants in a wool and silk blend. A bright-pink notebook made from recycled plastic bottles. A silver ring with an eye that wept a crystal tear.

The child woke up many times throughout the night, always with a whimper or a change in the rhythm of his breathing, prodding her awake a few seconds before him. She would lift him up and walk around until he settled down again, or pull him into her bed and feed him.

At night, Anna was a mother. At night, it could not be doubted. Aksel slept heavily and didn't wake up. The child was hers. She was Anna, she breastfed in the dark. She held him in her listening, she coaxed him to sleep, she did so with a serenity, an acquired instinct. When his body grew heavy, she knew it was time to put him back down. If she put the child down too soon, he would cry, if she put him down too late, he would wake up confused and cry even harder. There were thirty seconds in which she could put him down, in which he would let sleep wash over him.

When the boy had fallen back asleep, Anna crept out to check the digital clock on the oven. Winter was dark and long, and she couldn't guess the time by the light outside. From the kitchen Anna looked down at the snow on the road. The big plane tree was lit up by the streetlight below, each branch and twig doubled by a weightless layer of snow. She felt the snow in her mouth.

Almost as if he had sensed this bliss, Aksel decided that from then on he would take the boy when he woke up at night. This would, he believed, result in Anna getting more rest.

"You need to sleep."

At night she always woke up before Aksel, who now lay closest to the boy. She climbed over his sleeping body, gave the boy his pacifier and caressed him until he fell back asleep. Sometimes he cried long enough for Aksel to wake up and take him, under the impression they had all woken up at the same time.

Their both being up at night with the boy only deepened Anna's sadness. The nights had been hers, like a remnant of her pregnancy where it had only been her and the child. She had no words for this experience and didn't know how to explain to Aksel that in his attempt to protect her, he had only buried her deeper.

As soon as the child turned six months, Aksel began feeding him according to a schedule so he could beat the breastfeeding to it. He sighed with frustration when Anna put the child to her breast, as though breastfeeding were a bad habit, and Anna began asking him for permission to nurse the child.

I'll write a brief summary of these days, because I dislike being here.

After this has gone on for a month, the child is still nursing. Anna's breasts are taut and burning. Aksel believes breastfeeding is a choice, a simple matter of free will. Just like following a schedule. But her breasts turning hard as rocks every three hours is not a matter of free will. It just happens.

When Anna wants to breastfeed but Aksel forbids it, a curtain closes in her brain, as if she has hit her head. She cannot think.

Anna tries to explain it to Aksel. But the accumulating milk makes her dumb. She can only yell incoherent, strange words. She shakes Aksel. He holds the child out of her reach. The child cries. She believes she can tell he wants to nurse. She gets very close to Aksel, she does with her face what an animal does when it wants to threaten an enemy. She sharpens it like a weapon. She sees his mouth open with fright. Powerless, he lets her take the child. While she nurses, she can sense that Aksel is afraid of her. A rush of triumph courses through her with the milk and the blood. She is an animal. She is precivilization, preschedule. She holds the child, she looks at Aksel as though she intends to eat him. He must learn.

But when she has finished nursing, Aksel has shaken it off. He takes the child, and with the child, he has taken over again.

"Just go, Anna. It's not good for you to be here."

"You're the one destroying me."

"Don't say that."

The child spits up, distracting them. They fuss over the child and compete over who gets to clean up after him.

Because she doesn't like being here, I'll say it for her as quickly as possible.

Anna can't leave Aksel. First of all, she can't leave him because of the boy. She needs his help with the child. The flaw in her means that she would never be able to take care of him on her own. She also wants the child to have Aksel, she knows he has a right to him, a right to his father. She also can't leave Aksel because it would mean leaving the child, and she can't do that because, practically speaking, he needs her to survive because she breastfeeds him, and because they're in a foreign country where she doesn't know anyone. She would never be able to take the child with her because her flaw would damage him if the two were alone together for too long.

Somewhere deep inside her, Anna also suspects that she can't leave Aksel because she loves him. But this love stands in the shadow of the child, of the birth and the pregnancy, where Anna understood that men and women are not equal. Loving her own keeper repulses her, her clichéd feminine heart repulses her.

Anna and Aksel are sitting on either end of the sofa, sunken into the kind of despondent silence that arises at the peak of an argument. The child is sleeping. Both are deep in thought about what they have become. It is at this moment Anna understands that for the first time in her life she has been destroyed.

Not even the birth destroyed her. Even though it killed her, she was not broken but resurrected as a whole person. New, different, maybe, but still intact. Now, on the sofa, Anna realizes that the man has destroyed her. She will not return to herself again.

He's saying something now: "You don't have more claim to the child than I do, Anna."

"Yes, I do."

"That's essentialism. We're equals in this. We agreed we would be equals."

"You're an idealist. You can't be an idealist here. We aren't equals."

"I'm just saying it like it is, Anna. The bond between mother and child is not sacred."

How are we to love him, Anna?

If I can't kill him, I'll remove myself from the picture.

The boy woke up at 5:30, they got up in the dark, Aksel was away at Uppsala City Theater, something about an actor with burnout, he had to rush off. A former Aksel—the playwright—came over him, a swift kiss on his way out the door, the child forgotten in the heat of his work life.

The snow illuminated the apartment, she changed his night diaper in bed and put him in the baby bouncer. He was easy in the morning, babbling and fiddling with a wooden teether that had a crocheted teddy-bear head. She made coffee, drank it while he lay on his belly on a blanket. Put him on the changing pad in the bathroom and took a shower as he watched, and she made silly faces at him.

It was warm in the apartment, like inside a small pocket. He fell asleep quickly in the stroller at naptime. The snow was piled high, she had to push the stroller down the middle of the road to get anywhere. There were other mothers with strollers outside, a couple trudged past, each dragging a wheelie suitcase. Everything was quiet, the light was low, yellow and gaseous, as if from a lantern. Pushing the stroller was strenuous. She parked it outside Santa Fé, but he woke up after five minutes, so she had to run outside and continue walking while fumbling to get her coat back on. There was no wind, it wasn't snowing. She walked home in the peculiar light. The child woke up and they went upstairs. As they ate lunch, it started to thaw, the trees dripped, the snowdrifts shrank. Anna wiped the high chair and table, swept the floor beneath the boy's chair. She unbuttoned her cardigan, pulled her wool undershirt under her breast and unfastened one side of her nursing bra. Then she lifted the child up to her on the sofa and nursed him. He was content after eating, he drank calmly, she filled him up, made sure he was completely full. Eating solids was still new to him. He pulled his head away from her breast, and she offered it to him again. When he rejected it a second time, she switched to her other breast, he latched onto her nipple and pulled it against the roof of his mouth. Anna felt the heaviness come over her, a melancholy deep within her, like a train running through an underground tunnel. The milk flowed. When he was finished, she rested his body against her shoulder and patted him on the back. She didn't know what he was looking at back there, his face so close to the wall. After a while, she heard a burp.

Anna was lying close beside him when he started to cry. Aksel got up, put on a robe, picked up the boy from the bed and closed the makeshift curtain so Anna could go back to sleep. She watched the snow falling among the pines.

"Fuck!" Aksel shouted.

"Did he win?"

"Maybe."

Anna got up to join them. She pulled the boy onto her lap. Through the living room window she could see how much it had snowed during the night. The world was quiet. The snow fell with unhuman patience. It was five o'clock, they were watching CNN.

At ten in the morning, it was official, all roads were closed, the temperature had fallen to -17 degrees and Donald Trump had won the American presidential election. It was too cold to take the child outside so they had to stay inside in the small apartment all day.

While the child was napping, they turned the chairs to face the big window and drank their coffee in silence while they looked at the falling snowflakes outside.

"If we're going to live as equals, you as the mother are going to have to give up some of your privileges to the father," said Aksel. "I think you should try going into the city sometimes, and I'll take him. I think it could be good for you."

Anna looked over at the child in the hanging cradle.

"You just nursed him. The timing is good. I can give him baby food."

"But is the metro running?"

"Yes, only the roads are closed."

Aksel closed the front door and Anna wept in the stairwell. Then she walked to the station through the mountainous snow. She took the metro too far and left through the wrong exit. She walked up and down Götgatan several times, not daring to stray too far from the station and get lost when she had to be home in time for the next feed. She went into Nitty Gritty, into Afroart, into the charity shop, into the supermarket, into a coffee shop on Bysistorget, into the stationery store next door. She didn't buy anything. Then she walked back the same way she came. There was snow in her hair.

When she got to Slussen, she stopped on the bridge to Gamla stan. The narrow canal was almost frozen, a boat glided by below her. Her urge to breastfeed was hindering the child's development, Aksel had said. That was why Aksel had asked her to go into town; secretly the child and Aksel wanted to be rid of her. Her role had been played out. The flaw in her drove them further away. They couldn't bring themselves to tell her the truth: she needn't come back. She looked down at the black water and clasped her hands around the black railing.

But the thought of something going wrong, of not succeeding, of waking up and seeing their faces after having exposed her wish held her back.

In the metro she could feel the milk tensing her breasts more and more with every station. She longed for the child's mouth against her, like being enveloped by water.

She half ran from the station, key in hand, but at the front door she hesitated, suddenly afraid of the rooms above. She turned and looked up at the trees in front of the building. She sucked in the cold air.

When Anna's mother came to visit them in Stockholm, Anna was miserable and the child refused to sleep. Anna pushed the stroller around and around the ice-cold city while her mother walked beside her, freezing in a thin coat; she wasn't prepared for the Swedish cold.

The child screamed more loudly and madly than ever before. She was afraid her mother would think she was useless, a bad mother, and that she would soon see right through Anna and realize there was something wrong with her bond with the child.

Anna had been so excited for her mother's visit she had kept the child up far too late, eager to pick her mother up at the station, eager for her to see the child, to see how big he had grown. Now he was screaming from within the darkness of the stroller.

"Maybe you should try picking him up?" her mother cautiously suggested.

Anna easily got lost in this foreign city but was at least slightly more familiar with the area than her mother, who suddenly seemed small and lost like a tired schoolchild.

"Do you think he can sleep when he's so angry?" she asked.

Eventually Anna had to bring the boy up to her mother's hotel room and lie down with him while her mother waited in the lobby. The child finally fell asleep, and Anna lay looking out at Katarina Cemetery. The black gravestones marked the white snow like an alphabet. Now Anna was gripped by rage.

This was the anger and resolve that hid on the other side of the child's cries.

Sometimes he cried for so long and with such intensity that Anna eventually crossed a threshold. She became cold, she walked around with the screaming child in her arms, silent and faraway, until he screamed himself to sleep.

But Anna had never crossed into this state in front of another person. The child had never been awake for this long before, for this many hours. Now he was screaming again. She put on his sweater, the thick socks, the hat, and finally the wool onesie. She carried the bawling child down the stairs into the courtyard and put him in the stroller. She closed the bunting bag tightly around him, tugged the hat over his eyes, pulled the folding top all the way up. Beneath the yellow hat, his little mouth opened and closed forming scream after scream. She pushed the stroller briskly and purposefully toward the cobbled side street she had registered subconsciously when they arrived at the hotel.

She pushed him down the street to the big stairway leading to the cemetery, turned the stroller around and pushed him back up, back and forth across the cobblestones until he fell asleep.

On the way to the train, Anna said: "I like Hammarbyhöjden."

Aksel said: "You like the safety and security."

"Yes."

"Deep down, you're a Christian Democrat. You love safety and traditions."

"If it were up to you, we'd have an aristocracy, not a democracy."

He laughed.

"Do you think your mom will have a Christmas tree?" said Anna.

"Maybe."

"I'm excited for him to see his first Christmas tree."

Aksel kissed her. "Do you think he'll understand what it is?"

Anna shrugged and smiled. The train arrived. The boy sat in the stroller trying to pull his mittens off.

In a bag Anna had brought stewed red cabbage, made in the Danish tradition, she had offered to roast the duck. It was the day of Christmas Eve. In the city center, Stockholm's streets were almost empty in the crisp frost. Aksel's family didn't plan ahead, and they didn't care for traditions; they liked to keep things unorthodox. Yet Anna had never met anyone as bent on structure as Aksel. His meticulous schedules for the child's sleeping and eating only became more detailed. Every day he ate the same thing for lunch: a can of chickpeas, a boiled egg, and two carrots. Every day he went for a run in the woods, and if it was snowing he worked out at the gym. He went to bed at 10:30 p.m. and got up at six, he was sociable at parties but couldn't drink very much, he always went to bed before two. Aksel didn't like feeling full, didn't like having a lot of food in the fridge. He liked exercising and feeling strong, he liked to sit the boy on his knee and tickle him and make him sputter with laughter. Aksel's mother had not bought a Christmas tree.

"Aksel," called Anna as she changed the child in her mother-in-law's bed. "There's no Christmas tree." Anna started to cry.

Aksel hugged her, picked up the boy. "Darling, I didn't know it meant so much to you."

"I'm so tired of everything being so highbrow and all this talk about literature and politics, and to top it all off you don't even have a Christmas tree!"

"But our family just doesn't care very much about that sort of thing."

"I know it's ridiculous, I just think it's weird not to have a tree. And on his first Christmas." Anna sobbed at the word Christmas.

"Well, we'll just have to find a Christmas tree then," said Aksel.

"You can't buy a tree now. Everything's closed."

"I'm sure we can find one somewhere."

"Won't your mother be upset if we drag one up here?"

"No, she won't mind. I have to take him for a walk at nap-time anyway, so I can find one then."

"Can I come with you?"

"Of course." He kissed her.

There were no Christmas-tree sellers. When they turned down one street, Aksel thought he could see pine trees up ahead and with increasing anticipation they pushed the stroller in front of them, but it was just a park. Anna wept. She felt foolish and alone. She felt nostalgic and talked about the smell of pine needles.

"That's lovely, darling!" said Aksel overenthusiastically. And finally he did in fact manage to find a scraggly little pine tree. It was poking out of a trash can, abandoned by a Christmas-tree seller on a deserted square.

"Perfect," said Aksel, pulling it out.

Anna smiled through her tears. "Look, sweetheart," she said to the child who had woken up and sat sucking eagerly on his rubber pacifier. "A Christmas tree!"

On the way home, they bought tinsel, red ribbon, and a few oranges in the local supermarket. They had to lean the tree against a corner of the living room, it had no foot, it shed needles.

"We found it on the street!" Aksel bragged to the guests, over and over.

After they had stood in the theater's foyer, smiling politely, Aksel shaking hand after hand, introducing Anna again and again, who had been met with an *oh, you're Anna* and *where's your son tonight* and had replied *yes* and *yes* and *nice to meet you* and *with his grandmother*, and after they had hung their new coats in the cloakroom, lifted a glass—*bubbles!* exclaimed one of Aksel's colleagues, whose role Anna couldn't determine, a younger woman in the Stockholm uniform: an asymmetrical white shirt and flared black pants, platform shoes, silver-rimmed glasses—which Anna sipped at, quickly growing hot and tipsy, Aksel pulled her into the theater, *this is our seat, at the back,* in a whisper pointing out reviewers and important theater people, celebrities and colleagues, and then the room went dark, a big pink sun loomed on stage, a figure stepped in front of the shining dial and in the glare began to speak lines Anna recognized from the pages Aksel had sometimes asked her to read at home, he took her hand in the auditorium, squeezed it, his face expressionless, all evening there had been this politeness to him, an almost grating, greasy grin that Anna had learned to recognize as a sign of suppressed hatred, and now he leaned toward her without taking his eyes off the stage and whispered, "imagine if this theater was bombed right now, there would be no cultural elite left in all of Stockholm," she looked at him in surprise, his eyes flashed, sweat made his face glisten in the dim auditorium light, his mouth pulled back into a derisive, almost evil smile that appeared to stretch forever until his face was nothing but mouth, shining teeth, spit, "everyone would be dead."

"Can't you see that I lose confidence in myself as a mother when you try to control everything I do?" she said when they got home. "It's your fault I question whether I can trust myself, whether I can trust my own judgment."

"I was only asking whether it was a good idea to nurse right now."

"But you always ask me that."

"Sorry," Aksel said, but he had on his actor's face. It was the obedient son who apologized, the rhetorician, the diplomat. Apologizing now was the right thing to do, and Aksel knew it, but he didn't mean it.

"You always say sorry," said Anna, "and then you keep doing it." She believed it to be a general problem. Aksel believed it depended on the specific situation.

"But you do the exact same thing. You criticize me too when I'm taking care of him. Don't you think it's just part of parenting?" said Aksel.

"You always do this. You come and tell me *I'm* doing something wrong when I tell you *you've* done something wrong. Sure, I mess up, but that's not what this is about right now. It's purely rhetorical. I could just as well say: Yeah, I did something stupid, I made a mistake, but the Jews were murdered."

"Come here." He pulled her close. "I just like talking about stuff," he said. "Maybe parenthood wasn't always like this, people discussing, but that's the way I am."

"Don't turn this into something general," Anna said, "as if you're someone who likes to discuss things and I'm not!"

"No, you discuss things too."

"Yes, exactly."

"All I'm saying," said Aksel, "is that maybe it's a general parenting thing, the need to communicate."

"I feel like this conversation has become very abstract."

Aksel's mother came to congratulate him on the premiere. She offered to take the child for a walk. As soon as grandmother and child were out the door, Anna and Aksel were arguing again. Never in her life had Anna argued this much or this hard. They didn't have to argue for long before the urge came to stick her hand in the drawer of knives.

Aksel said: "You never touch me anymore."

Anna said: "How do you think I can have sex with someone who takes my child away from me?"

Aksel said: "You only think of yourself, you don't think about what's good for our child. You're so self-absorbed."

Anna said: "Aksel, I can't take this, I can't take it anymore." The words seemed to stop in her mouth.

They could argue without saying anything. Furious, they waited in silence, they repeated the same meaningless sentences: "Yes, you do," and "No, you do," and "Yes, you did," and "No, I didn't."

Anna was inside the wool mitten; she could see but couldn't see, she could speak but couldn't speak, she could hear but couldn't hear. It was the hissing of the trees, but the trees were quiet outside the windows, dressed in snow. It was the coffee in the cup at the café that shook like an earthquake, but the coffee just sat in the cup. She took hold of Aksel and shook him, she pushed him against the wall. "Now you listen to me," she screamed, about to split in two. "I'm the one who breast-feeds him," she screamed. "I'm the one who gave birth to him," she screamed. "I'm the one who carried him," she screamed. "I'm the one who took care of him when he was little and you went to work."

"I could have taken care of him when he was little," screamed Aksel.

"What do you mean?" screamed Anna. "Of course you couldn't, he had to be breastfed."

"I could have bottle-fed him," screamed Aksel.

"What do you mean? What do you mean?" screamed Anna. "He had to be breastfed."

"He didn't have to be breastfed," screamed Aksel, "I could easily have taken care of him."

"What are you saying?" screamed Anna, she shook him again, she stared at him with all her might. Aksel tore himself away.

"That's enough, Anna, you've gone too far," he said, trembling. "You're scaring me." He put on his coat, quickly. "I'm leaving."

There were different degrees of sedation. The first was simply to hold the knife in your thoughts. The next was to go into the kitchen. She pulled out the drawer and placed her hand on the knives. The boy sat in the living room on a blanket, sucking on a wooden teether. He had a new tooth on the way and drool ran down his shirt.

They didn't live high enough for a jump to be effective.

Carefully she drew the knife across her underarm. Then she heard the key turn in the lock. Hastily she put the knife back and closed the drawer.

"Hello, sweetheart," she heard Aksel say to the child. She joined them in the other room. He stood with the boy on his hip, avoiding her gaze. His other arm hung by his side, but his hand opened toward her.

"It's time to go back home to Denmark," he said. "I think you need it."

Second Continuation

5–8 months after the birth

*

an old woman in a black wool hat

bent at the waist
walks very slowly
across the hard-trodden snow
down the street
slick with ice
in Hammarbyhöjden

it's the end of November

and now
with this small child by my side

with this Swedish man by my side
the thought comes to me

coolly takes shape
like a flower or a path

between the tall
pines the woman
passes by

that I did the same thing

to carry on
writing
last time I was depressed

wrote on top of
someone else's book

that's how I wrote
my first book

and now
at the age of thirty
with this small child by my side
with this Swedish man by my side

I think the thought again
I did the same thing
last time I was depressed
this last
the doctors

I stand
in the hallway
with the laundry
in a bag over my shoulder
on the way
across the ice
across the hard-trodden snow
on the street in Hammarbyhöjden

lost to myself
but with direction

to the laundry room downstairs
where darkness falls
and I think
that's what I thought the last time
that's what I thought the last time

*
what I wanted
was to point out
that I have
two breast pumps

but before
I could write it down
you began
to argue with me

about wanting to go
into town
to buy
a new dimmer switch

these two
breast pumps
and so much more
I have acquired
to live
with the child

an electric pump
for 2,050 kroner
that can pump

both breasts
simultaneously
because it

increases milk production
by 17–18%
according to the nurse
at the hospital

and I was
required to pump
several times a day
the first weeks
hence this
electric pump

with its melodic hum

I write
about these pumps
to understand them
with that which isn't me

that in which I dress

that in which I come to rest

the pumps
so familiar
and this familiarity
this intimacy

with which
I place them against my body
this
foreignness
of the pumps
only I hold

and all women hold

while I pump
I think
about all the women
who came before me

when I
lift the child
hang the laundry
stand up at night
look outside

I think of the women
who did not get
the same amount of help

I think of the women
who had
the children to themselves
what joy

what horror

you say
you don't think

about the men
who came before you

you say
that's crazy
do you really think about that
about them
about all the women

and therein lies
the difference

it's not just
our bodies
that are different

but also
our history

you have so little to lose
and I despise you for it
I mean
you have everything to gain
as a father

you don't have to do much
to tower above

to do more
than the men before you

all the women
in me

their toil
throughout history

when you bend
over the child

you do not carry
this history

women's wageless
work

the birth
the pregnancy

you say
you want to be equals

but we are not equal

this sweet game
you play

us being alike

the other pump

is made of hard plastic
transparent
tinged with yellow

I bought it

at the pharmacy at
Gothenburg Central Station

it is a cheap
a simple
manual pump

for our journey
because the child

suddenly would not
latch

but I had to keep
production going

I work

my work

my work

it is beyond you

and should remain so

I prefer

the simple pump

it draws the milk out

in streams

with a tug and a puff

my manual pump

my little life

*
to imagine
a time where
I have no child no
husband
none of these
relationships
that have since shaped
my adult life
is very easy
when they are
inside the house
and I am not

a pleasurable
loneliness
made me

*

walking home from the station
the street light falls across my face

but not into the stroller

the child sees me
but the stroller lies in shadow

as if there were no child
inside the bassinet

only a solid darkness

and I push it
forward

through the
lamplit night

*

bending over the stroller to pick him up
I am embraced by his whole smell

*

as the child grows
becomes hungrier
more impatient
and strong
he begins to
reject the small breast
he cries inconsolably
wants food but will not take it
I am on the side of
the smaller breast
as if there were something evil
or ominous
about the bigger breast
as if it wanted to
decommission
the smaller one
I struggle to
keep it going
I pump it
massage it in the shower
the big breast and the baby
the big breast and the baby
an alliance
that excludes me

*
always suspicious
of a strength
I don't understand
I guest teach a seminar in December
a group of strangers
the big breast's
abundance of milk
I breastfeed my child in the breaks
a student wrote
I hope
a poem can be bad
and still
be part of something
good
and these lines
changed everything

*

today as my child
steps into his
seventh month
I'm sitting
at Coffice
in Stockholm
flanked
by two women
with the same black
baker boy hat with
military details
the concept of taste
is a class weapon
and it snows
on the second day
of November
a thinning but
persistent sleet
like a wet nylon stocking
pulled across Söder
the sloping streets
Slussen
Medborgarplatsen
and everyone has money
or rather no money at all

I want to breastfeed my child
longer
than his father wants
me to
you can't prevent
a woman from
breastfeeding her child
says my mother
on the phone
and then suggests
we have another child
to solve the problem
what is writing for
but to confess
where do I want writing to take me
a place
where I have no child
or is the child now
forever
present
in each thing I write

Third Continuation

Anna's journal, 2016

Tuesday, November 1, 2016
If a man tells you that you're worrying too much, ask him to
do the worrying for you.
    Today, my child is six months and three weeks old.
    Defeated and exhausted, I will perhaps go a little further.
    Incoherent trinketry.

Thursday, November 3, 2016
If Aksel sells his apartment in Stockholm, we can qualify for
a loan from the bank in Denmark and buy an apartment in
Copenhagen, and thus I'm facing a future as a property owner.
    I can't shake the feeling that even though the two of us are
taking the loan, it will be Aksel's apartment, and that with this
potential, disgusting but necessary purchase, I will become a
wife living off her husband's money.
    My mother asked, "Will both your names be on the deed?"
    "Yes, I think so."
    My mother said, "Hurry up and get married."

Today, writing is like walking into an expensive store where I
can't afford anything and the staff observe me with mild con-
tempt; my former teachers, the critics and the self-proclaimed
poets, the avant-gardists.

Friday, November 4, 2016
Fake flowers
Fake dewdrops on flowers

Croissants but miniature
Old nightgowns
The children's toys
An intoxicated woman
Doing things on the sly
is one of woman's greatest talents
a skill she has
honed since birth

Some people just love to be furious and I am one of those people.

20% OFF IS NOT A REAL DISCOUNT

Saturday, November 5, 2016
make money write poems lose weight starve apply eyeliner
the child

Monday, November 7, 2016
On this Monday in November when my child is seven months old, I am in an office among the yellow buildings of Södermalm, brimming with all the advice given to me about raising the child, pieces of advice that contradict each other, and it begins to snow outside the window on Stockholm's steepest street, Brännkyrkagatan.

All these men around me who say that women worry too much about their children haven't understood that everything around us installs women in worry machines, and that this worry is also a job, a duty. But how to phrase that?

To be a mother is to worry, and at the same time be dutifully ashamed of this worry. To be a woman is to know one must go hungry.

Today, a day when I can't gather my thoughts, I think I ought to write a long suite of poems about a postapocalyptic society where all the men have left the overpopulated cities to become traveling mercenaries guided by cryptic messages delivered by floating red balls, while the women are left behind, helpless and strangely elated, to shop and work in factories, and the light at sunrise and sunset takes on wonderful colors from the radiation.

Today, seven months since the birth, I can only understand the world in terms of men and nonmen, even though I know that's not how it is.

And on this Monday when it snows with insistent, Christmassy indifference, *I'm not writing a poem* about the bedspread from Hay photographed in every single apartment for sale on the listings site. And on this Monday, *I'm not writing a poem* about the emails I send back and forth with my bank to borrow money, *I'm not writing a poem* about the immense loneliness from before, that place where writing and anxiety reside, the place with no bottom or end.

And on this Monday when it's snowing in Stockholm, on Stockholm's canals and towers and on Stockholm's youths, who photograph the lights of the ice-skating rink at Kungsträdgården, I'm not writing about all the city's beggars; in Denmark begging is illegal and I have been spared poverty like a sheltered, sickly child, not writing about my country's new minority government formed without the popular vote, not writing about the doubts we harbor about each other after the child's birth, the overwhelming fear that our love can't withstand it, not writing about this fear, this destruction, the child's destruction that would be the end of our love. I'm not writing about what's behind this destruction, the knowledge that the child's destruction can never compare to the mythological destruction of our own childhood.

I'm not writing about something I read somewhere, about a philosopher who visits his mother with dementia in a nursing home, and his mother tells him she's in pain: "What hurts?" he asks, and she answers him, "My mother hurts." And he wrote that Alzheimer's patients often forget their own children, but almost never their parents.

On this Monday I'm not writing, not writing about the understanding that came with being a mother and not only a daughter: it's far easier to fail your child without feeling guilty.

Not writing about the relief that comes from understanding that I'm not attached to the child the same way I'm attached to my own mother. That the child is not my mother and I can therefore leave the child without falling apart.

Not writing that if I left the child, I wouldn't break but turn into a stone in order to do so.

Not writing about my love for the child which devours me.

Not writing about how the notion that the human psyche is established in the child's first three years in relation to the mother—in the symbiosis with the mother's body and the emancipation from it—the notion that the mother's absence or failures are fatally detrimental to the formation of our psyche and personality, is essentially misogynistic propaganda. And how this *arrangement* on this Monday when the snow is falling hard across the city, across Stockholm's buildings, the well-dressed Stockholmers, the platform-shoe wearers on the streets, how this *arrangement* prevents me from writing, from sitting on my own and writing on this day when my seven-month-old child is in the stroller with his father on a walk around the neighborhood so when the time comes I can return with my milk-filled breasts to feed him, how it makes me hate myself for hurting the child simply by longing to be away from him; how this notion of motherhood, this place, the mother-place, defined by performance and competition, prevents a natural connection between my child and me, prevents me from writing, prevents me from loving the child when the child is with me, prevents the child's father from carrying what could fall to him.

On this Monday, the day I have returned to my work: *to write*, here in a den of snow, the only thought that strikes me, again and again, is how my responsibility as a mother (and implicit in this responsibility, the warning that I could destroy a life far more easily than I could create one) prevents me from writing a word for fear that writing will shift not only my focus away from the child, but my whole being, and I *already* know that it is my duty to dedicate all of my being to the child, to make the child my life, to annihilate myself in the process. And with this annihilation, to annihilate the writer in me. But how?

The midwife who said, "Now we'll just have to wait and see how Mom's compulsive thoughts affect the baby."

I must stay in this not-writing writing place, neither writing nor not writing, on the edge of motherhood.

Wednesday, November 9, 2016
DONALD TRUMP: THE NEW US PRESIDENT
Dagens Nyheter

WORST SNOW IN STOCKHOLM IN 111 YEARS
Dagens Nyheter

Monday, November 28, 2016
Dear everybody,
I'm so sad and come to think of it, I don't even know what qualifications I have.

Sunday, December 18, 2016
I made spaghetti bolognese and the child tasted it for the first time, and was filled with glee.

It was a step into Real Mom territory.

It was a relief, and at the same time, like being stuffed into an ill-fitting form.

Fourth Continuation

Bottle versus breast

If I bottle-feed, the child becomes distinct to me and I understand that he's alive. I'm filled with tenderness for him, I'm bored.

When I breastfeed there is no such thing as time, and I feel nothing for the child. We're one and the same, and I don't understand that he exists independently of me.

It's the bottle that makes him human.

And with humanness comes devotion, impatience. Evening.

Bottle-feeding is like gazing at the sea, whereas in breastfeeding I become one with all water in the world. Without time, without love, without civilization. In the depths of breastfeeding, I'm lost and displaced, part of timeless nature.

As waves rush, the milk rushes through me with a patience only nature possesses.

This milk in me. In the child. A nonhuman language of nourishment.

If the child falls asleep at my breast at night, he lies still and sleeps deeply. But after a night bottle, he kicks off the duvet, babbles in his sleep, is like an underwater creature just hatched from its egg.

Fifth Continuation

Christmas shopping

*

once I earned 10,000 kroner
illustrating a department store Christmas catalog

they didn't declare it to the tax authorities

all the red mixing bowls
I had to draw
all the red things
on the Christmas pages

and the blue swimming pool–colored things
on another spread
for the men

about whom Marketing always complains
how are we meant to sell them anything

whereas women always buy things

a blue iPod and a towel
and a DAB radio
and a silver champagne cooler

we talk about male buyers
and male readers

about whether it's a book for men

they say it's women who read

down in Marketing

and in the newspapers

I don't know what that means

I just had to draw the red things on one page
and the blue things on another

and there were two pages with nothing but stockings
so I drew a bunch of legs
in the shape of a star

like a collection of past dismemberments

the nylon stockings' various
transparent and semitransparent patterns

the creative manager
absolutely insisted on
a photograph of a man and a woman
kissing and on the wall behind them
the shadow of their kiss
a sort of double kiss

I had to draw the storyboard
for the shoot
but it was impossible to draw

so I cried

I had three or four days
to complete the catalog

I learned many new words
words I have since carried with me
open-toe slingback

in the little staff room
where the creative manager
held out the shoe

the assistant took a picture with
his digital camera

and I made a note on my pad that said: shoe

I must have been twenty-one

this summer I drew Pogba on light-blue paper

in the garden

I hadn't drawn for many years

and then I drew him

the soccer star

drawing the things was easy

their shapes were conventional

an iPod a bowl

all the things to buy for Christmas

a baseball cap a stand mixer

a marzipan pig with a ribbon around its belly

I drew each purchase

all the purchases passed through my hands

the many socks and gloves

the reds and blues

all this for strangers

*
there were these girls
the institution taught me to hate

they stole from each other and the customers
and also from me

I could not
dress well be trendy

I could write bylines and
stay in the background

Cecilie was seventeen
and always said

she was on a cleanse

we circled around her in the office and said
don't you want some soup
don't you want some tea

they say she slept at the editor in chief's place
but that nothing happened

then she left for Los Angeles

with her parents

now she's in my poem
she probably wasn't expecting that

don't worry
I've changed her name

there was also Silke
with the big mouth

who would always criticize my family

as though she'd forgotten
I loved my family

despite their flaws

despite her never having met them

she only saw them once in the foyer

where my stepmother
had mentioned Shiseido mineral pearls
were her favorite beauty product

but the Shiseido mineral pearls
didn't do it for Silke

one morning Nikolaj
called me at the office

he wanted me to return
a bunch of cobalt blue
Comme des Garçons suits
to the boutique

because he had taken
too much cocaine

but I knew

that one of the lapels was stained

that they would lose their shit
at the boutique
in that strange glass and steel rotunda

on the border between
Hellerup and Østerbro

so I said
no Nikolaj
no I will not

and he was very astonished

don't know how
he got the matter resolved

I never understood
that the third part of a three-piece suit
was the vest

*

a bunch of people exit the delicatessen

each carrying a crate of clementines

a child in a pink puffer jacket her mother carries the bags

what one might call an elderly gentleman

each with their own crate of clementines

covering the clementines this little red net

like a veil or a mist

on the square

the city hall hovers in the sleet

and three girls sit beneath a marquee

at the café

watching me in the rain

I say I won't spend more than 300 kroner

but then I spend more

*

two hours later
and we buy a Christmas tree

in the courtyard I spotted
two very tall windows
next to ours
boarded up with Rockwool and foil

a secret life lives there

as though it were a waste
to be anyone at all

as if the very idea of a future had been discarded

decorating is my life
I love ornaments

a man and a woman
each at their end of the courtyard
in the courtyard in the rain
with blood in them
throw a glance at me
and each send their trash bag
down the garbage chute

its intestinal opening
or like the opening of rhubarb
pink-edged insides

I look at the things we call dead

I look at the things that barely live

I live as pure idiocy
the white milk like the dizzying interval

of not having eaten

I speak and burn myself on my voice

I carry fiction and its tropes
closer to my heart than facts

a flat-screen in the window opposite ours
is playing a documentary about the savanna
where big animals
lift their heads from the water hole
as if all living things came to life
in a pose

I'm the only one
who has made good use of myself
although both my employer and my partner
have tried

the years store their smell in me like a warehouse
the sky is the color of a cheap pair of silver socks

the air some kind of lavender

on the TV's savanna
the sun now sinks into the sea
like a star in a blue plum

birds flutter to rest in tall trees

a face speaks

the man in the window gets up and sits down at a desk

in front of the computer

he turns on a lamp as an offering

*

at the school for rich children
there was always a boy
who peed his pants
when he was picked up
I had a crush on one of the other substitute teachers
I wore this
really ugly
polyester acid-yellow H&M turtleneck

that accentuated my breasts
but was otherwise so hideous it hurt

this one time I took a shit
in the teachers' toilet
and it wouldn't flush

the toilet was located in a remote stairwell
between two of the school buildings
it was always chilly there

panicking
at the possibility of
my crush
finding my defecation
I fished it up and wrapped it

in toilet paper and threw it in
the wastebasket

I knew the cleaning staff
would empty the basket
at the end of the day

it was also during this time
I learned to use face powder

at the crosswalk my crush asked me
whether I was anorexic

we knew some of the same people
they played in the same band

later at the club
he got mad at me
for spreading a rumor about him

I said I hadn't
but he could tell
that I had

there was something about the brown color of the shit
and the scratchy yellow of the turtleneck

the two objects
entered into an alliance

that planned to eject me
from the world

a world
that would not accept me
as an object

now
the brown
and the bright yellowish-green
belong together
as an evil
only I know

*

inside the deli people are delighted by the snow

I buy the last jar of pickled red cabbage
two American men cautious and happy buy health food
and a lot of it

when I used to teach
I would always say

poetry wanted to initiate a conversation
with the world
only to realize
it was itself this world
with which it wanted to speak

and so it began to speak
of and with itself
and that was why
poetry
at its core
was more self-absorbed than prose

the students nodded and took notes

I'm not sure it's true but they understood something

they could later strip back off

apathy is the last thing I feel

after I started working in publishing
I realized
people don't buy books

Christmas pulls its teeth
through my nerves like a comb

I burn the way money burns

*

this was another job
it was at a café

there was no toilet
so you had to put up a sign

that read *back in five*
and go over to the stationery shop to pee

but I was afraid of the women there

some days there were almost no customers
the sun poured through the windows

I baked croissants and watered
the potted plants

and when I really needed to pee
I'd pee

in the back room

in a cup

the back room

was no bigger than a closet
there was a sink and a bucket and a mop

I squatted over the cup
but it overflowed

and the urine ran across the café's floor
I wiped it up as best I could

really I just wanted to be alone

Sixth Continuation

2 years, 9 months, and 4 days after the birth

I'm no longer afraid of the book, so I think I can finish writing it.

I can see in my mind what the final text will look like, and this vision is like an itch. I have to create a passage for this inner vision so it may become concrete, so I can give it away and find peace.

So much of this book has been about writing it. At no point did the form fall into place and write itself. The entire book had to be forced out. As though the book were a force that wanted to exist. And yet it is formless, and most of the time I have considered it a threat. I must start over, read every single word, adjust them, step inside, into the delivery room where the child was born.

Seventh Continuation

Dear Anna,

Does my work live up to the final text you envisioned? The one you've been writing about? I don't think so. I think a lot about what you would have done differently and am full of doubt.

Do you remember all those times when we would check whether he was breathing throughout the night? And we thought we wouldn't be able to tell if he was dying? And so he was always about to die without us being able to tell?

Today at the scan we heard the fetus's heartbeat for the first time. The boy is growing, he's doing well.

YOURS

Eighth Continuation

11-12 months after the birth

*

I've come down with it again
the maternity sickness
the tension in me
the deep envy
of everything that travels
that I have to stay
for so long in the worry
over the slightest thing
the child's clothes diaper coated tongue
long nails toys
with this useless
but apparently inescapable
tension and
disgust
with adult men
this morning
where we live in the wet fog
inside the mouth of the fog
he is on his way into the mist
in the window I watch him
and this disgust
I harbor
is impersonal
it is the sickness of women

in this time

the time of fog

the final days of maternity leave

an impersonal poison

*
all day
I carry around
the dream
in my ear
as if my ear
were plugged
with hair conditioner or
sperm
in the dream I was
pregnant with my
second child
and about to give birth
but the labor dragged on
for several days
the contractions weren't intensifying
we paced around the living room
called the hospital
at regular intervals
I felt strong
in the dream
in dreams
we had heard
that my ex
wanted to assume paternity
although there was no doubt

you were the father
we had heard
he had a rifle
there was a knock at the door
I had contractions

I know
what it means
to carry a
human being
inside my body
I know what
it means
to feel a human being
move
inside my body
among my organs
I know that
love
that's the difference between us
nobody can take that away from me

you opened the door
it was my ex
he barged in
he was hiding something
behind his back
it was a big
white syringe
and he squirted its
contents into my ear
screaming

you tried to stop him
it's an anesthetic
he shouted

I started to go numb
we have to hurry
he screamed
I've prepared the surgical instruments

we understood he was insane
he couldn't understand
there was a child inside me
there was a living child

he wanted
to operate on me like
in dreams
I began to lose
consciousness
because of
the medication
in my ear
I watched you fight
I drifted further away
as if my ear were pulling me
toward the ground
you screamed and shouted
I knew my child would die
while I was
unconscious
the catastrophe had caught up to us
all day long

with this medication of dreams
in my ear
so much anxiety
today
my heart in my throat
in the fabric store
in the checkout line
as if the man
from my dream might come
running and
attack me
any moment
the anxiety so acute
I can almost
extricate myself from
half of
what is me and
see it from the outside
as something
downright absurd or
amusing
playing out
in front of
the fabric store
April
one of the first
truly sunny days
I know these dreams
are the first sign
I am going mad

*

what I hate
about maternity leave
is not the child
not the housework
not the lack of sleep

but the moment
my husband
returns

and filled with
a whole day's longing
I go to him

so he will
take us
into his arms

the moment
he sinks into
the chair
exhausted

gone again
but present

toil surrounds us

onesies
matte plastic bottles
greasy pillows

rage destroys me

Ninth Continuation

2 years and 3 months after the birth

Very little to write today. It's 9:30 p.m. My husband is at work, the child is sleeping, tender-skinned and sweet. He said: Cuddle, and meant for me to stroke his fine hair.

Now, pouring in through the open kitchen window from the dark courtyard, half-hearted shouts of men watching soccer and the clattering of dishes being washed. I'm also washing dishes by the window, framed by the night and the housework.

Why am I trapped in the belief that writing about motherhood is shameful when I know that creating life where once there was none, creating flesh where once there was no flesh, is one of the most radical and outrageous things a person can do?

Tenth Continuation

Anna's journal, 2017

Friday, January 20, 2017
We've moved back to Denmark.
The child is 8 months and 15 days old.
Donald Trump was inaugurated as the US president today.
I constantly read the news online.

Thursday, January 26, 2017
SCIENTISTS CREATE FETUS THAT IS HALF PIG, HALF
HUMAN
Politiken

Monday, February 6, 2017
It's as though everything around me can enter into this journal. As soon as I go out onto the street I experience something that should go in the book. It overwhelms me so much I can't write. I become paralyzed and instead read the news online. It's as though life itself is literature. As though what I am living is text. Who is Anna?

My maternity leave is over, and I try to get out the door quickly in the morning so I can work in the early hours. I don't have any employment right now but am trying to write. Aksel is surly, almost sad when I leave, he always exits the room as soon as I hug the boy goodbye, and I end up sitting with him on my lap when I ought to leave while Aksel races about making banana pancakes, cleaning up, calling the nursery to check our place on the waitlist, and then I remember how we used to work like mad before the child was born, before I got pregnant.

At Emmery's Bakery on Nordre Frihavnsgade, the builders are arguing, they puff themselves up with imposing authority when their clients from the neighboring buildings walk in. Children wearing expensive sneakers pass by.

Tuesday, February 7, 2017
I bid on a hundred-year-old art deco sofa online even though I couldn't afford it. I don't know why I did it.

Anxiety gripped me. I can't gauge the state of my finances.

If something reaches a high enough price, I'll pay anything for it. The object's value becomes incomprehensible and the price stops making sense.

Friday, February 17, 2017
In the dark, when I put the boy to bed and nursed him to sleep, his little hand squeezed my breast repeatedly to make the milk run quicker. He milked me.

Did it feel more uncomfortable because he's a boy, a man-to-be?

Would I have viewed the situation differently had he been a girl?

The infant's greed.

These thoughts in the dark made me sad, and I was ashamed of them.

The child doesn't know he has a sex, only that he's hungry.

Writing about this makes me nervous.

Do I look at my child differently because he is male?

Must I always be honest with myself?

I've started thinking of my thoughts as sentences that must

be written in a journal. But then they drift away, and I don't write them down.

It's as though another Anna thinks these thoughts and I regard her emotions with curiosity from a distance.

Thursday, February 23, 2017
A dirty book, a misshapen book, a book cut wrong. A book that can't keep thought clean, time clean. A book written in the child's time. A chopped-up, stuttering book. A book with bottomless holes to fall into, like never-ending breastfeedings. A book full of doubt. A book struggling with achievement. Not a book that is an achievement. But a book that came of pleasure and horror. A book that either illuminates or erases its tracks?

Not a book about the right thing to do, to think, to be, but a book that creates space for pain and from this space engenders a possible future happiness.

A book that can save me. A book I write to survive.

Friday, February 24, 2017
Something that is not the child, from before the child was born, I call this something writing.

But is writing only a ritual for living?

Not to be a bad mother, not to be a good mother, but a living human being in the world.

Sunday, February 26, 2017
Is there a single thing happening in my life that has not been happening all my life?

Today, only this thought: the dolls were preparation.

Wednesday, March 1, 2017
Health and well-being should not be assessed based on an individual day, but the child's health and well-being overall. Is the child

happy? Is the child growing as it should? Does the child eat? Is
the child clean? Is there a strong bond with the parents? Meaning
should not be derived from the particular, but from the whole.

Thursday, March 16, 2017
I realized that in order to survive I had to eradicate the deep-rooted idea that everything would become easier when my husband came home from work.

All of the child's life, I have believed the work would stop when he came home, but the dirty dishes are still piling in the sink, and the child is still screaming, and dinner still needs to be cooked.

I need to stop thinking that my husband can see all these things that need doing and instead understand that I alone read the apartment as a to-do list that needs completing to sustain the child's standard of living. In this way, I have entered into a quiet pact with the objects, like being a child among toys. As a child, my toys always wanted to tell me something. The rubber pacifier's honey-colored latex, boiled and drying off in the orange colander, and under the holes of the bowl, the dark wood countertop, like an abyss. I live with these images of the child's things inside me.

Friday, March 17, 2017
What's worse: a child dressed in rags with a well-dressed mother, or a well-dressed child with a mother in rags?

Monday, March 27, 2017
I was taught that the partner, the husband, was supposed to see and share my innermost feelings, that I should live life turned toward him. That I, fierce in my loyalty, should live under his protection.

But when the child was born and my husband had to return

to work shortly after, when I cried on the phone in the early months, when I did this work—making a child—about which he was clueless, a work no one saw; when I had to lie to him about how his minimal efforts were equal to mine while I bled from wounds in inner organs he did not have, had to show him gratitude to make him stay, soothe his nerves, I understood there was no one with whom to share my innermost feelings. Our paths diverged. And after motherhood, the dream of an absolute romantic love was lost.

Our love now seemed like a mere ripple on a lake, at the bottom of which I live. I can breathe underwater. And no one shall know me.

I was taught that my husband knew me, and that I should turn my whole heart toward him, and now here I am, a dumb water lily under the water's glaze, and I see that it was all a lie. There is no man to turn my heart toward. It makes me furious. To become a mother is to lose the dream of a husband.

Wednesday, March 29, 2017
I kissed the boy and lifted him up in the pale winter sun, his little face beaming at me.

Thursday, April 6, 2017
I must rescue as if from a fire the parts that are still important to me, the parts I wrote while I was still there; as if time were a bonfire devouring memory by memory the person I was so I can no longer remember, much less understand what happened.

I walk into the future with a fire at my heels.

Eleventh Continuation

Dear Anna,

I don't know why I'm writing to you, seeing as you won't read it. Maybe somehow I'm hoping that if this book is ever published, you'll read it and find this letter among the pages.

I'm now in my fourth month of pregnancy. It has gone well so far, but in the past weeks something has crept up on me which reminds me of the things you describe.

For every day the child grows, I feel how I'm opened toward the world, how every sense is sharpened, and it's unbearable. The whole world is an inferno of sound and light pouring into me like big torrents of water. I become irritated, and everything scares me. Is this where you were, Anna? Is this how it was for you? Will it be the same for me? Are you what awaits me?

It's becoming increasingly difficult for me to pay our bills, and I have an agreement with the tax authorities to pay back 10,000 kroner a month. It's August, and I have almost no money left. I need 100,000 kroner to get me through this year if I'm to pay the taxes I owe. I don't know where I'll get the money. I'm thinking I'll have to sell these papers to a publisher and make a book of it. Maybe that's my only option.

I'll have to bluff and demand a big advance. And hope more work will turn up later. But whose name do I put on the manuscript?

The boy is doing just fine.

YOURS

Twelfth Continuation

The pregnancy journal

September 3, 2015—Week 6 + 0
I write this only for myself, though it's nearly impossible.

I'm seven weeks along.

We're looking for a place to live and have rented a studio apartment on Amagerbrogade for a month.

Something very strange is happening.

At night I get up and look around. I can't understand who Aksel is. I don't understand that I'm pregnant with his child. It's not too late to leave the apartment and Aksel and have an abortion. Something very strange is drawing to a close, and I feel I'm confronting death. I'm not filled with fear, but with an almost malicious emptiness, like the pause before a raised hand strikes. I'm by a gray sea on a damp beach in cold weather. I go to the bathroom to pee.

In the morning, very little of this remains, and I know I want the child.

Some days I've had brief spells of extreme nausea, but mostly I've felt as if I have the flu, for almost two or three weeks. My breasts and nipples are sore, my appetite is weak, and then there's my teeth: the gums around my wisdom tooth are infected, it has spread to my throat and jaw, and even though I have a fever and intense pain, I don't dare take painkillers because I've read online that they can cause ADHD in the child. The dentist won't pull the tooth as long as I'm pregnant, but has prescribed penicillin.

Yesterday Aksel chipped the bottom of my front tooth when we were having sex. His teeth knocked against mine, I spit out a shard of tooth, we laughed and carried on, the chip was an old injury. They easily glued it back on.

I think the child is taking all my energy and nutrients, I'm very tired and sickly, feeble.

September 6, 2015—Week 6 + 3
Still have a cold, but less so.
I've been invited to speak about my books at a creative writing school in Gothenburg.
I don't know what to say. I can't write.
Is my relationship to language changing?
I no longer know whether writing is important.
I don't feel up to it.
Is it because of the pregnancy?
I have slight morning sickness, tender breasts.
I have no appetite.
Perhaps I should think of writing as a *Sims* game I play at night, where books are tomes placed on a bookshelf in the avatar's house in its *quest to become an author.*
I feel outside the world.
Now I have to take stock of what I have previously published, and it's like nausea.
I miss drinking.

September 8, 2015—Week 6 + 5
Catastrophic thought no. 1
I tell my dad I'm pregnant. He's shocked and disappointed. He doesn't think Aksel is good enough to be the father of my child. He says he thinks I ought to carefully consider whether

I want to keep the child. He says: If you must, wouldn't it be better with someone else? He says: Are you sure it's a good idea? He encourages me to have an abortion. I'm forced to cut contact, tell him I don't want to see him again.

Catastrophic thought no. 2
My parents don't want me and therefore don't want my child. My pregnancy grieves and disgusts them.

Catastrophic thought no. 3
It's my own fault I feel so horrible in the first trimester because I never exercise.

Catastrophic thought no. 4
When my dentist tells me to relax my shoulders, it's not because she wants me to relax, but because she thinks I have bad posture.

Catastrophic thought no. 5
When my dad tells me to relax my shoulders, it's not because he wants me to relax, but because he thinks I have bad posture.

Catastrophic thought no. 6
I am bad.

Catastrophic thought no. 7
I'm going to lose the child.

September 9, 2015—Week 6 + 6
Lightly persistent, all-pervading nausea.
    Or am I just imagining it?
    On the train to Gothenburg, I feel plastic-like and minia-ture, like a child's toy ring.

Are all these notes merely about writing?
Have I forgotten the pregnancy?
I carry it with me like a star waiting to shoot.

When I look at pictures of myself, I always look innocent in the photographs where I felt the worst.

September 11, 2015—Week 7 + 1
Almost every night I wake up with this surreal feeling. I get up to pee. I don't understand who Aksel is. What I mean is, I don't understand the concept *another person*.

September 16, 2015—Week 7 + 6
Catastrophic thought no. 8
Each time I eat or drink something, I'm overcome by the fear that what I just consumed is toxic to my child, and that I've forgotten or am too irresponsible to keep track of what you are and aren't allowed to eat, and now it's too late.

Catastrophic thought no. 9
When I go to the hospital to have blood tests done, the nurse will be able to tell that I'm crazy, she will have me committed on the spot, a man will come to diagnose me and assess whether I'm fit to keep the child.

Catastrophic thought no. 10
When Aksel and I get divorced, in court he will emphasize my acute anxiety and the fact that I'm hiding a grave insanity and thereby gain custody of the child. Deep down I know it's best I be freed of the child as its existence exposes the madness I conceal. This thought scares me to death.

Catastrophic thought no. 11
The more my anxiety intensifies, the greater the chance of miscarriage.

September 24, 2015—Week 9 + 0
Whenever I have an anxiety attack—and they're getting more and more frequent—I've started to check for blood. The panic is like a stranger inside me who wants to exorcise the child. Or it's my double, the other Anna, who has no control, no desire or will, who is only fear. A fear that kills and lies fallow.

The pregnancy is not a child possessing me like an evil spirit, but a terrible destruction that has flown into me. An enormous hand of darkness that can rake its fingers through me like a comb through hair. But I don't think the evil spirit entered with the child; it has been hibernating, and the child's presence has awakened it.

September 28, 2015—Week 9 + 4
When 2 become 3—sex after birth

Pregnancy is natural and normal
During pregnancy, a number of physiological and hormonal changes may cause uncomfortable side effects in the form of fatigue and nausea. For both men and women, pregnancy may be a time of increased reflection: Am I satisfied with my life? How was my own childhood? What kind of parent will I be? And what will my partner be like?

These are all good questions to consider, but they may leave you feeling more vulnerable, more insecure or fearful than usual.

If your sex drive disappears
Some women—and men—may lose the desire for sex at the

beginning of pregnancy. For the woman, this may be due to increased fatigue and/or nausea, but just as often the reason is a fear of sex hurting the child or leading to miscarriage (sex during pregnancy is generally considered safe and does not cause miscarriage). Another explanation could be that the physical and emotional demands of pregnancy cause the woman to develop a greater need for privacy in relation to her body. During pregnancy she shares her body with the child and some women require a period of time during which the partner does not also make claims on her body.

For the man, it can be difficult to understand that the woman pulls away. Since he is not pregnant he may, in contrast to the woman, crave physical connection to feel he is part of the pregnancy and the expected child.

September 30, 2015—Week 9 + 6
Phone appointment
Pt says she suffered from depression in 20xx and was treated with Citalopram and Mirtazapine. Pt believes the depression was triggered by anxiety symptoms. Pt experienced another period of instability in 20xx after breakup with boyfriend. Pt received medication for eight months. Pt has not taken medication for the past year. Pt is aware of anxiety symptoms during periods of acute stress. Pt offered support via the Perinatal Mental Health Clinic. Pt is open to additional treatment options during pregnancy.

Pregnancy worries
Pt expresses high degree of worry about:
    "My housing situation," "Something being wrong with the child," "Ending up in the hospital," "The risk of miscarriage."
    Other worries: "Becoming mentally ill, being a bad mother."

Interpreter
Reads and understands Danish, nationality Danish, languages Danish, English, Swedish.

Employment
Employed

October 6, 2015—Week 10 + 5
Always this fear that when they see me they'll lock me up and at the same time the conviction they will soon tell me that nothing is wrong with me and all I have to do is pull myself together.

October 22, 2015—Week 13 + 0
Risk of Down syndrome is less than 1:300 therefore CVS and amniocentesis have not been offered. Screening test for defects not performed.

October 24, 2015—Week 13 + 2
If I gave birth today, would the fetus have any chance of survival? No. The first twelve weeks have gone by without losing the child, and without me choosing to lose it. Aksel said: Aren't you happy? Isn't it great? But I could only smile a little, as if the happiness couldn't fill the bottle inside me. A quiet joy that ran through me like a river in a landscape of unease.

October 25, 2015—Week 13 + 3
Only when I turned twenty-five did I start taking an interest in women. Until then, I couldn't understand what good they were to me.

What I'm learning now, in the madness of pregnancy, is that men and women are not equal. Suddenly all women look like wonderful, lost territories to me. Paradise upon paradise.

October 27, 2015—Week 13 + 5
As I write this, I'm standing beneath the park's reddening trees. It's evening, a foggy October, the streetlights have damp halos. A smell of rot from the bushes. I am one of the women who exist in secret.

November 5, 2015—Week 15 + 0
Tomorrow is our first appointment with the midwife. I have to ask her why I can't sleep when I'm so tired. About childbirth class, the child's size and weight and my weight, when our next appointment is, the pain in my left side, my loss of appetite and nausea, constipation.

What if she can tell I'm going mad? What if she tells me I'm asking for too much? What if she opens a door to a distant room where young women sit on chairs weeping with disheveled hair and violet dresses; what if my midwife points at them and says: Surely, now you can see that you have nothing to worry about, you're not wearing a purple dress, you've showered and are able to smile. These women, they're the ones you're depriving of help when you come waltzing in here with your complaints, your small problems like droplets of rain on a window you can easily wipe away, Anna, pull yourself together, Anna. It doesn't actually hurt, you're only pretending, a childhood game you couldn't let go of. I am appalled, Anna, by your impatient, spoiled heart that believes it's entitled to my help.

November 6, 2015—Week 15 + 1
Supplementary information
Pt encouraged to resume psychological treatment. Looks forward to having a child, happy to be pregnant. Afraid that she, the child, or the child's father will die.

November 7, 2015—Week 15 + 2

The midwife said by week 25 you should be able to feel signs of life every day. I haven't felt anything yet, but it's still early. Maybe the child is dead. I went to the doctor and cried. I said: I'm afraid I'm going mad. It took all my strength to say it. I felt immense shame. The doctor slowly turned from her computer to me and said: That's a very common symptom of anxiety. I felt dry inside, a static crackle, as if my skin were shriveling. I was in the gray room before darkness falls, where everything is gray but you can still guess its color. Is the child in there? Is it alive? It's impossible to see. I forced myself to go to a secondhand store on Jægersborggade and buy a sweater for a newborn.

November 8, 2015—Week 15 + 3

Do I understand all major life events primarily through shopping?

November 18, 2015—Week 16 + 6

Hilma or Elma, if it's a girl.

November 19, 2015—Week 17 + 0

At night, the child's first life sign.

November 21, 2015—Week 17 + 2

Precautions during pregnancy: dos and don'ts

—Buy ecolabeled products (see what the labels look like on page 12).

—Minimize the use of personal care products.

—Study the list of ingredients before buying personal care products.

—Consult the manufacturer's website to study the list of ingredients before buying cleaning agents and detergents.

—If you're concerned about a certain chemical in a product, you can look it up online.

—Remove the packaging of any newly purchased items for your home or child and air out the items for at least several hours before using them. Additionally, the items should be washed and cleaned, if possible.

—Wash new clothes before wearing them.

—Avoid large, predatory fish when pregnant or breastfeeding, and consume organic foods.

—Read this pamphlet.

If you experience unexpected leakage or letdown, nursing pads can prove helpful. Since the pads are placed directly against your skin where the child will nurse, it is important that the pads are chemical-free. To ensure that the nursing pads do not contain fragrance, dyes, moisturizers, or chlorine, purchase brands certified with an ecolabel. Consider purchasing and using rewashable and reusable pads.

If you experience sore nipples from breastfeeding and are concerned about the environment and your health, consider purchasing a nipple cream that is certified with an ecolabel.

You can use a nursing pillow to support your arms while breastfeeding. However, the fabric and foam filling of nursing pillows may contain halogenated flame retardants linked to fetal defects, cancer, endocrine disruption, decreased fertility, and environmental damage. Repeated exposure to formaldehyde can cause cancer and allergies.

Using ecolabel-certified wet wipes for your baby ensures minimal exposure to fragrance and other chemicals. Alternatively, make your own wet wipes by packing moistened washcloths or disposable washcloths into plastic bags. Use caution when selecting plastic bags. Garbage bags and brightly colored grocery bags are not suitable as they contain harmful chemicals that can leach into the wet wipes.

Voluminous hair, a signature perfume, a beautiful tan, silky skin, and eye-catching makeup. The world is full of products to pamper yourself with. But these products may contain toxic chemicals that are hazardous for the environment and for you and your child's health.

Many spray products contain aerosols, which can lead to lung damage when inhaled. To avoid this, consider not using spray deodorant and hair spray.

If planning to become pregnant, consider letting your natural hair color grow out as the chemicals in hair dye may be absorbed into the mother's bloodstream and passed on to the fetus.

Shellfish and predatory fish can contain a higher amount of heavy metals and other harmful chemicals in their bodies. However, fish remains a key source of nutrition so pregnant women are advised to continue eating a variety of fish, except predatory fish. Pregnant women, breastfeeding mothers, and children up to three years of age should not consume shark, swordfish, and large predatory freshwater fish. Follow the Food Authority's advice online.

Baby products such as mattresses and electronics may contain flame retardants. Halogenated flame retardants have been linked to endocrine disruption among other effects. Unfortunately, the use of these retardants has not been banned in all children's products. Use caution and contact the manufacturer to ask if their products contain these chemicals or find information about the product online.

During pregnancy, exposure to organic solvents may cause harm to you and your baby. Solvents can, for example, be found in shoe polish or waterproof sealants. If you need to shine your shoes or boots or waterproof your clothes or shoes while pregnant, consider asking someone else to do it. Outdoors is best.

Perhaps you have plans to renovate or decorate a nursery or children's room. If pregnant or breastfeeding, consider asking someone else to plaster, paint, or wallpaper and, of course, make sure your child does not enter the room until everything is dry.

The home is full of things a baby comes into contact with, and many of these common household items contain hazardous substances, for example cables and wires contain plasticizers. Even a marker pen may prove harmful. Consider avoiding contact with objects that are not intended for small children and babies.

Many common household items release various chemicals. For example, chemicals from flame retardants can leak from electronics into dust and into the air inside the home. And new furniture can off-gas formaldehyde for years. Therefore, frequent vacuuming and dusting to keep your home clean is advisable. Airing out frequently is also recommended, if doing so two to three times a day is not already part of your daily routine.

November 22, 2015—Week 17 + 3
Annihilation of Anna through repetition.

December 4, 2015—Week 19 + 1
I'm vomiting again. But it's a different sort of nausea than in the first trimester. I feel I may be losing my mind.

December 5, 2015—Week 19 + 2
While I was cooking in the kitchen, a knife went through me, severing me from the child in my belly. I was filled with a dark desire to go to Vienna and stay at a hotel, drink spritzes and have lovers. Now we're tied to each other through the child, Aksel and me. I can't deny the beauty in that. We say we will be equal, equals in raising the child. But we aren't equals, I'm the one carrying it. I'm the one carrying the fear inside me.

December 7, 2015—Week 19 + 4
My doctor repeats that thinking you're going insane is a very common symptom of anxiety, but that the nausea is concerning. It's impossible to get an appointment with the psychologist.

December 8, 2015—Week 19 + 5
Don't tell men that pregnant women can't think. That they can't read. That the devil is an invention that originated in a pregnant woman.

December 11, 2015—Week 20 + 1
My midwife has referred me to an anxiety program, an out-

patient offer through Rigshospitalet. We also offer treatment here, she said, but it's intended for girls who have trouble developing an attachment to the child. The alien expression scared me and it has haunted me ever since. Attachment to the child. Attachment to the child. She should never have told me.

December 18, 2015—Week 21 + 1
Supplementary information
Pt feeling unwell. Experiencing increased anxiety and trouble sleeping. Pt's nausea has also returned, presumably due to increased fatigue. Has been referred to psychologist by GP, but waitlist is long. Pt has practically given up on making an appointment. Conference with coordinator XX who advises that Pt is given referral from own GP via Psychiatric Assessment Center for evaluation re treatment for anxiety. Pt accompanied by child's father today. Is supportive of Pt.

December 29, 2015—Week 22 + 5
At night fear grips me. The darkness in the apartment is like walking into a curtain of chiffon that cuts my eyes, like the finest raw mesh, I'm pushed through it; the colorlessness before dark falls. I throw myself to the floor and roll around, hissing, eyes rolled back, flickering. Aksel is sitting on the floor, hiding his face between his knees. Help me, help me, I wheeze. But what can he do to help? The child is living in me, and I live beside it, like a split body sharing the same skin.

January 7, 2016—Week 24 + 0
Psychiatric assessment
Consultation with XX
Clinic for Anxiety and OCD

Psychiatric history

At age 10–11, Pt began experiencing symptoms of anxiety, recalls it being very difficult to cope with already then. Pt describes difficulty eating as a teenager, was underweight, weighed around 40 kg. Pt has been in treatment for eating disorders and fears relapse after giving birth, but not currently. In 20xx, when Pt turns 23, Pt experiences severe depression, is treated with Citalopram and Mirtazapine. Weight loss down to 42 kg as result of depression. Subsequently experiences feelings of anxiety. In 20xx Pt's breakup with boyfriend is followed by anxiety and insomnia. Pt was treated with Mirtazapine for sleep, which helped. Pt also saw a psychologist, 12 sessions, CBT. Pt meets new boyfriend, and in June 20xx Pt is feeling well enough to stop taking Mirtazapine. In Oct / Nov last year 20xx, Pt experiences relapse of anxiety symptoms. Pt is 24 weeks pregnant.

Current symptoms

Pt describes panic attacks in which she experiences sweating, heart palpitations, difficulty breathing, tension and numbness.

Typical behaviors include crying spells, screaming and rolling around on the floor. Pt has started avoiding coffee, exercise, long trips and cinemas.

Sometimes Pt avoids social situations, especially situations with many people.

Thoughts

Pt expresses fear of pain and fear of losing her mind when she feels anxious. Interprets her anxiety symptoms as evidence of insanity.

Fears these feelings, fears scaring her close friends and family or pushing them away. Fears losing social status, experiences discomfort at feeling this way at her workplace and often feels performance anxiety at work. Pt also fears that friends, colleagues, and family will lose respect for her. Pt also describes a pang of social anxiety, is afraid that people who don't know her will find her ugly or strange, also worries about the embarrassment of having panic attacks in front of other people. Pt's diagnosis: F41.0 panic disorder and F41.1 generalized anxiety disorder.

Social history
Pt lives with partner of past few years. Freelances as author of fiction. Has published books. Says finances are fine but fluctuate. Pt says she has a handful of friends and a few close female friends, which is new to her and has only happened in recent years. Has not previously mentioned wanting to form relationships with peers.

Mental status examination
Pt initially presents as nervous, but calms down over the course of the session. Exhibits strong formal and emotional contact. Pt receives psychoeducation during session and quickly responds positively. No sign of cognitive distortions, tone of voice is neutral.

Pt's personal goals
Pt wants to be less impacted by anxiety in day-to-day life. Pt wants to do something about panic attacks and her fear of these.

Summary incl. suicide risk assessment
Pt is a 29-year-old woman, 24 weeks pregnant, referred for panic disorder and generalized anxiety disorder with onset in

early adulthood. Previous eating disorder and underweight, not a current issue. Pt experiencing relapse of anxiety-related symptoms brought on by first pregnancy, not currently assessed as depressed or suffering from eating disorder.

Suicide risk assessment 1, no increased risk of suicide.

January 9, 2016—Week 24 + 2
There is a flaw in me that will spread like a disease to the child. Is there no room for a mother to be in doubt? Is there no room inside her? How have I become this temple of flesh? I have been hidden away behind a curtain in the back room, where I sit in the dark and damp, chewing bay leaves, raving mad. I ought to be outlawed. They should outlaw me. Pt is a 29-year-old woman, 6 months pregnant, who may contain hazardous chemicals that could be harmful to the child.

January 11, 2016—Week 24 + 4
I took a flight to Oslo for work, no one gave me their seat at the gate or stood aside for me on the plane. No one gets up for me on the bus. It hurts to stand and walk. I am a 29-year-old state-owned milkmaid. I am a campaign. I am not real. The entire population of Denmark is entitled to my body.

January 20, 2016—Week 25 + 6
Referred to physiotherapist for increasing back pain. Ball exercises followed by Pilates.

February 4, 2016—Week 28 + 0
at the Clinic for Anxiety and OCD
on Nannasgade
everything is shabby
and the doctors smile
apologetically

they look like
normal people

I disinfect
my hands

we want to
help you
but there are
only so many of us
to go around

behind a door
group therapy

calm voices
the young people
talk about
hopelessness

the chief physician says
everyone with anxiety
has a sprinkle of something else

I don't want to
spread the bedsheet
across the frozen grass

hopelessness sure
says a young man

it's not my job
to inform you

any further

you must believe me
when I tell you
I'm six months pregnant

I am a resilient person

the clinic on Nannasgade
the shabby stairway
the shabby bathrooms

the girls with
flawless makeup smoke
by the entrance

February 20, 2016—Week 30 + 2
Carrying the child and feeling it move is pure bliss. I understood in my bones that my mother must love me. You can't
help but love what you have borne into the world. A few
months ago, when Aksel felt the child kick for the first time, he
yanked back his hand, startled, and said *oh*, he looked terrified.
I laughed, and then he laughed too. He became sentimental.
I could tell he was experiencing something important, but it
was still only a fraction of what I'm experiencing. I'm many
months ahead of him. He talks about going to a children's
theater festival soon after the birth, he talks about going to
Mexico, to Paris. He really has no idea what's in store for him.
I could try to explain it to him, but it's pointless. This knowledge that life is forever changed for the both of us, I carry it
alone, and it feels as though I have to protect him from this
insight. I'm tired of his happy, open face, of him not getting

it. He has no pregnancy hemorrhoids, no yeast infection, no sciatica pain, no locked pelvis, I told him: You can walk away from it all and I can't, that's the difference. He said: What do you mean? I can't walk away. But he doesn't understand that what binds him to the family is his moral duty and his love, while I can't afford morals, I don't have the option of choosing the child. Being pregnant is being subject to an impending, incomprehensible fate, spun inside a painful enigma. If only I had the option to say: *No, I don't want to after all*, perhaps the shame wouldn't be so great. If I think that way now, it's the same as wanting the child dead. Why do I feel forced to want the pregnancy at every waking moment? How does a pregnant woman step away from her pregnancy? How does she put it aside in order to breathe, to grasp the scope of what is happening? The answer is that she cannot. There is no respite for the pregnant woman. She is a constant in creation.

When Aksel and I go to a screening or a checkup at the midwife's together, no one speaks to him. When we're given a pamphlet on food or nursing or sex after childbirth or harmful chemicals in the home, I'm the one they hand it to. Everyone around us lectures me, tells me what to do and what not to do, gives me tips and advice, and hardly anyone says anything like that to Aksel. As a result of all these tips and advice, I'm constantly thinking about infant care, about the various sleep techniques and theories, about childcare philosophies, about co-sleeping and hanging cradles and cloth diapers and baby carriers.

I wanted Aksel to buy some luxurious organic cloth diapers at the department store because I was in too much pain to walk but craved the cloth diapers with a deep hunger. He chose the color, green. Although I would have chosen a different color, I felt he ought to have the experience of buying something for the child. I have bought all the clothes, all the toys until now, although we're still missing a few things. When I described which floor Aksel would find these cloth diapers on and told him what they cost, he said: "Why can't we just use dishcloths? I really don't get what they are, these *cloth diapers*." And I rolled my eyes, I couldn't explain it to him, couldn't put it into words. Far too many feelings and far too much significance was folded into these cloth diapers, they were an entire language I could not translate for him.

February 27, 2016—Week 31 + 2
What I thought was a good man. Month 8. Who is he? That I am alone with the child.

March 24, 2016—Week 35 + 0
Individual session
Pt attends session. Acceptance- and mindfulness-based psychoeducation and is given homework. Pt is strongly motivated but also finds it demanding. Is increasingly aware of own catastrophic thoughts and self-criticism, which reinforce anxiety.

March 31, 2016—Week 36 + 0
One month until the due date today.

April 7, 2016—Week 37 + 0
The evil spirit, sleeping. I am embroidering.
   The child at once less fathomable and more flesh than ever. I can't walk. My belly finally big. Braxton Hicks. All day alone in the apartment. Every day the same now. Wanted to fetch milk from the store. A liter. Nothing else. Waddled off in pain, my belly tightened, then grew hard. The large muscle is practicing.

I can't go to work, but must lie down as much as possible for the remainder of the pregnancy. The doctor used the term: full bed rest. In his office, I suddenly thought of this expression: a pound of meat. And then imagined a handbag of meat. We shook hands. This blue milk carton, cold with condensation in my hand under the leafless trees along the boulevard, and above me the March sky, pale and open like a roll of gauze. I pour the milk into me, into the muggy darkness of pregnancy, so Satan falls into a deep sleep. A little dog. As was intended. I bathe my face in the light falling from the day. It's noon. I'm pregnant. Pt is a 37-week-pregnant female. And the child unfurls calmly in my belly like a hand or petals in red water. I'm a container and also what I've always been: a soul. How to play both roles at once? How does a handbag speak? This is my story. This is a mother speaking. A mother-to-be. Your mother, mine. She is not happy. Her happiness does not depend solely on her child. At times she must turn away from her child. And your mother's happiness, her big smile when she walks toward you, you're eight or nine maybe, waiting outside school, you're a girl or a boy, you're wearing a rucksack, and this radiant face comes toward you, you think that your mother's longing is longing away from you, and that her wanting something else is proof that she doesn't want you. You're wearing a red beret, and she a yellow coat, together you're colorful, she runs her fingers through your hair, you know that there is a plastic comb at the bottom of her bag made of imitation bone, your mother's hair, now you remember the smell, your stories are inextricable, if she walks in a direction that isn't toward you, it doesn't mean you'll lose her. You think that a child must be a mother's all, and who taught you that? No wonder you're afraid of annihilation. You think that if your mother wants something other than you, it's a sign of your inadequacy, and who taught you that? You think you've got to be everything for your mother, and that she must be nothing else but you. And who taught the two of you that? No wonder you're afraid of annihilation. It isn't true. You walk hand in hand.

April 14, 2016—Week 38 + 0
Individual session
Pt employs and benefits from cognitive restructuring but has difficulty using acceptance-based strategies due to emotional evasiveness.

April 24, 2016—Week 39 + 3
Braxton Hicks contractions—
18:51
19:02
19:10
19:19 (strong)
19:28 (strong)
19:36 (weak)
19:39
19:41
20:25
20:42

April 25, 2016—Week 39 + 4
Braxton Hicks contractions—
20:50
20:56

April 28, 2016—Week 40 + 0
Individual session
Pt came to session. Has passed due date, not yet given birth.

Today worked with restructuring of negative automatic thoughts regarding childbirth and parenting abilities. New appointment scheduled for next month.

Week 40 + 6
Braxton Hicks contractions—
9:32
9:43
9:49
9:53

MDT meeting
Pt has had 8 individual consultations with me for the purpose of relieving anxiety symptoms brought up again by current pregnancy. Pt has improved panic disorder symptoms and it has become clear that these are linked to unstable sense of self and relational difficulties caused by fear of being unwanted and judged as abnormal and unfit to be a mother. The therapy form has initially been cognitive, but Pt has profited most from talk therapy when working with relational difficulties. It is agreed that Pt will complete current treatment within the next three months. Referral to further treatment encouraged in which Pt can work on strengthening sense of self and improving relational difficulties. Currently no grounds for concern for the unborn child.

Thirteenth Continuation

2.5 years after the birth

After I picked him up from the nursery, the boy ran into the kindergarten's playground and hid.

The older children weren't out. I walked beneath the trees and saw him disappear into a playhouse at the far end of the playground. Once I was inside, he was already gone, but on the wooden floor was a big chalk circle the children had drawn, and it looked like the remnants of a magic ritual.

I heard the boy's voice and I answered. He keeps calling for me, only to ask that I turn around or leave. I have to respond each time so he's assured that I'm there on the outskirts of his lonesome game.

I picked up a piece of chalk and drew a circle around the children's circle.

Maybe the book I'm writing when I write about motherhood is actually my life.

I'm not shattered, but suspended in air, exhausted like autumn leaves falling from the tree branches.

Fourteenth Continuation

Dear Anna,

I've met with the editor a few times. Each time, we have discussed which name should be on the book. They hope to publish next year. The editor wants my name on the cover because you're not here, but also because I have already, as he put it, "written a couple books." (Maybe that's why you left the papers to me? Perhaps you thought I knew what a book was?)

It would be a bit strange for me to be the author of the book since I didn't write it. But he's insistent, and I don't think I can change his mind. He also asked me to change some of the texts he thought were badly written, and I let him believe that I would, but of course I would never do that, Anna!

If things go as the editor says they will and this is published, and one day, somewhere in the world, you step into a bookshop and pick up this book and see that it's yours, and if you get so far as to read these words, even though I know the chances are slim, I want to thank you. If you hadn't left the papers with me, we wouldn't have got through this year financially. When you gave them to me, I had no idea they were so valuable.

The boy is doing well in kindergarten, but he misses his friends from the nursery. He chipped his tooth on the playground the other day, but you can hardly tell. He eats well and is developing as a child should.

I'm hard at work with your papers. Though I'm the one they call the author, I don't compare and I think we've both always known that. That's why there was always this pain between us which verged on devotion.

I can only imagine what you're writing now, Anna.

YOURS

Fifteenth Continuation

Anything meaningful she preferred to do in secret. Like an animal, she would quietly approach all the world's objects and with a touch dissolve the boundary between them and her, become a leaf in the wind or an abandoned tricycle on the lawn in front of an apartment block, disconnected from people but connected to everything around her in an endless exchange of material.

She regards woman as an antiquated form. She thinks motherhood is designed for a woman who no longer exists. A woman who is entirely dedicated to her child, her house, who stays at home while her husband goes to work. But even though she can see that the form is false, this idea of the mother is lodged so deep inside her it can't be extricated, so she's left hating herself for not spending her life staring deep into her child's blue eyes while drying off a billion plates with a dish towel.

The only area in which she can't tolerate the second-best is poetry. She can eat the cheapest tinned food, watch bad TV shows, and buy fake designer copies, no problem. But she can only stand the very best poetry, nothing that is *okay* or *ambitious* or *promising*.

When she emerged from the fugue of early motherhood and started to look for employment, she began to feel ashamed of this attitude. She thought it was ridiculous, elitist, and snobbish, and also devoid of humanity.

Life was hard enough as it was, there was no reason for inaccessible art. She found herself caught between wanting to create art that was accessible to all, and creating the art that she was able to create which always revealed the part of her that was not normal. She sat down to write during her lunch break, and what she saw was an aberration. No reason to overcomplicate. No reason to overdramatize. She hated herself for what she wrote. She felt miserable. She went to a café, what would you like? A small latte.

She wanted to buy a glass jug so the boy could pour his own milk at meals. She had seen these jugs at the nursery, and all the children used them. She had to help the boy help himself. It was almost always a bigger task than doing it for him.

"When you have a child, something else in life has got to go so the child can get in," the Danish poet Benny Andersen once said in a newspaper. She had no problem letting go of friendships, trips to the movies, nice clothes, going to the hairdresser's, reading many books, her freedom and sleep, her sex life, and so on, but did writing really have to go as well?

The question was whether Benny Andersen had his own private study when he had small children. It's not improbable.

When Marx wrote that work should be outsourced to machines so the worker could instead write poetry in the morning, who did he imagine would change the diapers?

Could the revolutionary subject, in Marx's eyes, be anyone other than the man at the factory? Other than he who received a wage for his work? THE ANSWER IS NO, Anna wrote, suddenly infuriated.

Then she wrote the sentence: "I thought I could maintain modesty by writing prose."

She was quoting the American poet and essayist Anne Boyer. Maybe I should imagine that Anne Boyer is my only reader, Anna thought, that only Anne Boyer and no one other than Anne Boyer will read what I write. Maybe it will help, she thought. Then she remembered Anne Boyer couldn't read Danish.

Each time she started reading a book she liked, she would fill with fear, shame, and endless sadness because this good book was whole, and the thing that was Anna's book would not become whole, would never become one with the world, one with these books and their wholeness, and because Anna was not whole, could never be so, could never become this person who was one with the world and sure of their place in it.

In an attempt to feel at one with the world, she went shopping. That was the closest she could come to joining a global circuit. This chain of production, of sales and purchases and carrying goods home in bags necessitated people in certain places. Shopping was like touching these people with an invisible hand.

The next best thing to connect her to the rest of the world was watching live-transmitted TV, like soccer or the Bake-Off, which everyone watched at the same time as her.

After that came writing.

Anna didn't know whether it brought her closer to or further away from other people.

Why did she wish to portray herself as such a helpless and pathetic figure? Wasn't she an intelligent, strong woman? What therapists called *resourceful*? And perhaps she was also what people always wanted children to be: *resilient*.

Was Anna resilient? Was Anna a horoscope?

Anna hated when people talked about their books as if they were children. That the *conception* had been difficult. That it was a life-changing experience *to birth something into the world*. That the book was the author's *baby*. A book is not a human and an authorship not motherhood. You do not have a proprietary right to your child, you do not own it. It lives its own life, unknown to its parents. You can't compare books to infants, Anna thought. It was gross. Anna could only assume that the comparison had been thought up by someone who didn't have children, or who had at least never given birth to a child. Sometimes it felt as though Anna was practically the only person in the world who knew what it was like to give birth.

Why couldn't she keep her thoughts collected, her book collected as a whole? Why did she always have to start over? Why did it always have to be something else? Shed its skin and take a new form? She didn't *feel* fragmented, and she didn't consider her writing to be so, it merely couldn't be contained in the forms available to her.

So she kept on breaking the forms, even though it wasn't destruction she sought, even though all she longed for was a whole, a solid form, normality. Something she could present to others without having to explain herself, without meeting resistance. She wanted to achieve unity, to achieve a gentle order the way everyone else did, but no available form could contain her.

The forms were old, stiffened, adapted to an outdated reality, to the nuclear family, the stay-at-home wife. Experiences that would lock Anna up and thereby lock up the text in a form that required a way of thinking that wasn't her own. A form in which Anna could only appear as a ghost. A form in which Anna could end in disaster.

There was nothing Anna wanted more than to write a normal book.

She wanted to write a normal book because she wanted to speak to normal people, mothers who were too tired for complicated poetry. But she kept on writing increasingly complicated poems.

No matter how much Anna tried, she kept on writing strange texts that jumped all over. The writing in her wouldn't resign itself to Anna's plans. She couldn't see herself and had to grope in the dark.

Over the course of her education, Anna got the impression that any art made by a woman except Virginia Woolf was a secret, because no one referenced or engaged with it, and therefore Anna too was a secret—just as the child had been a secret inside her, and also the birth, now that it was distant; a place she no longer had access to but that had forever changed what she was.

When Anna got pregnant, she began seeing pregnant women everywhere on the streets. She had never noticed them before. It was natural enough to notice them while pregnant herself and while the child was still young, but even after he had turned one and a half she kept on seeing them, noticing pregnant women everywhere. What was I seeing before, Anna wondered. I didn't know what a pregnant woman was.

Sixteenth Continuation

That morning, Anna put on a new beautiful dress she had saved for a sunny day like today. But Aksel didn't notice. And who else would? Anna had no contact with any other adults anymore.

Anna sat on the bench in the shade of the tree, the child slept in the stroller beside her. Aksel sat under the café's umbrellas, drinking coffee and talking on the phone. No one had warned Anna of the loneliness once a couple had a child. Or that the time they had spent on each other, their togetherness, would erode. Or else everyone had told her but she hadn't understood it, wouldn't listen.

Really, the only thing truly wrong with Anna was that she sometimes wanted to die.

At times her feelings grew so strong, so all-encompassing, that death seemed like the only deliverance. It was a matter of finding the line where her emotions went from being intense to being deadly. For Anna, this was the border of normalcy.

On one side of the border was the good mother, on the other the bad mother.

On one side health, on the other sickness.

Here, her thoughts began to escape her and Anna became light-headed, as if she had been left in the sun for too long.

Now and then, Anna would say she just wanted to be normal. The most common reply to this was that normal people didn't exist and that the very concept of normality was debatable, or even that Anna ought to be grateful she was special.

Anna tried to incorporate these statements into her own way of thinking but after hearing them enough times she had sufficient data to conclude that the people who say they can't understand why anyone would want to be normal or that normality doesn't exist, these are in fact the normal people. These people are so normal they've never felt deep horror at their own difference; they don't know what it's like to be weird.

The child woke up in the stroller. She lifted him up into the sun and he laughed. Aksel stood up and walked over to them.

"Honey," said Aksel. "Are you okay?"

"Yeah, I'm just feeling a little introverted."

"Well, can you be introverted toward me?"

"I think you've misunderstood the meaning of introvert."

He got up, the child said "Pappa."

He sees two types of weakness in me, Anna thought as she watched Aksel coax the changing bag out from under the stroller, and he responds very differently to each of them.

The first weakness turns him into my protector, Anna thought, watching Aksel hand the child corn puffs from the bag. And he gladly plays the role of the strong, capable man who takes care of me. The child was warm in her arms and sweaty after his nap. Excited like any other one-year-old, he grabbed the little puffs.

He likes this weakness in me, Anna thought. When I'm melancholic, and the melancholy originates from a time before him, he finds my weakness attractive and romantic.

The sun strained through the tree's leaves, mottling Aksel's face with shadow and light, like clouds hurrying past.

This weakness, my melancholy, may make me difficult, Anna thought, but the emptiness stems from a previous life, and Aksel believes he can fill it. I become the sad girl Aksel can take care of.

The other weakness stems directly from our life together, Anna thought. There was sand in her yellow patent leather shoes, the child ate another corn puff, the air felt cool by the trunk of the tree. From the outside, we probably look idyllic, she thought, and then: Aksel did not care for this other weakness because it could threaten his freedom.

If Anna forgot something at the store, for example, or broke down when he worked too much. If she thought he was being harsh, told him he hurt her feelings or offended her, he would refuse to accept her experience of what had happened. He would not allow this weakness.

"That's your subjective worldview," he said when Anna asserted he had been cruel.

"But everything is subjective," she replied.

It was pointless. She could only be weak with him if she was the sad emo-girl. And she could not be emo-girl and mother at the same time. She had to turn the mother in her away from him. He could not, would not, see it.

Now he took the child and put him down on the cobblestones. The boy had just begun to walk. Aksel took his hand, together they waddled out into the sun.

In Aksel's eyes, he was still the protector while Anna was weak and helpless, and so he couldn't see the hardness with which he met her; she could only be weak with him if she turned it inward, became small, self-harming and melancholic, and never dare not live up to his standards. And if she did, they would quickly have to agree that her *sensitive nature* was to blame.

"Don't forget his hat," she said to Aksel, handing the child's sun hat to him.

"You're so sensitive," he said affectionately, putting the hat on the child. Anna was repulsed. Sensitivity was a shackle.

"Woof," said Anna.

"Woof!" replied the boy, pulling off his hat.

Aksel couldn't handle her witnessing his shortcomings. He saw himself through her eyes. She had to carry all his Protestant self-hatred so he could flog her in place of him. She was never allowed to be someone who could help him. Was this love?

In that moment, while Anna was convinced he had condemned them both to a life as two stones, the three of them, soft in the sunlight and nestled in the tree's shade, were turned toward one another in a bliss Anna did not see.

She bent over to shake the sand out of her shoe, and, not noticing the child, knocked him over with her elbow. The boy began to cry and Aksel scooped him up.

"Mommy!" the child cried, stretching his arms toward her.

She hesitated, but then went over to comfort him. When she did, she saw Aksel's eyes flash with envy; he turned his back to her with the child in his arms and said "yes, that was bad, Mommy hit you."

Suddenly, Anna understood that Aksel had imagined that they would both be mothers to the child. That Aksel had assumed he was going to be a mother. All this time he had competed with Anna to be the mother. In the absence of role models, he had rejected fatherhood and reached for motherhood instead.

Anna's mind retracted like a pupil in the sunlight, she felt pleasure and surprise. Anger at what he had said to the child. She stood still, unable to move.

"Aksel, you can't say that."

"You don't get to decide what I can and can't say."

She had only seen him cry once before. And that was when they watched *Gladiator*. But now he was standing there crying in the sunlit square with their child in his arms.

"Mommy!" screamed the child.

"I'm Mommy," he said, hugging the child close to him. "I'm not going to die."

"No," said Anna, shaking her head. A heavy tiredness poured over her and she sat down on the ground, the hot cobblestones burning her thighs. The boy had stopped crying. Now Aksel sat down too. The child crawled from his lap over to Anna, who hugged him.

"What are we going to do?" she asked.

"I don't know," he said. "But you can't leave me."

A man approached them.

"You forgot to pay." He worked at the café. Aksel found his wallet and handed the man some notes.

"I didn't know you had cash on you," said Anna.

"Soon we won't have any money left."

"We could sell the apartment?"

"Yes, but we still need somewhere to live."

"I could ask for more hours?"

"Do you think they'll give you more?"

"Yes, Asta has just gone on maternity leave."

Lovingly, she took his hand in hers but underneath lay a bitter seed; once again she had to be the one to initiate. Everything seemed to sink into the cracks between the square's cobblestones, which shone like molars in the sun. The child opened his mouth and sang.

Seventeenth Continuation

She is tormented by the thought that her love for the child, for her husband, is deformed. She is tormented by the thought that when she is not with the child, the child is in danger. She is tormented by the thought that when she is enjoying her time alone and is late to pick up the child from the nursery even though she has nothing important to do, she is willfully putting him in danger. She is tormented by the thought that this means she is indifferent to whether or not he lives or is subjected to pain. She is tormented by the thought that this means she wants her child to die. She is tormented by the thought that she is this person having these thoughts.

She is tormented by the thought that no man will ever love her passionately again. That that time in her life is over. That no man will ever hold her again when she cries. That no man will ever love her tears again, the way some men love to take care of crying women whose sadness they can't comprehend. She is tormented by the thought that her husband only wants to have sex with her because he is horny and wants a warm body, that she is interchangeable.

She is tormented by the thought that her husband doesn't love her anymore. She is tormented by the thought that she will get a divorce. She doesn't want to get a divorce, so she is tormented by the thought that she will live in a loveless marriage for the rest of her life. She is tormented by the thought that no man will ever love her again. That that part of her life is over. She is tormented by the thought that not only is that part of her life over, but her entire life is over.

Eighteenth Continuation

The doctors teach them how to watch for the signs. Is the breathing shallow, is there tenderness by the ribs, beneath the collarbones, is the child lethargic and uninterested in playing?

Anna cannot spot the signs. She stares and stares at the child's ribs, but doesn't understand what she's meant to be looking for. Something inside her suspects there is perhaps nothing to see, but then the thought transforms: it's her eyesight that's poor.

The boy has attended the nursery for just over a month. At the hospital, he's fitted with a nebulizer hooked up to a saline solution. He's checked for diseases that can't be cured with antibiotics. The family is sequestered in a room, the boy is checked and prodded and poked until he throws up. Aksel and Anna take turns holding him down.

"Is that blood?" says Aksel, the fear in his voice audible for the first time at one o'clock in the morning at Hvidovre Hospital when blood appears in the tube from the boy's throat. They're taking a sample to test for something but Aksel and Anna don't know the details.

When the tube is removed, the boy screams. Anna has him in a tight grip so she can keep him still. She lets go and he hops down from the bed and plays with a toy phone on the floor, suddenly full of energy for thirty minutes around two, eats yogurt, runs around and says hi to the others in the ward, then vomits up all the yogurt, goes limp.

Anna and Aksel are sitting across from each other in children's chairs. Aksel reaches out and strokes Anna's cheek. Anna covers Aksel's hand with her own. She cries. He kisses her. He's warm.

The test results come back. There's nothing wrong with the boy, he's just on the small side and is hit especially hard by the various bugs going around, and perhaps also has a case of asthmatic bronchitis.

"Do you mean childhood asthma?" asks Aksel, using the Swedish term.

"I believe that's what it's called in Sweden, yes," replies a doctor.

"That's what I thought," says Aksel, his face darkening. Anna takes his hand.

When they return from the hospital for the third time, after the boy has gone through yet another night with the saline nebulizer, Anna cannot think a single thought. It persists. She cannot think, she cannot write, she cannot return to the part of herself where writing resides.

She finds herself in a stiff panic. She goes to work. She goes grocery shopping. She picks up clothes off the floor. She ruffles a head of hair by her hip.

She doesn't want to write about the child's hospitalizations for fear of him reading it one day when he's older, for fear of scaring and retraumatizing him, but also for fear of him being upset with her for using his story. And she doesn't want to write about the asthma attacks because she thinks these hospital visits may be the first steps of the boy's obliteration.

Maybe the boy won't care about these hospital visits when he's grown up, maybe he won't remember them at all and it'll turn out to be nothing but a few bad episodes in his early life, and Aksel and Anna will think back with relief at it being over.

Even though the distance between the child and Anna has started to grow, their stories are so intertwined that Anna can't separate hers from the child's, and therefore can't tell what she has a right to talk about as part of her own story, and what she must omit out of respect for the child.

Might these hospitalizations carry far more significance in Anna's story than in the boy's?

The fourth time the boy is hospitalized, they have to wait in the ER for a long time. Anna stands with the sleeping boy in her arms. It's almost midnight. She can't sit down. Her shoulders hurt.

"When the doctor comes to get him, I might collapse," she tells Aksel.

"Okay. That's completely okay, Anna."

The doctor comes, takes the child, Anna doesn't collapse. She's filled with adrenaline and starts to giggle. They follow the doctor down a long corridor, she sits down with the boy in her lap, they bring the nebulizer, she holds him down, it's the same as last time, she watches his condition improve, she loses her sense of time, is very awake, it's one o'clock in the morning again. The nebulizer is hooked up to a machine that creates a fine mist, which is dispensed via a tube into the mask. The machine makes a rhythmic, whirring sound, like the sea or something that cannot die. A breast pump of improbable dimensions that emits mist instead of sucking up milk. In the room next to theirs, a chubby boy, nine years old, hospitalized with an irregular heartbeat. Each time the nebulizer comes off, the boy toddles out into the hall and says "hi!" very loudly to the other boy. He sits with his legs dangling over the side of the bed and waves but doesn't say anything. In the night, the boy says "hi!" loudly again. It's the only word he knows besides "woof," "caw-caw," "Pappa," and "iPad."

Each time they come home from the hospital, Anna and Aksel hate each other more intensely. The battle over time has begun. Anna walks across a field in the fog. She is lit up by an early sun. Late summer arrives like a slight, persistent sweat. They work full time. The nursery has called—someone needs to pick up the boy right away, he's sick again. Anna is at the office, waiting to see who will give in first. She envisions the boy, feverish on the lap of a nursery teacher. She clenches her fists beneath her height-adjustable desk. She thinks about the meeting with her boss she's meant to attend in a moment. The meeting has been scheduled for a long time. They're going to discuss her salary.

Anna and Aksel work as much as they can in the hopes of being offered permanent positions, say yes to all the side gigs to make ends meet.

Still, the work of the other seems like nothing but an obstacle. And the other's purchases are frivolous. Those expensive shirts they used to indulge in together in Stockholm, now they hide the price tags from each other and each quietly thinks they contribute the lion's share to their joint finances.

"I'll pick him up," Anna writes, "but it will have to wait until after my meeting with Mathias."

Walking up the stairs to the office on her first day of work, Anna had felt free and happy. She had finally gotten a job, the child had just begun nursery. The timing couldn't have been better. The joy of the new job stood side by side with missing the child and fearing he would be neglected, and Anna had realized this was her new reality: the dual state of missing and happiness, but after a few months, the freedom slipped away. It was soon the same old job as before the child. Emails.

Anna had previously worked at the publishing house in short-term positions with less responsibility than she had now. Back then, she didn't get home until late at night. Now she has told Mathias that it's her intention to leave at four seeing as she has a child and therefore cannot work late without remuneration. And she is proud that she has managed to communicate a clear boundary to her boss. She will work the hours she is paid for. And if they need her to work more hours, she expects to be compensated. Those are the union rules. Mathias doesn't know that Anna isn't a member of a trade union, at least she hopes so.

At the meeting, Mathias informs her they intend to cut her salary by 5,000 kroner. As Mathias sees it, Anna herself has requested her hours be reduced and that must naturally be reflected in her salary.

"You can't be serious," she says. There is a silent pause in which he chooses to study the landline telephone on his desk. Then her stomach rumbles loudly. "Um …" Anna says, as if answering her stomach. "No, seriously."

"Alright, let's say 2,500 kroner instead," Mathias eventually offers and turns his gaze from the landline to her. His shoulders are up by his ears, as they have been the whole time she has known him. "You can be proud of that." He smiles. She stands up and tries to exit the office without turning her back to him.

When Anna gets back to her desk, she's cold with sweat. The nursery has called three times, and Aksel has responded "ок" to her text.

Anna will never have sex with him again.

She grabs her coat and rushes off. When she arrives home with the boy, she undresses him and he falls asleep in her arms. She has no feelings left in her.

She's still sitting with the boy when Aksel lets himself in. She hasn't turned on the lights. She just looks at him. She has started avoiding everything that angers her. She has started sitting very still. She will never sleep with anyone again. She does not want to be embraced. To touch another adult is to descend somewhere she cannot go. Thoughts of knives come to her.

Nineteenth Continuation

1 year, 5 months, and 19 days after the birth

*
something small
I can fit myself into
a poem
the muffled
clinking of
coins in my pocket
when I hang my coat
in the empty apartment
a piece of music
the weather
like a piece a part
the gray clouds
the cold
who I am
to survive
the smallest component
to survive
where I can put
a song
mine
an outward-reaching
the small things
the small living things
I become
a poem
to carry myself forward

in order to love
time transformed
in the sounds
my own mouth
my own hands
to survive
the writing
to survive
the colors
not deftly
but to survive
live
continue
the poem
in the poem's hand
here
I will believe
an upward-rising
in the night
his voice
the voice that
offered shelter
and later destruction
a divulgence
a bird's body
against the gray clouds
physical pain
a swath of fabric
red with
yellow flowers
human-drawn
like a letter
these things

that hold me
the black table
the white closet
the red dresser
the hint of rot
along the leaves' edges
a footstool
a piece of chewing gum
the balcony
he seldom speaks
of forgiveness
where am I
if not here
held up
by the object poem
a poem
to stay
where I am standing
without purpose
must continue
like the pocket's darkness
unseen homelike
but alive
among all
these things
in their
endless lives
continue
among them
like the poem itself
I carry
forward
I carry

to stay
without
destruction
I put myself
into each and every thing
around me
in the empty apartment
alive
who I am
among those
those who are not
human
who hold me up
toward the world
the blossoming trees
by the bicycles
where the child ran about
and spoke of the branches
the petals on the ground
between the wheels
like me
I should
not hate
what holds me in place
what separates me
but carry it
face
forward
love it
believe
the child disappears
into the nursery school

Twentieth Continuation

"It's not my fault your life is shitty," said Aksel, zipping up his bag.

"Please don't go," Anna said. "I don't think I can cope on my own."

"You have to cope," he said. He'd been hired to put on a play in Gothenburg and stood with his back to her. "This is a really important job for me. And we need the money."

"But I don't know how."

"Why don't you call your mother?"

"She lives too far away."

"She could come and live here."

"I don't want that."

"It's okay to ask for help sometimes, Anna."

"But I'm asking you for help."

"I can't be everything all the time."

The boy woke up in the next room.

"Hello, sweetheart," she said, lifting him up, "let's go say bye to Daddy." She heard her mother's voice in her own, as if she were programmed.

The door shut behind Aksel. For many months now, she hadn't been able to concentrate on anything. Books seemed lifeless, they turned to dust when she opened them. She grew angry at herself for not being able to read. So far, no one at the office had noticed. Her job mostly consisted of answering and forwarding emails. The child cried at night. She tumbled out of bed to comfort him. There were five days left until Aksel came home. Inside her was a feeling she couldn't reach. It was hidden under a pile of other feelings. One of these feelings was the feeling of not being able to read. Beneath this, something angry. Like wanting to become a knife. It took a long time for the boy to calm down. When he finally fell back asleep, his face wet with tears, Anna was wide awake.

She sat in a chair and watched the night's traffic. The headlights of the cars drew fingers of light across her face. Anna knew for a fact she would soon fall and carried the horror of this impending fall within her. The premonition kept her awake, she sat shivering in the chair and felt its approach, the fall, the moment when everything would change. The sun rose, the boy awoke in his bed at six o'clock, he sat up and looked at her.

"Good morning," she said. He rubbed his eyes. She had to be ready. Each day she felt it, and still she did not fall.

From the outside, it doesn't look like much. She's sitting on the balcony. She's wearing her red wool coat. The coat is big and heavy, she sinks into it so only her hair peeks out. Two fingers stick out between the lapels, balancing a cigarette.

Below Anna's feet, the trains run toward Høje Taastrup and Køge. The exhaust from the locomotives lingers in the white haze of early autumn, the air is thick and milky.

Behind the glass doors of the balcony, the boy sits at the end of the dining table in his high chair and eats, still clumsily, with a spoon. At times he looks at Anna with wonder. Inside Anna is the thought of letting the red coat fall to the ground, and inside the coat, her body.

Anna sits for a long time in the greasy light, hunched over in her own silence. Why do I want to die, she thinks. She sits in her red coat on the balcony while the boy eats his food. Trains and cars pass by. Nothing more happens. She considers it for a long time.

She imagines it over and over again. The red fall, in a loop. The sounds, a brief rush of wind and then the thud. How long the child would sit alone in his chair, unable to get up, unable to see her, before he would start to scream.

Something passes through her. She gets up and looks out across the tracks. The railing is cold against her hands, they're overheated by coursing blood. She can feel the boy's eyes on her back. She flicks the cigarette butt and watches it fall.

She goes inside. She hangs up the coat and washes her

hands. She lifts the boy from the chair.

"Come on, honey, let's wash our hands."

He runs off squealing because he loves to wash his hands, almost as much as he loves to climb up onto the stool Anna has set out for that purpose.

He is still wobbly on his feet and she keeps watch as he climbs, worried he will fall and hit his head against the tile floor. She can see the open skull, the pink flesh. He gets to the top and she turns on the water, they splash and laugh, she washes his face, he sticks out his tongue and repeats "flippedy-flop" to himself in the mirror. She thinks of blood.

When it's bedtime, Anna lies down next to the child in his crib and holds him until he falls asleep.

In the dark, his sweet-smelling breath beats against her face. Just as he passes from awake to asleep, a shift occurs in both of them. Anna gets the same feeling as when the milk used to come in, a tingling in the nose, a drowsy pleasure, a sting in each breast even though there's no milk. A weight pulls her downward, as if her heart were a stone falling down a well's warm, shady shaft.

The sleepy happiness flows between them like a language. Together in the bed in the dark they remember they once were one. The child falls into a deeper sleep, their pulses synchronize. Anna lies awake by his side, engulfed by love. This space between them, the wordless union, is what keeps Anna alive.

As soon as the thoughts subside, Anna forgets it all after a day or two. The memory fades, it's like a sore muscle or an old wound. An adjoining room in the house that Anna forgets exists.

Is Anna's story the story of a woman's inner life?

And is the story of domestic life, of the child's first year, of housekeeping, a story driven by internal events? And therefore a narrative arc without any major dramatic climaxes?

If Anna's job is to bring children into the world, to keep the house clean, the food healthy, and the heart warm, to care for and strengthen her body so that it is at the disposal of future fetuses, of children who want to be carried, babies who want to be breastfed and men who want to be loved—if this is Anna's work—is her writing about her body and home not precisely workplace literature?

Anna turns on the radio, and a British researcher explains that the word *economy* comes from the ancient Greek word for *household management*.

She changes the channel. "Thought is action," says an author, his voice echoing in the kitchen. Anna takes out a chicken breast and begins to cut it into thin slices. While she coats the pieces in flour, dips them in egg wash, and covers them in breadcrumbs before frying them in oil, the author on the radio proceeds to explain that if you get stuck with your manuscript or experience writer's block, then it's because the text is trying to tell you that what you perceive to be its problem, its flaw or blockage, is in fact the key to it becoming something greater and more beautiful.

It's a nice thought to apply to people too, Anna thinks. That her mistakes, her anxiety and stupidity hold the key to her transformation into a greater and more beautiful human being. On the sofa, the boy is watching a film. The chicken is sizzling in the pan. The potatoes have already been put on to boil. But if thought is action, then what action is the thought of death? Who owns a mother's life after she has brought a child into the world? thinks Anna. Am I free to give and take my life as I please once I've given birth? Or does the concept of *life*—my life, the child's—change after birth?

Anna couldn't understand her death wish. Just as she couldn't understand what it meant to create life. There was something preternatural about these two states, as though the mind couldn't hold them and therefore resorted to categorizing them as fiction. Like a film in which you see yourself from the outside. Another Anna, another Aksel, another doctor in another office at another hospital where a possible diagnosis was discussed and a course of treatment decided on.

"I'm not a real person, I'm made of plastic, I don't know myself," said Anna as she walked in the quiet rain from the bicycle shed toward the Psychotherapy Clinic in Nørrebro in Copenhagen, as if she were now about to overstep the boundary between reality and film; as if the clinic were a fiction, this smell in these wards, anyplace on Earth, and the wet city that shifted and swayed around her.

Twenty-First Continuation

Dear Anna,

At our first visit to the midwife the other day, I asked whether I could see my records from the five days I was hospitalized with our first child. The midwife sat down at her computer and pulled up my records. As she skimmed them, she told me there were no notes from those five days, not even a discharge summary. She apologized profusely and said they must have been too overburdened. The only record from that time is this short note on sleep medication, which the midwife printed out for me:

Prescribed for insomnia and anxiety
Rx: Tabl. Imoclone 3.75 mg *1
Hospital: RIGSHOSPITALET
Department: OBSTETRICS CLINIC Y, 24 HOURS

It feels strange that nothing has been written down. As if these five days are five empty pages in my life, without notes, and I'm suddenly unsure whether it was five, six, or seven days we were hospitalized. I envision the empty days as a staticky, blank image, as unreachable, sleeping faces. I carry them with me like white noise. I can't remember very much and wanted to know what the hospital staff had observed.

When we left the midwife's office and stepped outside into the bright August sun, I caught myself thinking that I had to use your papers to fill out those five missing days, as if we shared a biography.

The publisher has now scheduled the book's publication for September next year. I'm working like mad to finish it before the child is born. I'm tired and nauseated and dizzy and find the second trimester much worse than the first, contrary to what everyone says.

The boy is doing wonderfully, chatters nonstop, and has started climbing up high in trees.

YOURS

PS
Last night I awoke with the thought that nothing calamitous happened in these five days, but I now have the chance to fill them with lies, make up anything at all, magnify the madness, turn the pain into a story. Is this the gift of fiction, Anna? Or is it that I don't trust my own memory, don't trust my own instincts, but solely wish to come into being through the language of doctors?

Twenty-Second Continuation

Anna's journal, 2017

Thursday, October 5, 2017
Tomorrow I start group therapy. A walk with Aksel yesterday, along the canal. Hardly any people, everyone at work. He had the day off, and I didn't have to. I managed four months at the publishing house before ending up here. A blessing in disguise, I told him, since now I'm entitled to sick leave. His face winced with a mixture of tenderness and aversion, I recognized my proclivity for self-humiliation.

I dropped off the boy at the nursery, and on our way there we both felt the coming frost, the day was brisk and it bit at our cheeks, I left mittens in his cubby. A blue fog on the trees at the playground. I don't know where to put all my shame.

Wednesday, October 11, 2017
At the nursery, a flock of birds in the white hawthorn pecked at the bright-red berries. The boy in the stroller and me by his side, we stood watching them, gripped and quietly delighted.

After dropping him off, I sit down to read the news. This open time, the calendar of illness.

LIBERALS' NEW SPOKESPERSON IN COPENHAGEN WANTS
GANG MEMBERS' FAMILIES FIRED
The Liberal Party's new spokesperson in Copenhagen wants to put an end to what she calls "misguided benevolence" in municipal policy, arguing it is detrimental to integration and

children's education. She therefore intends to close schools and penalize the families of criminal gang members.
Politiken

Friday, October 20, 2017
POLICE RELEASE PHOTO OF SHIRT DEAD CHILD'S BODY WAS FOUND IN
DR

Saturday, October 21, 2017
INSECT DEATH FORETELLS "ECOLOGICAL ARMAGEDDON" —ALSO IN DENMARK
Information

Sunday, October 22, 2017
CHINA BUILDS DIGITAL DICTATORSHIP TO MONITOR PUBLIC BEHAVIOR AND DOLE OUT REWARDS AND PUNISHMENTS
Politiken

Wednesday, October 25, 2017
The trees by the nursery, one in particular, radiant yellow, dropping its leaves in a continuous downpour like computer-programmed snow. I lingered and breathed in the fresh air.

INTERNATIONAL RESEARCH UNCOVERS BLIND SPOT: PESTICIDES CAN HARM CHILDREN'S BRAINS
Politiken

Saturday, October 28, 2017
JUVENILE CRIMINALS IN KOLDING TO FIGHT FIRES AND CLEAN TRUCKS
DR

Friday, November 3, 2017

In group therapy today, we were asked to look at a drawing and offer possible interpretations.

These strange, perfectly normal people in Group Room II and the things they say:

"The mother is lying in bed sick, about to be operated on, and the children stand around her, afraid."

"The mother is in a coma and her children are afraid."

"A random couple see a woman in a hospital bed and are glad they aren't sick."

"The family gathers around a sickbed, and everyone is glad the patient survived."

"A new mother is lying in bed and next to her are her husband and mother-in-law."

"It's two parents who are afraid their daughter won't survive."

"The mother is dead."

Monday, November 13, 2017

At my individual session today, the therapist told me I might want to consider reading the news less. She also encouraged me to delete several apps.

I cannot and will not step into the place where I am destroyed. I don't want to feel anything. I just want to be up-to-date.

I may be a piece of garbage, but I will endeavor to at least be a well-informed piece of garbage.

THERAPIST: But how do you think the stress you experience from following the news impacts you? Is it your responsibility to keep track of everything going on in the world? Do you think a single person can bear all that?

ME: No, but if I don't, I'll be a bad person.

THERAPIST: A bad person? Could you elaborate?

ME: If I turn away and refuse to see what's going on in the

world, refuse to try to understand other people's misfortune, it must mean I don't care whether they live or die.

THERAPIST: I understand. That must be difficult.

ME: It's not like I actually do anything. I just read. I'm not politically active.

THERAPIST: Do you wish you were?

ME: I have too much anxiety to be politically active, but then I think it's just an excuse I use because I'm lazy.

THERAPIST: Do you think having anxiety is the same as being lazy?

ME: Um...

THERAPIST: Maybe one has to forget all the world news once in a while to stay somewhat levelheaded?

ME: Somewhat?

THERAPIST: Yes, just once in a while. Take a deep breath and look out at the world as it is around you, the trees and the parking lot down below, for instance, and don't look at the world as it appears in the news. Besides, the picture painted by the media isn't always representative of how things really are.

ME: No, that's...

THERAPIST: It's not uncommon to feel frightened by the news. It's a societal issue.

ME: People read the news without taking it in. Is that what I should do?

THERAPIST: Maybe sometimes?

ME: When I read the news, I guess I assume most people read the same stories I do...

THERAPIST: *(interrupting)* But I don't know that they do, Anna.

ME: *(continuing)* ... and then I think that they must either, well, they either understand it, or do they just go numb? People can't bear it, so they push it away.

THERAPIST: One has to learn to filter some things out.

ME: But it isn't just that the news is full of horror, it's also that you can't handle the constant stream of horror. You can't bear being aware of it all the time. So you've got to become a barbarian or an idiot or … an aristocrat. I mean, don't you think people know that they … that we live in a society on the verge of collapse, that it's all coming to an end soon, but we go on pretending nothing is the matter, because maybe it's already too late, don't you think so too?

THERAPIST: Well, this isn't about me. But no, I don't believe that I do.

ME: I think people think they shouldn't think about it. And at the heart of all their feelings lies the sanctity of private property. And their love for their fellow human—it's unripe, it can't deepen, it's been hijacked by capitalism.

THERAPIST: I think you should take a break from the news.

ME: Is that what you're prescribing me?

THERAPIST: You could say that.

ME: So how much news can I read? Per day, that is?

THERAPIST: I think you should set aside time to read the news—say, ten minutes in the morning and ten minutes in the evening, no more than that. Then we'll see how that goes, and maybe you can cut down even further in a few weeks.

ME: But how will I stay up-to-date?

THERAPIST: I think you'll find that you'll manage. In fact, I think you'll find that if you stop reading the news entirely, nothing will happen. And what does happen, you'll be able to figure out based on what you already know.

ME: Are you saying that if I stop reading the news, the world will stop too? That with my reading, I can start and stop world events?

THERAPIST: No, Anna, that's not what I'm saying. I'm saying that you can learn—if not to control, then at least to understand—how the world moves through you.

Leaving the session—always those strange brief moments on the stairs and in the lobby and in the parking lot in which I shift from the clinic's reality and stuffy air charged with the nerves of all the patients and reenter the world, pausing beneath a tall chestnut tree on the street corner to regain my bearings—it occurred to me that I'm part of the logic of war, an accomplice in a hegemony of destruction.

But now, writing it, and reading what I've written, the words aren't strong enough to hold the experience. It's left there beneath the chestnut, a bodily knowing that I perhaps always had, but only truly saw then: I am part of the war, but as a weapon that cannot point itself the other way.

Tuesday, November 14, 2017
In addition to a pamphlet titled "Supporting Patients with Anxiety," which the therapist asked me to pass on to Aksel, she gave me a slim blue book called *The Earth Almanac*.

THERAPIST: *(rummages in her bag, takes out the book and hands it to me)* Here, why don't you try reading this?
ME: What is it?
THERAPIST: It's just an idea I had. My mother-in-law gave it to me and I haven't really ... figured out what to do with it. But perhaps you can read it whenever you feel like reading the news.
ME: You're prescribing me something called *The Earth Almanac*?
THERAPIST: Well, technically I can't prescribe you anything. I'm not a doctor.
ME: Right, okay. But I don't think I can completely stop reading the news. I mean, it's hard to avoid.
THERAPIST: I understand. But see if you can keep it to just a single headline, for example.

ME: Don't you think I'll just start obsessing about which headline to choose?

THERAPIST: You need to learn to filter things out. Let's just try and see how it goes.

I *need* to have something outside of me which orders time or which time can be filtered through so as not to be left to my thoughts and destructive sense of duty.

"Chickweed with its small, white blossoms cannot tolerate frost but otherwise flowers nearly all year long."
The Earth Almanac

DENMARK TO SEND 30 EXTRA SOLDIERS TO IRAQ
DR

Wednesday, November 15, 2017
"The yellow-billed whooper swans arrive from the north and their calls can be heard in the November fog."
The Earth Almanac

MÆRSK UNDER HEAVY CRITICISM FOR STORING 450
TONS OF RADIOACTIVE WASTE
DR

Friday, November 17, 2017
"Moon in last quarter at 10:11 p.m. —Lichen adorns branches and trunks in striking patterns and bright colors in the wet November weather."
The Earth Almanac

The patient expresses:
I feel anxious.

I'm worthless because the anxiety prevents me from doing anything.

I'm disoriented, angry, afraid.

The panic attack continued for a few hours, for a few hours I didn't believe that anyone could love me.

Saturday, November 18, 2017

"Mute swans make their way to the coasts. Here, they will spend the winter in large flocks, often alongside fellow species that have migrated from the north."

Friday, November 24, 2017

Outside by the bike racks in the rain, they leave the clinic one by one. Some of us sick, others healthy. I watch them. And the sick will cure the healthy. I don't know whether I'm lying when I tell them the truth about myself. Each time I tell a secret, it feels as though the secret is retrieved from a bucket inside me that's filled with fiction. And as soon as the secret is spoken aloud, it hangs above the table between us like a mobile of mirrors and suddenly seems made up. Maybe I believe I can't live without my secrets. Group therapy is just a theater in which we play the role of the sick and others play the role of the observers.

What I'm trying to say is that the sickness itself feels artificial.

And I find myself in a constant, paralyzing doubt. Each Friday I sit there and am deciphered. We act sick.

Sometimes when I step into the room, when it's my turn to speak, it's as though I'm falling back into my chair, into a role in which my emotions, made pathological, are of medical interest, and it's a relief.

I don't like being sick. This choreography disgusts me, but then I soften to it.

Everyone plays their roles in Group Room II with such tenderness. Brutal honesty, fearless strangers. Their simmering presence. Each of us, about to burst.

Saturday, November 25, 2017
"If the winter is mild, the yellow blossoms of the poisonous, prickly gorse grow along the coastline during this time."

At this point in my life I must accept that I am a diary.

Monday, November 27, 2017
"Hundreds of thousands of long-tailed ducks, greater scaups, common scoters, and velvet scoters migrate to Danish waters to spend the winter."

Wednesday, November 29, 2017
CHILDLESS COUPLE BOUGHT BABY BOY FOR 5,500 KRONER IN POLAND
DR

Thursday, November 30, 2017
"If the weather is mild, some white anemones may become so confused that they bloom."

Friday, December 1, 2017
In a group room next to ours, a circle of empty chairs, on the floor in the middle, three boxes of tissues.

A fellow patient told me she spends an extortionate amount of time on job applications and writing her CV. She says: "I feel my lips pulsating so strongly I'm afraid they might explode." I immediately became enthralled with her. The beauty of Group Room II.

Sunday, December 3, 2017
Full moon.

Monday, December 4, 2017
I want to write myself as if I were a stranger. And I want to listen to who speaks in these sentences, not because I believe I'm an invention, but because I know I'm full of deceit. How to see oneself as anything other than an image, spoken into being out of nothing?

Friday, December 8, 2017
We were asked to reframe our catastrophic thinking.
 Not, for example: "The ferry will sink" but instead: "It's normal for the ferry to rock when it's very windy, and it's normal to feel nervous in such a situation."
 The state-funded psychiatric treatment for anxiety is basically a visualization workshop.
 I've seen it happen.
 The atrocity of it working. The humiliation.

Monday, December 11, 2017
Two adults, Aksel and I, turned toward this child like naked trees toward the moon.

Friday, December 15, 2017
To the therapist's question about what I'm avoiding, I could reply that I'd like to avoid being alone with the child.

Tuesday, December 19, 2017
This cannot be about me. It must be about someone else. Someone else who lives inside the book and who doesn't have the same hair color as me.

Monday, December 25, 2017
PREMATURE LAMB FETUS KEPT ALIVE IN ARTIFICIAL
WOMB
Politiken

Wednesday, December 27, 2017
I told Aksel I was afraid my writing was too pretentious, and he assured me: "The last thing you need to worry about is being pretentious, Anna."
    Compliment or insult?
    This coming from a man who pronounces Paris without an *s*.

I watched his serene face while he slept and saw the child's face in his, but suddenly also my own. For a fleeting, blissful moment, I believed in his love.

"The common brimstone hibernates in ivy and other evergreen plants, where it can survive the frost."

Sunday, December 31, 2017
The last day of the year and the last day of *The Earth Almanac*: "The flat water scorpion is active all winter long on the shores of small ponds."

Wednesday, January 10, 2018
even though there are
eight of us in the room
as well as two therapists
I am alone
alone with the anxiety
and everyone else is me
everyone a screen

on which I read myself
fear of open spaces
fear of abandonment
fear of anxiety
fear on behalf of the child
fear of sickness
fear of others
fear of public transport
fear of exercise
fear of going to the theater
fear of grocery shopping
fear of being alone
fear of picking up the phone
fear of the phone not being picked up
fear of flying
fear of nausea
fear of distressing thoughts
magical objects
safety behaviors
the patient has started to avoid:
cinemas, coffee, cycling
she describes feeling
intense discomfort
when picking up her child
states that she
is afraid that
the staff the pedagogues
and other parents can tell
something is "wrong"
with her
as a mother
or that

the child will not want
to be picked up by her
because he "doesn't like her"
the patient says
she sometimes thinks
it would be best for everyone
if she did not exist
the patient is informed of
medication options

Sunday, January 14, 2018
POTENTIAL SALMONELLA SCANDAL: INFANT FORMULA
RECALLED IN 83 COUNTRIES
Z

Friday, January 19, 2018
Today is the last day of group therapy.
    We were told we will also have one final individual session.
    Anne-Lise passed around biscuits.

Wednesday, March 21, 2018
Yesterday they screened me for a personality disorder and
forwarded me for further assessment. "I think it sounds like
borderline." And then my name, "Anna," as if the name were a
fish swimming around in her mouth, something pale blue and
translucent, a piece of sky.
    In the evening, this dryness in my brain. I collapsed in the
bathroom. Something fell to the ground and broke inside me
and I heard sounds without seeing.
    I thought this was a part of me, but since I began group
therapy the flaw in me slowly became obvious for what it was:
a sickness.

That night this inner flaw broke away painlessly and hovered above me, never more than 10–20 centimeters away, as though still tethered to me, or like a satellite. I saw it there in the bathroom, it was late and Aksel came in and had to hold me up. For the first time, I understood that there were perhaps two of us. There was something that was not me, which I had tried to integrate into me for years. And when I realized I consisted of not just one but several illnesses that I had lived with for so long I had merged with them entirely, I was so devastated I again thought of taking my own life.

But the thought was new, clearer than before. Not as revenge or escape, not as a last grasp at power, but because it had become impossible to be alive. Because I was dissolving and disappearing.

I tried to think of the child. But it didn't help. I was filled with shame. Not even the thought of my own child could convince me I could go on living, and it felt as though there was not a single person worth staying alive for, seeing as I was not...whole?

Perched on the child's stool in the bathroom, I finally remembered the book, and in that gutting moment, I felt something there, welcoming me. Both the sickness and what was not the sickness, and their combined weight. The book was a place of deep ambivalence, or the precise sliver of space that must exist between me and the sicknesses, and after some time I was able to get back up.

Tuesday, March 27, 2018
A letter summoning me to an appointment at Frederiksberg Hospital, where I'm to be assessed again, because the treatment team at Therapeutic Center Copenhagen has asked for a second opinion. They also informed me that I require a new diagnosis to be eligible for further treatment.

Tuesday, April 10, 2018
The architecture made the illness seem more possible. The trees above the hospital's low buildings blossomed. It was the hospital's heavy, automatic glass doors, in the corridor the sound of a running toilet, the hospital smell, hospital signs, the hopelessness and the rainy trees, bushes, the green veil in every window.

Another office. A black-haired woman, she asked me to take a seat. I held out the child like a waxy white flower in my hand.

Saturday, May 5, 2018
The child turns two today.

Monday, May 7, 2018
What does it mean to be an Anna?
Does she speak with one voice?
I am a bowl of blood, still in the delivery room.
Carrying this destruction while being a mother; it seems criminal.

Thursday, May 10, 2018
Today a message notifying me that I haven't been diagnosed with a personality disorder, and an official discharge from the outpatient program at Rigshospitalet.

Saturday, June 23, 2018
From the open window I heard a child crying for a long time in the courtyard below.

I went down and discovered a boy in a stroller. I gave him his pacifier and rocked the stroller. No one came to get him. He continued crying. I had never before met such a small person unaccompanied by parents.

Based on his four teeth I estimated his age to be eight, maybe nine months. I found within my body a knowledge of this small child from when my own son was the same age, and this knowing enveloped him, and he felt it, soothed, whimpering. I didn't know how to get hold of his parents, I spoke to a neighbor in a window up above, asked whether he knew the child. More neighbors I had never met opened their windows and chimed in, the boy fussed, I rocked the stroller in the courtyard, the neighbors in all their windows. Finally a woman opened her balcony door and came out to see what all the fuss was about and she was the boy's mother.

Had he been awake for long? No, not more than fifteen minutes. Fifteen minutes! The baby monitor must not be working, my husband is on his way down now.

Why didn't I know her? We shared a courtyard, but I had never met her or the child before.

What's his name? I called up to her while the other neighbors began retreating from their windows.

Hans Christian, she said.

Hans Christian, I said, and looked down at the boy who had finally quieted. His father arrived and lifted him out of the stroller.

Evening came.

Twenty-Third Continuation

Dear Anna,

I'm now halfway. My muscles and pelvis have begun to stretch and grumble. The child is supposedly growing as it should inside me. Last Monday I went by the publisher to show them how far I've come. The marketing and sales department were under the impression I had written the whole thing, Anna. That it's only mine. I opened my mouth to tell them that that wasn't the case but stopped before I managed to say anything. What could I say? That there is never just one person writing? I had no language they would understand. Whatever I said would have been turned into something precious, brushed aside as an emotion; an artificial pond in a garden with fallen leaves swimming on the surface. "So cute!" exclaimed one of the staff members and showed me a picture on Instagram, a fluffy owl with red eyes. Outside the publishing house, autumn's last birds diving in the streets and chirping, I touched my cheeks, I felt like a painting. I sank into myself, looking for you, found you there, could go on. The child kicked in my belly, several hearts beat.

YOURS

Twenty-Fourth Continuation

One early morning I went to the playground with the boy, who had woken at five o'clock. I found a seat on a bench in the sun with a cup of coffee. The boy was playing near some yellow bicycles. No one else was there.

Here, I read a short story by Margaret Atwood called "Giving Birth," which I feel compelled to share. Jeannie has just given birth. The morning after, she wakes up in a hospital bed, stands up and walks over to the window to open it:

All she can see from the window is a building. It's an old stone building, heavy and Victorian, with a copper roof oxidized to green. It's solid, hard, darkened by soot, dour, leaden. But as she looks at this building, so old and seemingly immutable, she sees that it's made of water. Water, and some tenuous jellylike substance. Light flows through it from behind (the sun is coming up), the building is so thin, so fragile, that it quivers in the slight dawn wind. Jeannie sees that if the building is this way (a touch could destroy it, a ripple of the earth, why has no one noticed, guarded it against accidents?) then the rest of the world must be like this too, the entire earth, the rocks, people, trees, everything needs to be protected, cared for, tended. The enormity of this task defeats her; she will never be up to it, and what will happen then?

Anna looked up at the trees and the sky and the apartment buildings, there were no people in the windows, it was almost seven o'clock, she couldn't remember if it was a weekday. A big, black formation slid over one of the rooftops like a bedsheet or a cloud of smoke, only to disappear just as quickly.

Anna squinted up at the roof. She turned toward the boy, but out of the corner of her eye she saw the same black shadow glide weightlessly across the roof and then fall away again. She looked up. Was she hallucinating? The black shape was lifting and falling like a breath.

The boy called, and she went to him. What did he want? He just wanted to have her nearby. He was digging with a shovel in the sand. Threw it away. Strutted over to a basketball, picked it up with two hands and carried the big ball around in front of him with short steps.

Slowly Anna turned her head up toward the building's roof to see whether the black shape was still looming. A wind blew through the playground, the trees rustled, a plastic bucket scraped across the asphalt, and there, again, the black shape.

She was most likely going mad. She was all alone with the child. She looked around, but they were still the only people at the playground. Anna hardly dared look up at the building again, she lifted her head.

She saw the black shape again, but now it was a loose plastic tarp covering a hole in the roof. Each gust of wind lifted the tarp up with a wave and let it drift back down over the hole. Anna took a deep breath.

The feeling that she was losing her mind stayed with her. She was relieved it was only a tarp, but saw her uncertainty as proof that things would soon go wrong. She looked over at the boy, he didn't seem to have noticed anything.

The first thing I did when I got home was to write down the scene. It had a surreal quality to it which I almost immediately recognized as literary. Was this impulse to turn it into writing a means of protecting myself against this opening into madness, or rather a way of digesting the event and giving it space?

Often when Anna saw things that did not exist, she told

herself: *You can write about it*, and in that way she tied it to the real world.

Anna parked the experience with the tarp in her notebook and didn't tell anyone about it—that is, anyone apart from me, who now, more than a year later, is writing it down for her before we go grocery shopping.

ME

Really, I'm interested in the gap between the established truths we tell each other about pregnancy, childbirth, maternity leave and childrearing, and how people actually feel. I think a lot of unnecessary problems arise from this place. The incongruity between the story about childbirth and childbirth itself.

ANNA

Are we having steak?

ME

That's why we're writing this book, isn't it? To shrink the incongruity, to make it easier to become a mother?

ANNA

But we're already a mother.

ME

Yes, but easier in the future, and retrospectively.

ANNA

You're talking about healing.

ME

Yes, Anna, is that so bad?

ANNA

I don't think I can be healed. I mean, I'm what you need to be
cured of.

ME

But that's not what I want!

ANNA

I know.

ME

But should I be worried?

ANNA

No, there's no need for that.

ME

Good, then I can rest easy.

*(Anna takes out a knife and proceeds to stab me to death at the
supermarket.)*

ANNA

Sleep tight, sweetheart. *(turns away from the corpse)* Hello,
everyone! My name is Anna and I am a knife! Such poor
wretches, the load of you. Painted queens, vain flowers! Why
do you sprinkle sugar on the pickled spiders in whose deadly
webs you're trapped? Fools! You whet every knife that wants
to kill you. The time will come when you'll beg me to help
you curse these poisonous toads you call housekeeping,
motherhood, birthday cakes, love. Slash it open! Is that understood? AS FOR THE BIBLE, in John CHAPTER SIXTEEN,

verse TWENTY-ONE we find JESUS saying: "A woman when she is in travail hath sorrow, because her hour is come: but as soon as she is delivered of the child, she remembereth no more the anguish, for joy that a man is born into the world." And I'd love to know, what does Jesus know about that? *(addressing me)* Is it just me, or are you groaning in your pool of blood over there? Aren't you dead yet? *(returning to the point at hand)* And what does John know about it? In my experience at least, great joy doesn't necessarily exclude pain. One doesn't rule out the other. But anyway, that's what we've been walking around telling each other for approximately two thousand years, so it's a little tricky to quash. Oh, look, now she's waking up. Resurrecting, impossible to kill once and for all. That's how much she loves life, unbelievable, the laboring mother over there, look how she goes on and on about her experiences for years.

ME

(gurgling own blood, smiling) Good morning.

ANNA

Another thing about THE BIBLE, which kind of contradicts John's Gospel, but then again it's the Old Testament, which of course is a bit old-school, one could say. Here, it's God speaking *(clears throat)*: "Unto the woman he said"—so this is God speaking to women now—"I will greatly multiply thy sorrow and thy conception; in sorrow thou shalt bring forth children; and thy desire *shall be* to thy husband, and he shall rule over thee." And then they're kicked out of the Garden of Eden. Not a dull moment. That was Genesis 3:16. So far, so good. ANYWAY, let's take a CLOSER LOOK at these two pieces of INFORMATION the Bible gives us about CHILDBIRTH.

According to the bit I just cited, SPOKEN BY GOD, it HAS to hurt because as a woman, you've got to be punished. But AT THE SAME TIME, don't forget, ACCORDING TO JESUS, *(addressing me)* Hi, Jesus …

ME

(still lying in pool of blood at supermarket, propped up on arms) Um … you mean me? Okay then, hi!

ANNA

(continuing) … Yes, well, don't forget, ACCORDING TO JESUS, at least it won't hurt anymore as soon as the child is born, AND YOU WON'T EVEN REMEMBER IT. No, no, not at all. So you've got to suffer, because that's God's will, and not complain about your suffering, because you've forgotten it. That means that the pain of childbirth is both there and … not there. It's only there for a split second, about which you can't speak, because you have to talk about this delightful child, the miracle that it is, its lovely fingers and its little pink seashell nails, and THE PENIS, my goodness, how lovely it is, and how the testicles have dropped, and if it's a girl, she might bleed from her vagina after birth, the boy's scrotum might be swollen and red, both girls' and boys' nipples could be swollen and secrete a bit of fluid known as witch's milk.

ME

And it's completely normal and stops on its own!

ANNA

But when visitors come to your hospital room, where you're drenched in sweat from all the fucking work you've done, don't mention the pain, merely smile your sweet motherly smile and say:

ME

Oh my, that was hard.

ANNA

Your grandmother says: Well done, my girl.

ME

Thanks, Granny.

ANNA

And Granny says: Although you were given anesthesia, so it couldn't have been *that* bad. And then you say:

ME

You're right, Granny.

ANNA

And the child flails silently in the hospital crib like a pack of vibrating pig's tails, and your mother says:

ME

Now, remember not to bottle-feed in the beginning. It can be very dangerous.

ANNA

And you think: dangerous how? But you nod and smile and in your little meek voice, you say:

ME

May I have some juice, please?

ANNA

And:

ME

Were you able to find good parking?

ANNA

This is where one becomes the knife. The knife that cuts open the belly. *(Anna walks over to me, raises the knife, the blade glints)*

ME

(propped up on arms) Seriously? … *(Anna stabs me again, I die)*

ANNA

WELCOME TO THE CHILD'S SECOND YEAR OF LIFE!

Twenty-Fifth Continuation

Mixed anxiety   *Group Room II*

1 year, 5 months, and 1 day after the birth

A SCENE. THE GROUP ROOM. A COFFEE VENDING MACHINE, A SIDE TABLE WITH PAMPHLETS, A NUMBER OF FADED POSTERS (KIND OF CHAGALL-LIKE), A WEIRD SMELL. THREE WINDOWS FACING A PARKING LOT, OUTSIDE A CLUSTER OF WILLOWS IN A SOUNDLESS BREEZE. SIX PEOPLE GATHER AROUND A RECTANGULAR TABLE IN THE MIDDLE OF THE ROOM. THEY EACH HAVE A FOLDER IN FRONT OF THEM. INSIDE THESE FOLDERS, *PSYCHOEDUCATIONAL MATERIAL.*

Welcome to Mixed Anxiety, a group therapy treatment at the Schiller Clinic.

The group consists of four participants and two therapists. The group meets for two hours a week for twelve weeks.

A doctor is assigned to the group and is responsible for overall treatment.

Attendance is mandatory. All participants in the group are bound by confidentiality. You are therefore not permitted to talk about the other members of the group in an identifiable way.

You will be taking part in a transdiagnostic cognitive behavioral therapy treatment for people with anxiety disorders and unipolar depression.

The treatment is intended to help you challenge unhealthy coping strategies for managing emotions and develop more healthy strategies.

In practice, this means you will learn that you are capable of tolerating strong emotions and handling the situations in which these arise.

The aim of our treatment is for you not to avoid emotions, but instead to change your reactions to them.

That means you must approach your emotions instead of distancing yourself from them. This will allow you to live the life you want once again.

"So, maybe this is nothing, and if you think it's stupid you can just forget it, I mean, I don't even know whether it's an issue, it's just, if you tell me to spin around in circles a bunch of times, for example, I wouldn't want to because I might get dizzy, I mean, I hope you're not thinking it's because I can't see it myself, because I can, I can see I have a problem, I just don't know how *big* the problem is."

A SCENE. MORNING. ONE OF THOSE HORRIBLE MORNINGS;
COLD, COLORLESS, DAMP, A POORLY DRESSED MORNING.
A PATIENT IN THE GROUP ROOM. SHE IS IN HER SEAT,
WAITING. SHE HAS PLACED HER FOLDER ON THE TABLE IN
FRONT OF HER ALONG WITH TWO PENS, A BOX OF MINTS,
AND A BOTTLE OF WATER, FROM WHICH SHE REPEATEDLY
TAKES SMALL SIPS.

THE PATIENTS
A woman with a nose piercing: Arazo
A woman who never takes off her Saks Potts fur-trimmed coat:
Amalie
A woman with a narrow face: Alberte
A woman of childbearing age: Anna

THE THERAPISTS
Mette
Mimi

EXAMPLE OF CONVERSATION

ALBERTE
On a scale of 1–10, where 10 is the worst and 0 is none at all,
in the past week I've experienced anxiety at a level of ZERO.

METTE
So no anxiety at all?

ALBERTE
I feel no anxiety at all. Which leads me to question whether this
treatment is even beneficial to me. The rest of you obviously
benefit a lot from it. But I sat still for ten consecutive hours to
figure out whether I felt anxious. And there was nothing.

METTE
You sat still for ten hours straight?

ALBERTE
Yes, five days a week.

METTE
I think it's time you introduce yourself to the group.

ANNA
But we already know Alberte.

ALBERTE

Hi, my name's Alberte, and I suffer from emetophobia, also known as fear of vomit and nausea. Most people who suffer from emetophobia don't like *(enumerating the following)* the sound of vomiting, hearing people talk about vomit ...

ARAZO

(interrupting) But I talk about vomit all the time.

ALBERTE

(continuing) ... feeling nauseated, seeing vomit on the street or elsewhere, being with people who might be contagious, eating food that may or may not have expired, eating in public, taking medication with side effects that may cause nausea, being with people who are intoxicated, being in waiting rooms at the doctor,'s going to the movies.

AMALIE

No, I don't like that either.

ALBERTE

But at present I don't have any symptoms of anxiety.

METTE

No symptoms at all?

ALBERTE

No, none. None at all.

ARAZO

That is, besides sitting still for ten hours at a time.

METTE

And how does that feel?

ALBERTE

It feels completely fine. I'm worried I'm not benefiting from this treatment, seeing as I, UNLIKE THE REST OF YOU, am not anxious.

ARAZO

Yes, extremely anxious. None of us can sit still for ten hours at a time.

ALBERTE

Five days a week.

METTE

And Alberte, how does it make you feel when you think everyone else has anxiety and you don't?

ALBERTE

Well, it ... it makes me a bit nervous, I can't deny that.

METTE

And how does that feel?

ALBERTE

The nervousness? How it feels?

METTE

Yes.

ALBERTE

Well, sort of ... pressure in my chest and ... nausea ...

METTE

And how does that feel?

ALBERTE
Well ... well, I don't want anything in my mouth!

METTE
And how does that feel?

ALBERTE
I'm telling you, I don't want anything in my body. Just ask my dad!

(pause)

ALBERTE
You don't understand. I'm thin and have to be thin.

(pause)

AMALIE
Okay, Alberte.

ARAZO
(full of admiration) Just look at her.

ANNA
Alberte?

ALBERTE
I don't like food entering my body.
I don't like the sensation of food in my mouth.
I don't like the little grease stains, the black seeds.
I don't like taking the world in.
I don't want all these objects from the world inside me.
I want to be outside the world.

I want to be a roll of fabric leaning against a whitewashed wall which is maybe bleached by the sun and wind but is otherwise unchanged and unused.
I want to be me and nothing more, not a rice grain more.

ARAZO
What do you want to be?

ALBERTE
I want to be very thin.
I want to be very little.
They can't get me.
They can't touch me.
I don't want to be of use.

AMALIE
What do you want to be?

ALBERTE
I want to be very thin. I want to be hard.

METTE
What do you want to be?

ALBERTE
Very thin. Very small.

ANNA
What do you want to be?

ALBERTE
Something hard. Don't look at me.

A LONG, EMPTY CORRIDOR. WHITE. NOT A SOUND. A DOOR
TO AN OFFICE OPENS. IN THE DOORWAY, A BLUING WIN-
DOW. A VOICE SAYS: COME IN.

would it be alright if
I send you downstairs?
asks the psychologist
we're on the floor
for anxiety and OCD
downstairs is personality
disorders
and suicide prevention
yes, that's alright
I say
you tick a lot
of boxes
she says smiling
my horoscope
is never right either
am I choosing the wrong apps
group therapy
Tina the nursery teacher
Tina talks about
the imaginary
teddy that will
make the child sleep
I gave him the
same bunny
every night
for four months and

it made no difference
he doesn't become attached
to stuffed animals
I am a woman
in need of
supervision
she asks me
what my compulsive
thoughts are about
clothes
sex
motherhood
death
doesn't that sound
like a woman

as soon as I
stepped into the room
I saw they were
all women
and I thought
what's wrong with society
and
what's wrong with me
I'm much worse
than any woman
the worst woman
thoughts of grandeur!
beware!
immediately I thought
you don't
belong here
you belong with
the truly mad
but no one has
found out yet
I want to be found out
and not found out
I want to
be penetrated
by a man who
isn't human

they drew
a graph on
the whiteboard
what am I to do with
another education
psychoeducation
I am critical
of the way
they separate
thought and emotion
I said to the woman next to me
after they had drawn
the *cognitive diamond*
on the board
later she said
to the entire group
that she was
skeptical whether
anxiety was
biologically conditioned
as suggested
by the
teaching material
clever girl
I thought and
then I thought
am I the one who has
planted those
critical thoughts
in her have I
already
contaminated her

destroyed her
chances of
recovery
beware!
thoughts of grandeur!
I am bound by confidentiality
so I can't talk about the other
three women in the room
and the two female
therapists
all social classes
were represented
but I can
talk about myself
I have decided
to keep a journal
after each session
every Friday
because I think
what they're up to
at the Schiller Clinic
is fucking bullshit
and yet
every Friday
I return
I tell myself
it's of
anthropological interest
but still
I hope

THE GROUP ROOM. DECEMBER. AWKWARDNESS. SOMEONE HANDS OUT CHRISTMAS BISCUITS FROM A BIG TIN. POLITE SMILES. COGNITIVE BEHAVIORAL THERAPY FORMS ARE FILLED OUT AND SUBMITTED TO THE MUNICIPAL EMPLOYEES. OUTSIDE, DARKNESS.

"I began thinking about what to buy at Waterfront. It's as if each time there's something I ought to get off my chest, my thoughts immediately turn to shopping. And then I replace the conversation with shopping. Maybe I buy a gift to try and say something with that instead. Then I might spend a long time picking out an outfit and finally put on some clothes, and then I go out, and when I've driven around for a while, I look down at myself and think, no, this won't do at all, and then I find a parking spot and go inside the shop and buy a whole new outfit and change in the changing room, and I feel better straightaway but I also feel bad because I've spent all that money, but I think if I look like someone who has it together then I can become that person. Usually I change in the car, and each time there's that same moment when I look down at the price tag I've just torn off in my hand and I think: God, you're so fat and ugly, Amalie, and then I start the car, and I'm only able to drive very, very slowly through town, because everything has closed in on me, as if the trees' reflection has engulfed the car windows, and I drive down a street that's so long and endless, and my ears are completely clogged with all this day, and I look down at my clothes, and then I disappear into the thought of how, for instance, lilac is a color, but the color is also fuzzy because it belongs to a sweater."

"This project of yours, it's like rewatching an old TV series—here comes that scene as expected followed by another predictable scene only I'll have forgotten some detail, like 'what are your compulsive thoughts about?' or 'anxiety attacks on public transport.' The illness is always the same but with some degree of human variation. Sometimes I think the variations are so minor that I doubt that humans are real or else it's the illness I doubt, and then I think we've all just made it up, and then I think, no, no, Arazo, the others are sick, it's just you who has made it all up, and then I think, no, no, the others are just these little things, these little squealing piglets that can't get it together, and you're much better than them, much madder than them. So why can't you get it together? Get it together, Arazo. I want to be penetrated by a man who isn't human. I belong with the truly mad. I am a very weak person but hide it well. I am a haystack and around the haystack is my breath. For a long, dark winter I breathed at the top of a windswept mountain and my breath formed condensation that froze to ice on the walls of the house and the ice slowly grew thicker on account of the glacial temperatures, so each time I breathed, the ice inched closer to the haystack that was me until the wind finally blew the house away, leaving behind a house-shaped block of ice with a haystack inside, and I had to go on living that way. A pile of cut grass, maybe still smelling of summer, and inside, something hard.

"And I've just been informed by that doctor down the hall—you aren't doctors, you do know that, right? Mimi and Mette, they aren't *doctors*, they're just therapists—but the doctor, right, he says I have what's called Pure O, and there's a pamphlet about it right over there. So this doctor, he says I'm mainly obsessive, that is, OCD without the C and D, right? It's perfectly normal, but also a kind of illness. I know, right? That's a strange thing to say to a psychiatric patient. But never mind him, it's pure obsession, Pure O, purely obsessive thoughts. You just can't tell by looking at me. Can you tell by looking at me? I'm mainly obsessive, apparently, mainly obsessive. But you can't tell by looking at me. Everyone must think we're crazy, I mean, absolute lunatics. But I don't know that we are. It's perfectly normal to have all these thoughts, you know? It's not being able to let go of the thought that's the problem, really. Or thinking that since you've thought it, it must be true, right? Or—and I think about this often—that the most unpleasant thought or dream is the truest? Meaning unpleasantness per se is an indication of truth. Meaning suffering is the only concrete thing I've got. But then this doctor says, no, no, Arazo, you're just mainly obsessive, but you can't tell by looking at you, can you? Then he gives me this pamphlet and I just recognize all of it, you know? It was so annoying. If you're Pure O, there are no compulsive behaviors. The compulsive behaviors take place *inside* your head, so you can't tell by looking at me, which is probably why it's gone so well, right? You know, my life? Even though it's also gone quite badly, actually. I have thoughts like: What if I'm a pedophile? What if I kill someone I love? And it says that right there in the pamphlet. Plain as day. Examples include thoughts of killing one's partner, child, or sibling. Or how about this? The compulsive thought: Am I going mad? I mean, that one's hard to swallow when you're at a psychiatric clinic, that is, you know, *a café for crazies*. We're all at a crazy café, I've seen it before, and right now, as I'm speaking, I'm thinking, what if I jumped out the window? And at the same time I'm thinking: Am I even capable of having real feelings for my partner? But you can't tell by looking at me. He said I was mainly obsessive, he said I could experience thoughts of having cheated on my partner without remembering it. But while he was saying that, I was thinking about whether I could have killed someone and buried the body without remembering it afterward, and I told him that, and do you know what he said? You know what the man said? He said: 'Those are some of the typical thoughts that may come up.' And he says it's just an anxiety disorder, and that it doesn't say anything about who I am as a person. And I just think: What an idiot. 'It's perfectly normal to have unpleasant thoughts,' he said, and I'm just thinking, what if I steal something from Amalie's bag, right? Will I ever be allowed back to the café? Does animal sex turn me on? Do I not love my mother? Was I raped just now? Could I push someone in front of a train? Am I not made of ice? Is that just something I made up? The summer hay and all that? Maybe it's just something I conjured with words, out of thin air. I mean, how do you know if you're actually deeply miserable? So what I want to know is whether I'm living a lie. Rationally, I understand that it's impossible to know. But I still want to know. But you can't know. But I want to know. But you can't know. But I want to know."

A SCENE. LATE AFTERNOON. THE GROUP ROOM. EVERY-
ONE IS GATHERED AROUND THE MEETING TABLE. A LONG
AND UNCOMFORTABLE SILENCE. THE RUSTLE OF PAPERS.
A CHAIR BEING PULLED OUT, A SINGLE POLITE COUGH.
PATIENTS AND THERAPISTS TURN TOWARD THE COUGHER
BUT SHE SHAKES HER HEAD AND LOOKS DOWN, DOESN'T
HAVE ANYTHING TO SAY AFTER ALL.

the kitchenette
next to
Group Room II
is noisy
they're talking about
massages
I felt
megalomania
I was a
natural leader
of the group
at the same time I
experienced self-judgment
for having a
small life
a small pain
compared to
the others
again
this
I am
artificial
a plastic bracelet
flung

when the two therapists
play
a piece of music
for us
so we can
practice our emotional
awareness
the tune they
choose to play is
"Jaws"

anxiety is a future-oriented feeling
it says in the
blue folder
we've been given and
one of the therapists
asks who can
describe
what anxiety
feels like
oh dear says a woman
anxiety is like:
I don't want to
uh-huh says the therapist
drawing it out
good says the therapist
anyone else?
she is looking for
a particular answer
and the answer
is in the pamphlet
right in front of us
we must be coached
violence is part of
the family structure
heart racing
on public transport

fear of traveling
fear of being alone
two young women
experience anxiety when their
boyfriends don't
come home on time
and share that
they have crying fits
and storm about
the apartment
young women who become
pathologically anxious
without men
in the house
heart racing on
public transport
when I
leave the room
to cry
the therapist follows
and I say
you're not going to be able to help me
this isn't going to work
she says
the worst that can happen is
you'll waste your time

"I don't like being sick."

"It's awful."

"But also alright."

"Each of us, about to burst."

"We're almost done for today."

"Do you think Group Room II can heal us?"

A SCENE. MORNING. THE GROUP ROOM. LIGHT LIKE FALL-ING WATER. A PATIENT IS WAITING IN HER SEAT, READY. SHE HAS PLACED HER FOLDER ON THE TABLE IN FRONT OF HER ALONG WITH TWO PENS, A BOX OF MINTS, AND A BOTTLE OF WATER, FROM WHICH SHE REPEATEDLY TAKES SMALL SIPS. ANOTHER PATIENT ENTERS, OUT OF BREATH. SHE IS WEARING A BICYCLE HELMET.

EXAMPLE OF CONVERSATION

ANNA
I've come straight from drop-off at the nursery. That's why I'm so early.

ALBERTE
I'm always early.

ANNA
I know.

ALBERTE
Would you like a mint?

ANNA
Having to pick up the child at a specific time in the afternoon drives me crazy. It's as though all time in the world shrinks and by nine in the morning I'm already stressing about picking him up on time, so I spend so much energy thinking about what time is.

ALBERTE
What do you mean?

ANNA
I don't want to neglect him by picking him up too late.

ALBERTE

What do you mean by that?

ANNA

And at the same time, I never want to pick him up again.

ALBERTE

And what do you think that means?

ANNA

Whether I never wanted a child in the first place. And I feel sorry for the boy for having to love me.

ALBERTE

Is this where the anxiety comes in? You sure you don't want a mint?

ANNA

Yes, please *(accepts mint, but holds it in her hand)*. No, the anxiety comes long before that. It's there when I wake up. I get up, I bathe him, I make porridge, we get on the bike. The whole way to the nursery, when he's so quiet in the seat behind me, I'm afraid he'll be dead when we arrive, all limp and blue, and images of his dead body flash through my mind so I hardly register whether the lights are red or green. We arrive, I'm shaking, I drop him off, he's so sweet, I'm afraid the teachers can tell I'm carrying his dead body inside me. To give birth to a child is also to give birth to a future corpse, you make a death, have you ever thought about that?

ALBERTE

Um ... no ... ?

ANNA

Once I've dropped him off and walk back to my bike, the day is both open and empty. Time ties itself into a knot around the day's expiration, and my thoughts are never free but end at pickup time.

ALBERTE

I'd like to have a child one day.

ANNA

Alberte, don't tell the others what I told you, okay?

ALBERTE

I'd never do that, you know that.

ANNA

I'm glad you're here. I'm glad you come every week.

ALBERTE

Do you think we'll see each other once this is over?

ANNA

Probably not. Do you?

ALBERTE

I don't think I can. It's the nausea. It's very insistent.

ANNA

You can have my number, if you want?

ALBERTE

I don't think so. No, I … I think I would like some time to consider it.

THE STRAW METHOD

Physical symptoms of anxiety: Racing heart, shortness of breath, dizziness, nausea

Everyone breathes through a straw for one minute.

Everyone spins in circles for thirty seconds.

Everyone does jumping jacks for one minute.

Everyone breathes through a straw for one minute.

Everyone spins in circles for thirty seconds.

Everyone lies down flat on their stomach, stands up, shakes hands with someone else, lies back down. The exercise is repeated for one minute.

Everyone lies down.

Everyone breathes through a straw for one minute.

this fever

how anxiety
has no root

only a bodiless
crinkling

my face

my story

my hand
as I reach out
to the child

and he takes it
lets it go

we walk
beneath the
covered pathway
toward the bicycle

THE GROUP ROOM. JANUARY. INCREASING UNEASE.

EXAMPLE OF CONVERSATION

MIMI
I see here in my guide that there are a few concluding questions we need to cover in conclusion. To conclude. Um.

METTE
Can you name a few things that are important to you which don't relate to men, children, or work?

MIMI
But that's not the question.

METTE
Well … no matter. Can any of you think of anything?

AMALIE
Grass … textiles … tongue-and-groove pliers … That's it.

ANNA
But in large parts of my life I am all alone.

ARAZO
The part of me that is determined by my life circumstances, which I won't delve further into now as I must admit I want you all to forget me as soon as we leave this place and I'll prob-

ably be coming back and doing this all over again with others, but anyway, the part of me that is determined by my life circumstances, the part of me that has always existed, innate or fostered in childhood, these are the deep-rooted tools that will keep death at bay.

AMALIE
I'm alone when I'm on my way from the supermarket to the grassy area where the car is parked, for example.

ALBERTE
Where I am entirely my own. Where no one owns me. And I am of use to no one.

ANNA
Where the entrance to the kindergarten is.

Twenty-Sixth Continuation

Anna embroiders a star on yellow fabric. She titles the embroidery "The birth of my first child." Does that mean I'll have more children, Anna wonders.

In the middle of the star she embroiders a blue eye. The star's uppermost arm is red and pink. She embroiders the upper left arm in two different shades of gray, the upper right arm is dark blue with two bloodred droplets. The lower left arm is brown with yellow crosses and dots. The last arm, the lower right, she leaves empty.

It takes her a long time to finish the embroidery, several years, she abandons it for long stretches.

Anna thinks: What kind of book am I writing? A monstrous book for a monstrous feeling. A monstrous experience: giving birth.

Anna steps out onto the balcony for the first time in months. It's February, she's freezing, she sits down. She doesn't want to die.

Anna thinks about always having to choose between denying herself and her wants, or denying the child and what's best for him.

Anna doesn't want to keep all these things she has written about the birth and the weeks after the birth, because she doesn't want to remember what it was like. They must be transferred to the realm of dreams. Since giving birth, Anna cries so easily. She doesn't want to look at the words because she doesn't want to remove herself from her experience. To look coldly at her own child, to view her child, her love, as writing, Anna will not do it.

She tries to write something about the part of her life that has nothing to do with men or children.

Anna thinks for a while, then she writes:

Garden
Textiles
Tongue-and-groove pliers
Cooking

What is this? Anna thinks, looking at the list she has written. It appears incomplete.

There are large parts of my life where I am alone, all alone, Anna thinks. For example, when I'm on my way from one place to another. Where I am entirely my own person. Where no one owns me. What writing comes from this place? I think this place will save me.

Anna recalls a night a few weeks ago when she cried and told Aksel: "The two of you are devouring me."

Very soon I will have to leave to save myself.

The part of me that is determined by my life circumstances, the part of me that has always existed, innate or fostered in childhood, these are the deep-rooted tools that will keep death at bay.

Anna stops writing. She listens for something inside and waits.

Twenty-Seventh Continuation

Summer in the big man's house

2 years, 1 month, and 24 days after the birth

DAY ONE

1.
My new rule: As long as I'm in this house, I'm not allowed
to go back and read what I have previously written. Nothing
will come of it but getting stuck in the already-said. I must
continue to the end. Although I have tried putting it off and
haven't touched the manuscript for a year, I can't avoid this
work any longer. Completing this book is somehow tied to
my life and well-being.

More rules: I must sit down and write for two hours every day.
     I can't write in secret, but must inform my family of these
hours I'm taking to write.
     Every day for the next ten days I must write.

There are three of us here: the woman, the man, and the child.
     We're spending ten days in a house in Spain.
     The stay is part of a residency program that I applied for
under the guise of doing work, but we have agreed to spend it
as a holiday instead.

When we arrived at the house, I began to long for a life in
which the man takes care of the child all day while I write.

There is a study on the second floor which remains in the same state the former owner left it in.

When I stepped into the room and closed the door behind me, it was as though this former owner flew into me, and I told myself the smell in there was his. I sat down at the desk, in front of the window with the heavy, red drapes. Dust whirled up and glittered in the sun. There were floppy disks and an old hat. And while I sat in the shade of the study, looking out at the sun-scorched mountains, I was again struck by this yearning for the man to cook, to drive, mind the child, clean, for neither of them to spare me a thought while I sat here working and could disappear.

I tell myself that my writing is not depriving them of anything. That by choosing to write, I am not demanding any sacrifice of them. This is the life the big man who built this house, a famous author, once led. I can't bring myself to demand this of my family; that they sacrifice themselves for my art. Yet in this study, in another world, the temptation is enormous and I allow myself to feel it completely: The family is insufferable.

How am I to love this man downstairs in the kitchen who both annihilates and protects me? I cannot live without the love of a man. This is both pathetic and wonderful. There are very few men in the world I can stand. The man in this house is one of them, and he loves me. Now the birds of prey are gliding above the mountain ridge in the bright sun.

I must demand two hours of them. This is my task. To demand time to write. To demand that they forget me.

Implementing writing as a necessary part of our shared life will change my writing, the way I write.

No longer writing in secret.

No longer writing furtively.

No longer writing in the shadow of shame, incoherent notes when everyone else is asleep.

I must tell them that writing is work but also not work. It's more like a personal sport. No one questions the fact that my husband wants to go for an hour-long run each day. It's good for him, and he takes the time to do it whenever possible.

That's how it must be: to create a family life where writing is included.

And not a life in which writing lives in spite of the family.

And not a life in which the family gets by despite a writing member.

2.

How does an author of childbearing age write after she has had children?

If becoming a mother has been the most life-changing experience of her life, must she refrain from writing about becoming a mother in order to be a good mother?

Is writing about becoming a mother *being* a bad mother?

Does it subject the child to writing's destruction?

Does it mean choosing oneself, one's writing, instead of protecting the child?

Must she kill the writer inside to become a good mother?

So much of what I write has been written in my head on the short walk beneath the pergola from the nursery to my bike after dropping off the child, and from my bike to the nursery in the afternoon.

Why do so many authors write about writing? Why do their readers, who are not authors, want to read about it? Is it because writing is a metaphor for life? And if so, what does it mean to write about becoming a mother? Is writing about motherhood a way of becoming a mother? Is writing itself an act of mothering? A place where the child is and is not? Or, let me rephrase: Is it through writing I become a mother?

When the child left my body, the whole world transformed, not a single living thing could be understood in the same way again. Among the world's objects was now my child, my own literal flesh, looking back at me. My connection to the world changed radically. Every single thing in the world revealed another, deeper side, because part of my body had left me and now existed among them. I was no longer the same. The divide between what is me and what is the world opened. Everything casts the same light as before, but now I see that it's living.

3.
I can no longer write in the third person.
   Writing in the third person was born of a powerlessness in the face of experience.
   To write in the third person was to create someone else to endure the pain.
   One invents her. Her name is Anna.

To unravel the suffering, I had to find a place to begin.
   Certain things cannot be written in the first person, so they are transferred to the second or third.

A woman looking at someone who looks like herself from a distance; she describes this person.
   She starts to walk. She crosses a field. As she moves forward, she walks into a falling snow, and there in front of her she sees the other woman. The woman who could be mistaken for her,

and she comes closer step-by-step. But when they reach one another and see each other's faces, she realizes they do not look anything alike, it only seemed that way from a distance. The woman she described is a stranger.

The third person is a helpless woman.

Look, I'm writing. I'm writing again. So something inside me must have changed. Is this change for the better? Are my muscles stronger? I'm sitting in the shadowy study. Soon the sun will reach me through the window. And the sun is hot and hard-hitting. I am writing on a mother's borrowed time.

DAY TWO

4.

Sitting down now, with two hours at my disposal, I'm so thirsty to be writing that the doubt quickly washes away.

A buzzard hangs in the air, the big palm outside the window swishes.

The man asked me: Do you write nonstop for two hours up there?

ME: Yes, pretty much.

But that isn't true, sometimes I just sit here. I try to reserve the time for not feeling guilty. I read.

The man asked me: How did he, this great author, get rich enough to build this house?

ME: I don't know how he became so rich and famous. Some just do.

When I schedule time for writing in the midst of family life, when I take these two hours to work and don't write at other times, I'm filled with thirst and happiness as soon as I sit down. Writing becomes a discipline, a relief, not an art form. When I don't go back and read what I wrote yesterday, don't edit, this act becomes a matter of creating space, not of producing.

Will I keep writing this book for the rest of my life?

5.

Which thoughts came to me when I stepped into this office yesterday?

That what I find interesting is not my own life but how a mother writes, and how becoming a mother changes a person's writing.

That when motherhood began, I found that I could no longer write freely. Writing was not accessible, and at the same time I needed writing more than ever.

And why was writing not free? Because to write is to be a bad mother. Because to write is to fail the family. To protect the child means to omit it. (How is this logical?) To protect love means not to write about its object. Not to write critically about the man. Not to show the child one's pain. Let the child believe he was brought into being in immense love.

Each time I come in here, I must grapple with these thoughts about writing with the child inside me. Or rather, not the child, but the traces it left behind.

And how do the traces of the child write?

The dull pain of scar tissue, the loose joints. The entire body altered by the child's coming and going yet still somehow the same as before.

The mountains in the big man's study.

I sit here.

Searching for the voice for years.

How to write this mother, this mother's writing? How does she speak? How does she carry the writing forward? This resistance, each time. I cannot hear the voice. It's locked inside the delivery room I no longer have access to.

Will I keep writing this book for the rest of my life?

DAY THREE

6.

In Charlotte Perkins Gilman's 1892 short story "The Yellow Wallpaper," the narrator has just had a child, and there is something wrong with her. Her husband and brother, both of whom are doctors, say her condition is not serious and at the same time they claim she is ill.

They also tell her she isn't allowed to write. She believes writing is precisely what could help her. The book consists of the notes she writes in secret after she has been told not to. In order to cure her, her husband has brought her to an old house in the countryside where she is eventually locked in a room with yellow wallpaper. Meanwhile, her child is tended to by a nanny her husband has his eye on.

The narrator says: *If a physician of high standing, and one's own husband, assures friends and relatives that there is really nothing the matter with one but temporary nervous depression—a slight hysterical tendency—what is one to do?*

My brother is also a physician, and also of high standing, and he says the same thing.

So I take phosphates or phosphites—whichever it is, and tonics, and journeys, and air, and exercise, and am absolutely forbidden to "work" until I am well again.

Personally, I disagree with their ideas.

Personally, I believe that congenial work, with excitement and change, would do me good.

But what is one to do?

I did write for a while in spite of them; but it does exhaust me a good deal—having to be so sly about it, or else meet with heavy opposition.

These men in "The Yellow Wallpaper" tell the woman there is nothing wrong with her while maintaining that she may not work until she is "well again." They tell her she is both healthy and unwell. This contradiction creeps into the narrator, because if she is not ill, but also not well, there must be something about her very being that needs to be tamed, something about her that is intrinsically wrong and not simply an illness she must be cured of.

Since they deem her incapable of telling the difference between what is illness and what is her, what is good and what is bad for her, they forbid her from writing, lock her away, and leave the child in someone else's care.

In the wallpaper's pattern she sees monstrous vines twisting and turning, and behind them a woman, creeping around. These wallpaper vines seem like a text; written lines covering a trapped female figure.

"The Yellow Wallpaper" documents the writing that the main character has been forbidden. When she concedes that writing is indeed exhausting, she doesn't mean writing itself, but the fact that she must do so in secret. That it's so strongly opposed, that it's forbidden—that is what's exhausting. And ultimately, it's the discounting of her experience and the objection to her expressing herself in writing that makes the woman lose her grip on reality.

In a gruesome but equally pleasing finale, the woman's insanity is portrayed as a chilling victory. She has finally become what the others told her she was: a sick, wild animal that cannot be trusted, the woman behind the wallpaper. Her husband's horror proves he has known all along she wasn't mad. She triumphs by exposing his lie. By mirroring their image of her back at them, she wins back the right to define herself. By courting madness, she courts freedom.

"The Yellow Wallpaper" can be read as a warning of what can happen to a mother if she doesn't bond adequately with her child, if she feels a certain sadness in its infancy. It warns that this place, a life with small children, can drive a woman mad. It can also just be read as a story about a woman who's driven mad by her husband's control issues.

When I read it now, I think the most destructive part of the story is that the woman is forbidden to write. What is dangerous is not writing, but the adamant opposition to it. That one is forced to be sly about it, to write surreptitiously.

That is why I ask openly for this time to write.

That is why I ask openly for this space to speak about becoming a mother.

"The Yellow Wallpaper" tells us how difficult it can be as a mother to insist on your own experience. How all too often attending to the needs of the child is conflated with forcing the mother into silence. And how attending to the needs of the mother is all too often conflated with forcing her into silence. How people believe that just by speaking evil, one makes it come true.

But the belief that it would hurt the child, and the mother herself, to openly speak about the pain of motherhood is a lie. And I don't want to be afraid of it any longer.

By writing it down on these pages, I relieve us both of the burden, the child and me. Here I put all that is horrible about becoming a mother. Here I put the mystery, everything I don't understand. Here I put the loneliness, the distance to the child's father that came with this new life. So neither he nor the child, nor I, must carry it. This book will be a container, a vessel for what a mother is not allowed to be: torn, in doubt, distraught, unhappy.

For as long as I'm writing this book, I think I will remain in a state of postpartum depression. Not writing the book is to remain in the anxiety. Not writing the book is to give power to the fear of words. Not writing is to not become a mother, to remain forever on the threshold of motherhood. To write is to step into it. Let's see what's inside. In there is my fate. To be someone's mother from now until I die.

7.

One poet who is radically reconfiguring the relationship between motherhood and writing, and exposing the idea that a mother is not permitted to write about her children as a culturally contingent belief, is Itō Hiromi.

Itō Hiromi, born in Tokyo in 1955, made her breakthrough in Japan in the 1980s with the long-form poem "Kanoko-goroshi" ("Killing Kanoko"), about a woman who kills her six-month-old child after the child has bitten her breast to the point of bleeding. It's unclear whether the killing was accidental or premeditated.

The woman in the poem receives visitors and is given gifts while to her it feels like a celebration of her annihilation.

Throughout the poem runs the refrain: *Congratulations on your destruction.* Surgical and spontaneous abortions, ectopic pregnancies, and the infanticides of previous generations run through the poem like a glistening trail. Killing small children has always been a part of human culture.

The poem ends by turning the celebration on its head so it's no longer the destruction of the mother that's congratulated, but the destruction of children and fetuses that's celebrated: *Kumiko-san / Congratulations on your abortion / Congratulations on killing Tomo-kun / Mari-san / How about getting rid of Nonoho-chan? / Mayumi-san / Was the fetus a boy or a girl? / Riko-chan / It's about time to get rid of Kōta-kun / Let's all get rid of them together / All of the daughters / All of the sons / Who rattle their teeth / Wanting to bite off our nipples.*

The poem becomes all the more radical when one finds out that Itō Hiromi's firstborn child, a daughter, is named Kanoko. That is, the child in the poem is Itō's own. It is Kanoko who is killed, not once but multiple times throughout the poem.

Many read both "The Yellow Wallpaper" and "Killing Kanoko" as texts about postpartum depression and postpartum psychosis, but to me, the diagnostification, the pathologization of the texts nullifies the women's experiences. I believe these texts are about what it means to become a mother for anyone who has experienced it, not just those who become ill along the way.

Precisely because it's fiction and not reality, there is no reason to classify the women as ill. All of us can become madwomen creeping along the walls when we read Charlotte Perkins Gilman, and when we read Itō Hiromi, we can all in our imaginations kill our infants together.

8.

In 2016 Itō Hiromi was interviewed by Swedish author Tone Schunnesson in the magazine *Bon*. Schunnesson asked her: "What does motherhood mean for your writing?"

Itō replied: "It means I have lived with children, and these children have provided me with plenty of material to write with. Throughout the years, people have been concerned about my children's integrity and well-being, particularly after I wrote that I wanted to kill one of them, but they're doing fine. They don't care, and they understand. If you're from a family of farmers, the children help their parents with the harvest. The same applies to my profession. I provide my children with food and a roof over their heads, and in return they provide me with material for my poems."

And later in the same interview: "The only time I've ever felt forced to explain myself was after I had written I wanted to kill my child. My message was: 'Kill your children because you yourself are more important.' I had to write essays about how even though you hate your children, you might look the other way and embrace them, because at least they have sweet, small bodies. [...] My problem is probably that I am too oriented toward literature, everything is fiction to me, everything can be written. But people aren't good readers, they often stay up there on the surface."

My problem is probably that I am too oriented toward literature, everything is fiction to me, everything can be written. But not for a mother. We demand of a mother that she does not write that way about her children, about her motherhood. For a mother, everything cannot be fiction.

One could say: A mother has no right to fiction. Or: To be a mother is to lose the right to fiction.

"A woman and her book are identical," wrote Edgar Allan Poe in a review of Elizabeth Barrett Browning's *A Drama of Exile and Other Poems* from 1844. Poe felt it was difficult to say anything bad about Browning's book, because it would be the same as saying something bad about Browning herself, and a gentleman does not speak ill of a lady. He then proceeded to copy the rhyme scheme from "Lady Geraldine's Courtship" in his canonical poem "The Raven."

If we turn Poe's claim on its head, we could say that a woman may not write anything that is not identical to her person. That's why Itō, when she writes about wanting to kill her child, is not granted the luxury of fiction. She must be identical to her book, and that's how she is read.

If we follow Poe's line of reasoning, this means that if a woman, a mother, writes an amoral book, she herself is amoral, and her abilities as a mother must be brought into question. A mother who has no morals is a mother who is willing to sacrifice the life of a future citizen. A mother without morals corrupts her child, harms it.

No one is required to exercise constant sound moral judgment the way a mother is.

I think most mothers, at least for a split second, must have had the thought that their own fallibility would lead to the forcible removal of their child. For those of us who received psychiatric treatment while our children were young, this thought is tangible, seeing as the well-being of the child was always discussed in relation to our illness.

We tell a mother she must sacrifice everything for her child, that it is her responsibility to keep it pure, in body and spirit, and at the same time we tell her that the child is not hers, and we will come and take it if we find her incapable of being the kind of mother we think she ought to be.

Why must a mother stay in the realm of reality? Why must a mother remain a reality? Is it because we're scared of losing her? Or is it because we fear for the children's health and well-being? Or is it perhaps, most obviously: because we wish to control her?

Is any writing mother condemned to represent the mother of every reader?

What misfortune! What a horrible fate!

If so, this book must be written for all fellow mothers. Those who do not read me as their own mother. Those who do not demand my protection. Those who do not believe that when a mother writes that she wants to kill her child, she has already, in some way, killed something in the child. That those who give life must be prevented from taking it.

9.

I must accept that this book most likely will not be well-formed. Just as I must accept that my parenting will be full of mistakes, is already full of mistakes. That the strangeness of life will also exist in every book I write and every child I raise. In this way, books and parenthood are inextricably linked. Not as images of one another, but as two forms of vital creation. My work is to make sure the creation of one does not overshadow the other.

Now the man and the child are returning from their grocery trip, I can hear the car in the driveway. I have written for a long time. The door opens, the child is calling. I'll have to continue tomorrow.

DAY FOUR

10.

A birth:

Now it's time. I throw the coverlet off my legs in order to watch closely how you, my sweet bastard, are coming into the light of this world. I can already see your red, wrinkled forehead surfacing between my thighs. You've got a black shock of hair on your fat head. Your face is smeared with my blood. Your nose is wide and flat, and your toothless mouth is wide open. You smell like the insides of my belly—a nourishing smell that seems like a meal to me. It looks insane: your head, sticking out of my lap. A thing like that should be forbidden. All births should be punished by the death penalty. If I had any say in the matter, then there would be no more people from today onward. Only cats and, of course, me.

Unica Zürn, The Trumpets of Jericho, 1968

11.

Every time I go up to the big man's office to write, I'm afraid of writing and drawn toward its happiness.

The child is two and a tyrant.

I'm reading an important book on motherhood, *Frankenstein* by Mary Shelley.

She was twenty when she published it in 1818. Four years earlier, in 1814, shortly before Mary turned sixteen, she eloped with the poet Percy Shelley and quickly fell pregnant. In the following nine years, there was almost no time in which Mary was not either pregnant or breastfeeding—including when she wrote and published *Frankenstein*.

Her first child, Clara, was born two months early and, much to everyone's surprise, lived for eight days. On March 6, 1815, Mary Shelley writes about Clara in her journal: "find my baby dead."

Two weeks later, on Sunday, March 19, she writes: "dream that my little baby came to life again—that it had only been cold & that we rubbed it by the fire & it lived—I awake & find no baby—I think about the little thing all day."

Mary Shelley's own mother, the feminist thinker Mary Wollstonecraft, died eleven days after giving birth to her daughter, who was given her mother's name: Mary.

Mary has her second child when she is eighteen. Her son William is born on January 24, 1816, barely a year after Clara's birth, and she describes him as follows in a letter: "Blue eyes— gets dearer and sweeter every day—he jumps about like a little squirrel."

Later that same year, Mary and William and Percy travel to Lake Geneva, where she is inspired to write *Frankenstein*. Back in England, she finishes the novel while raising her son.

In a letter to her husband, she writes: "The blue eyes of your sweet boy are staring at me while I write this; he is a dear child, and you love him tenderly, although I fancy your affection will increase when he has a nursery to himself."

The year after, in 1817, Mary gives birth to her second daughter, Clara Everina, her third child in three years. Mary is twenty. On January 1, 1818, she publishes *Frankenstein* under a pseudonym.

During a longer stay in Italy, Clara Everina falls ill, likely from dysentery, and dies at thirteen months old. Nine months later, in Rome, William dies of a form of malaria. He is three and a half years old. In a brief letter to a friend, Mary Shelley describes what it was like to sit with the child as he was dying: "The misery of these hours is beyond calculation—The hopes of my life are bound up in him."

It's June 1819. Mary Shelley is twenty-one. On Thursday, June 3, she writes in her journal that William is very sick. She then writes the date "Friday 4th," but the page is empty. William dies on June 7. On the following empty page is an undated note, "The journal ends here —P.B.S." When I read this, I think P.B.S. must be Percy Bysshe Shelley's initials and it is he who with these words ends this volume of Mary's journals.

By then Mary is already four months pregnant with her fourth child, and in November she gives birth to the boy Percy, who will be her last child and the only one to survive her. After losing two children in one year and giving birth to a third, she writes about her youngest son in a letter: "It is a bitter thought that all should be risked on one yet how much sweeter than to be childless as I was for 5 hateful months."

12.

Most of Mary Shelley's journals consist of lists of the books she is reading. It's quite boring, actually, but then, suddenly and unexpectedly, an undated note from 1815 (when Mary was around eighteen years old): "*a table spoonful of the spirit of aniseed with a small quantity of spermaceti.*

9 drops of human blood, 7 grains of gunpowder, ½ oz. of putrified brain, 13 mashed grave worms—"

A line from "The Yellow Wallpaper" wells up inside me; the husband, addressing his wife in the third person: "Bless her little soul! [...] she shall be as sick as she pleases!"

13.

I dreamed my one breast (the good one) was full of milk again, and I was so happy.

I can hear him playing with his dad outside in the garden.

He says a word only he can understand: "TEETOO! TEE-TOO!"

Then: "Meeeee!"

He rattles his tractor.

"Oh, more haaaair."

"What?" asks his dad.

"Wow! More!"

And then in Swedish: "Foten!"

Later: "Mommy? Mommy where?"

"She's working."

"Mommy?" *(pause)* "Two cars."

Writing is difficult today.

I'm looking for a quote I know I've saved on my computer but can't find.

Later, in Swedish: "Mama!"

"She's working."

"Working. Mama working."

Crying. Then a song. "Lala-leela."

Forty minutes have gone by since I came up here.

I'm convinced my husband thinks it's been an hour and a half.

For a couple with a small child, even the passing of time is often up for debate.

Now he's crying loudly: "Mama! Mama!"

Now he makes a delighted sound.

I am writing, listening to my child, to what he says while he misses me because I am writing.

How to explain it?

I open the books, and the poems I once read and memorized seem meaningless and empty.

Now they turn on a kid's show. It's *Paw Patrol*.

My exhausted partner.

A clanging of pots in the kitchen.

I must try to continue writing.

My two hours.

"All done," says the child at the table.

"Don't you want more sausage?"

"Beep-beep dee-dee," says the child. "All done."

"Would you like some more melon?"

"Nooo," sings the child. "All done."

"Try to drink a little more water, please."

"Nooo."

They wash their hands. He whines.

I want to add more people to this book, more characters, outside the family. But the truth is I am a lonely person.

How to fictionalize this voice, this position, so it starts to speak of its own accord? So I can create the necessary distance?

Write for seven more minutes.

This is a book without fixed borders, but time is fixed.

It's easy to describe a specific space. But how to describe a time? Is this entire book an attempt to describe a time? The time of the newly arrived child, and that time as it billows inside its mother?

The time before the child learns to speak.

Can describing time be work? And how are work and time connected?

If my work consists of: earning money, writing, cleaning, caring for the child, feeding it, giving birth to it, growing it, raising it, keeping it clean, keeping it warm, keeping it fed.

If my work consists of: loving my husband, loving my child,

keeping the house clean, staving off the worst fights, paying taxes, voting, taking responsibility for my health.

When the psychologist at the psychiatric clinic in Frederiksberg told me that if I was discharged I would be free to seek private treatment, she never took her eyes off her computer.

"I see you've used up all your allotted sessions."

"Yes."

"We can only offer you further treatment if we give you a new diagnosis, and given that I believe you to be on the subthreshold of such, I recommend you take the next year to pursue treatment with a private psychologist instead. For example, when you say you truly believe no one loves you, this indicates to me a potential for further treatment."

"But isn't that very expensive? Since I have to pay for it myself?"

"It's a snag in the system, to be sure."

"Like you said, I've used up all the free sessions from my doctor's referral and I don't qualify for more. It's going to cost a lot of money I don't have."

"Think of it as a good investment. If all your windows needed repair, you'd spend the money."

My health: a good investment.

"Would you come down soon, please," my husband calls, frustrated, and with these words I leave the big man's study.

DAY FIVE

14.
I ought to insert something in this house that isn't here.

What would Anna say to this arrangement?

It would undoubtedly make her very nervous. She would wring her hands. She would wish to wear a costume so as to know how she was perceived by others.

So now there are two of us here. Me and Anna. Anna and I. Anna arises. She arrives on foot, you can hear her steps on the gravel road. Now I see her, on her way down the driveway, carrying a small suitcase. Practically a doll's suitcase. I don't know what's inside, but it doesn't surprise me that her luggage is ridiculous. She has wispy hair, a long, pointy nose. She looks like a girl I knew in school named Lilje. She looks like a girl I've dreamed of many times who is always about to die. Is Anna sick? She looks at the man and the child playing in the garden. She looks up at the window of the big man's office where I'm sitting. Where will Anna sit? Can my husband see her? Can the boy?

If Anna is merely a ghost, and hence only visible to me, if I insert her as the foreign object in this house only I can see, then this will remain a story about my loneliness.

But I'm tired of ghost stories. She will have to enter into the whole world, so the whole world will change. I cannot keep her a secret.

So let's say I become the ghost and Anna takes my place? No, that won't work.

Anna must walk over to my husband, and she will ask him in Spanish what his name is.

And my husband will answer in Swedish: "Är du svensk?"

Between the leaves above them, the sky looks like it's made of rippling water.

And Anna will grin sheepishly, and say: "Yes."

Because apparently Anna is Swedish, and my husband can tell from her accent.

"Rock!" says the child and holds a rock up toward her.

The air smells of dry grass.

"Interesting," she replies.

And all the leaves turn in the wind with an imperceptible rustle. I regard the three figures.

"I'm Aksel," says Aksel.

"I'm Anna," says Anna.

Will they fall in love?

Will my husband leave me for Anna? He's very dutiful, it wouldn't be easy for him to betray me.

Anna takes a seat on a chair in the garden, sets down her suitcase and pulls the child onto her lap. He quickly slides back down and goes over to the rocks.

When I look out the study window now, I see the landscape has changed. We're no longer in Spain, but inside a novel and the vegetation here does not come from nature, but is pieced together from books. There is a Britishness to this new landscape, like a romantic manor house or Charlotte Perkins Gilman's rose garden.

It's true, there's something dangerous about Anna. She is my double, and therefore she can take my place, eviscerate me.

Should I preserve this danger or render her harmless?

This landscape in me, the garden of books Anna brings with her.

Deep and deciduous.

I hate her the way I hate the girl who teased me in school.

Together we carry the hatred forward.

I love her the way I love the girl who teased me in school.

We eat love.

Now Aksel says: "But it's you, Anna."

For if we follow the rules of fiction, Anna and Aksel have a child together. And earlier, Anna was Danish, but now she's Swedish, she just came walking down the driveway, and what is the reason for their separation, and why hasn't the child aged?

"Where have you been?" asks Aksel.

"I was at the butcher's," says Anna.

Her suitcase is now a plastic bag filled with meat.

"What are we having for dinner?" asks Aksel.

"Chicken drumsticks."

"Chicken!" shrieks the child, he only ever shrieks.

I am inside a tree. From the tree, I call for the child. He comes over, picks at the bark covering my face. "Dee-dee-doo," he says. "Tooth. Snack."

So I became a ghost after all. Am I doomed to write ghost stories my whole life? And must these ghost stories absolutely be set in a British countryside? And why does Anna wish to poison me? Now that I have poisoned Anna with my thought? Is this insanity? I have started to change. With Anna in the text, in the garden, I feel my voice changing shape.

And there is a felt hat.

And there is a pocket with something smooth inside it.

And there is a little red box for the child's rock.

And there is a roomy closet.

I know this closet from my earlier poems.

I don't know what this closet means but I know its smell. This place. Where the head is split open toward a sky swimming with darkness. I walk through the old chapters. The gardens. The salty shrubs along the sea. A window open to the night, and in the panel beneath the window an endless, star-filled abyss. And beyond that Anna, dressed in costume, so she knows how she is perceived.

Anna. She's at the hospital.

She's seven months pregnant.

There are six of them in the room.

All the others have diabetes, and another arrives under the cover of night with preeclampsia.

"I'm a medical student," she informs the nurse. "I just thought you should know."

"Well then, welcome." There's a smile in the nurse's voice.

Anna has had so many Braxton Hicks contractions she nearly went into labor. And her cervix is completely effaced. Anna is scared witless. Aksel has left, he wasn't allowed to stay, and night has settled over the hospital. Anna has never spent the night at a hospital before. Anna can't shake the thought that there is nothing wrong with her, but that she has somehow tricked them all.

That this isn't Braxton Hicks, just an invention of her own making. That if she pulled herself together, if she really tried, she would be able to make it stop. Not be a bad child. Be strong Anna.

She opens her little suitcase. The others doze off. Netflix plays soundlessly on their laptops on the nightstands. Anna feels nauseated and can't sleep. Her heart pounds in her chest. Why doesn't the writer want her to see Aksel again? Does Aksel no longer want her? She feels a muscle pulling across her belly, it's a contraction. A nurse comes in and sits by her side. She checks the CTG, whispers so as not to disturb the others.

"Try to rest now, and we'll reassess in the morning."

"Okay."

"Have you had any kind of childbirth classes yet?"

"No."

"I'm sure you can have a chat with one of the midwives in the ward."

Anna now realizes that they deem it likely she will soon give birth.

They have no crib, no changing table, nothing at home yet. That's her first thought.

Later, the next day, when Anna's mother visits her at the hospital, Anna says the words: "What if he dies?"

But Anna doesn't know whether she means it. Whether she actually fears for the child's life or whether it's just something she's saying. Is it because she knows deep down that the child won't die or is it because—and this is almost worse than the thought of the child dying—she wishes to heighten the drama around her?

And why should Anna wish to heighten the drama around her? As a game? Is it because this entire situation is a machine? A machine with dials Anna can turn? Then why can't she pull herself together and stop the Braxton Hicks contractions? Is it because she wants her mother's love and thinks the more Anna suffers, the greater her mother's love will be? Is it because Anna wants to feel the drama? Something is wrong with Anna's emotions. She's like garbage.

Here in the big man's house, I can hear the man and the child splashing in the pool. Anna is at the hospital and can't hear them.

But now, in the hospital night, the nurse tells her: "We'll

have to see how things look in the morning. If it's time to give birth, we'll give you an injection to mature the lungs. The child's lungs aren't fully developed until week 24, and in order for him to breathe on his own, we'll inject you twice, and then we'll see. Do you understand and consent?"

"Yes," says Anna, and: "Can I get something for the nausea?"

The nurse brings her a medicine cup filled with a thick, white liquid.

Not until around five o'clock does Anna fall asleep. A few hours later the other women in the room start to wake and begin their morning routines. They glance at Anna and at Pre-eclampsia, both of whom arrived during the night.

Across from Anna, a tall woman with an enormous belly is talking on the phone. Based on her conversation, Anna gathers that the woman's two children will visit her today.

"Sure, just come during visiting hours," the woman smiles, looking out the window, and Anna is excited to see what her children look like.

"Are your children coming to visit you today?" she asks once the woman is finished talking on the phone.

"Yes, I'm looking forward to it."

"How old are they?"

"Six and eight."

"So this is your third?"

"Yes, my third child and first gestational diabetes."

A nurse comes into the room for morning rounds, examining woman by woman, and the room goes quiet. After speaking to each patient, the nurse checks the numbers on the external CTGs all of them have belted onto their stomachs, notes down contractions and heart rates. Preeclampsia meticulously describes her pain. The woman next to Anna talks to the nurse about her C-section later that day, it's been scheduled for ages. The child in her belly is already very big. She also has diabetes. She starts to brush her hair. Afterward she gets out of bed and packs up her things. "He's coming today," she says decidedly.

Each woman fetches breakfast from the hallway.

The woman across from Anna chats to the nurse, it's clear she's been here for awhile, they joke and laugh. But when the nurse checks the woman's CTG, she frowns.

It all happens fast. She must have pressed a button, because immediately the room fills with medical staff. They confer hurriedly, one of them orders an operating room be prepared over a phone. The woman's face in the bed among the scrubs, entirely expressionless and turned toward Anna. They whisk her away. The staff disappear along with her. Only a few minutes have passed. None of the women speak. Preeclampsia turns onto her side with her back to where the bed just stood. Bright winter light falls across the linoleum floor. After half an hour a new nurse comes in and packs up the woman's belongings. She draws a curtain around the empty spot.

A third nurse comes over to Anna and checks her CTG.

"How's it looking?" Anna asks.

"It's still the same," says the nurse. "We'll have to see what the doctor says. Are you in pain?"

"No, not really."

Then Anna's mother and Aksel arrive. The woman from the empty spot doesn't return. Anna doesn't dare ask about her for fear of the answer. She doesn't even know her name.

Around noon, Anna is discharged with strict orders to stay off her feet for the remainder of her pregnancy. She's told that if she goes for long walks or otherwise exerts herself physically, she will go into labor. She's told that she just needs to make it past week 34, when the lungs will be fully developed.

"Can't someone do the vacuuming at home for you?" the doctor asks. Anna can't remember the last time she vacuumed anything.

"Yes," Anna replies and goes home to lie in bed until week 37, when the so-called birth window opens. That's almost two months away. When Aksel is at work, she orders takeout and onesies online. Every once in a while she walks down to the corner store for milk and alcohol-free beer. Her belly contracts sharply, it's the Braxton Hicks. She waddles. One time she takes a taxi downtown to buy baby things. After forty minutes she's sweaty and out of breath, has to hurry home. She doesn't like being this weak. When she reaches week 37, Anna and Aksel go for a long walk. During the walk, it starts to hail, they curse, each in their own world. Anna's feet get wet. Anna has a bloody show, but still no labor. She ends up going seven days past her due date, and on the second day of week 41, she gives birth.

When Anna and Aksel arrive at the delivery ward, the midwife on duty sticks her latex fingers into Anna's vagina to measure how far she has opened and says: "You're seven centimeters dilated. That's a lot. Well done! I'll prepare a delivery room."

"That's because I've been in labor for the past two months," Anna laughs, and she and Aksel high-five. They're still eager, glad that the day has finally arrived after all those weeks in bed. As if the worst were now over. How naive. The poor fools.

DAY SIX

15.

Today I was very tired after staying up all night with the fussy
child and getting up early, and decided to use "my hours" to
sleep. Resting was the better option. Now I'm writing while
the child naps. I can't go up to the big man's office because I
won't be able to hear him if he wakes, and my husband is out
for a run. So here I am, writing clandestinely again, not during
my hours, but in a gap left over.

Until now I haven't mentioned the wind, but today I find it
necessary. The wind has been raging for the past two days.
At night there was a storm, and this morning the wind was so
strong we couldn't leave the house. We've brought in all the
garden furniture, the buckets and flowerpots, and driven the
car into shelter behind the house.

Why, I would like to ask—I, Anna—will the narrator not allow
herself to finish writing this book?
   (Anna, it's because motherhood and writing eclipse each other.)
   Giving birth was a sorrow. With the sorrow came shame,
and the tragedy of the child bearing the mark of it.
   (How to say it, Anna?)
   You own your life, and you must not let the child carry it.
   *(Here I would like to insert a red flower, a geranium from the
garden.)*

If a woman is identical with her book, as you say, there is no balance between life and writing.

(*I didn't say that, Edgar Allan Poe did.*)

But you wrote it.

(*Okay, fine.*)

And if it's true that woman and book coincide entirely, she can only write as a destroyer.

(*What do you mean?*)

As someone who in writing overwrites, oversteps the limits of life.

(*But I don't want to. I want to stop writing.*)

You want only to write.

(*That isn't possible for me.*)

That's a lie.

(*I'm tired of writing to avoid writing, Anna.*)

This book must be written.

(*I won't let it cost me, I refuse to pay such a high price.*)

Then you'll have to negotiate the price.

(*How do I do that?*)

This book is such a negotiation. Today is such a negotiation. A negotiation of the price of writing in a mother's life.

(*What will it cost? What has the child cost me?*)

DAY SEVEN

16.

Does a fabricated story more accurately reflect human existence than the attempt to realistically render a genuine lived experience?

Does fiction, like a dream, depict experience far better than a writer's endeavor to directly reproduce her own life?

And what is this notion of *one's own life*?

Is fiction as I invent it not just as much my own life as, say, a drive down to the town butcher is? And maybe even more so?

Are my dreams not also my biography?

And if writing is comparable to dreaming, is the writing I produce not also my biography? My biography per se? And not simply a documentation of it?

And if dreaming at night is also living, is part of experience, and writing is also dreaming, then writing is twice as much living as anything else.

But life is doubled here, because the words remain long after they are written. Writing continues its own life. Is this life a real, living life? A life form? Or is it an artificial residue?

If what I want in my writing is to come as close as possible to reproducing a human experience, should I stick to pure fiction, since through its lies I'm nearer some truth of the human condition? And is this the reason why we humans have invented lying? Not to hide our intention, but to double it?

Or will emotion as I portray it in pure fiction (*Franken-*

stein)—in the invented, the fabricated, the fake—always be artificial emotion?

What I am asking is this: Where, in what form, is experience made real, and how do I recognize it? Where, in what form, do I know that I love?

17.

Reading *Frankenstein*, it strikes me that it's an intentionally artificial book. Mary Shelley assembled it out of elements from other literary forms; it's a pure experiment in genre, like Frankenstein's monster—made up of dead parts from various corpses.

Just as Frankenstein's monster comes to life, in the novel these artificial literary elements together create a tension that lights up the pages, a tension that appears far more *real* to me, closer to who I am as a person and how I experience the world than one hundred autobiographical novels put together. So what does that tell me about the role of art? About the purely invented story?

18.

I have been taught that originality is the artist's worst sin.

I have been taught terms such as "the inner necessity."

I have been given long books filled with so-called reality.

And I understood that it was a very particular reality art had to revolve around if it was to remain within these set boundaries.

And obedient as I was, hungry for praise, vain, I tried for many years to stay there.

But I cannot stay there.

I am a genuine rose made of paper.

I am a flesh-and-blood ghost.

Call me Anna.

19.

But does *Frankenstein*, in all its originality, its artificialness and horror, work solely because Mary Shelley was a genius? That she was only eighteen when she wrote it astounds me.

Should I take my cue from Mary Shelley and relinquish the idea of writing's necessity, relinquish the idea of the reproduction of reality as a particularly noble gesture? And instead rediscover myself in a long bibliography of invented, artificial monsters? Genre fiction. Should I let Anna write?

It's true, I loathe *psychological realism*.

20.

The question of whether the invented or the realistic comes closest to the truth gained importance when I realized that the story I had been fed about childbirth being the happiest moment of a mother's life was a lie. But it wasn't like that. It was an abyss. Since the child's arrival I have fought this story. I want this story to admit that it's a lie, and then I want this story to bless me.

Step-by-step, I have recognized this story as fiction. The story of the happy mother. And it has led me to the question: Why has this story been necessary?

It has given mothers a story to hold on to, a fixed form to pour their experience into. But it's also a story that serves *the common good*. It's a story that is part of the overarching narrative that a woman is made to produce children. That it's every woman's greatest desire to have children, and that it is this act above all that gives her value in the eyes of society.

According to this logic, not being happy at the moment of birth is to fail as a member of society, to fail at one's assigned task, to lose one's value and identity.

The moment motherhood begins, the role of mother is taken away from her, because her happiness is what defines her.

This story and its accompanying abyss of not feeling the right thing have made it easy to control women and their lives. And if one is interested in such control, the child's arrival must of course be staged as a happy event.

But it was not happy.

I believed the story.

I stepped inside. I expected to find happiness. But the entire room was made of pain, built by it. Blood ran from my nipples, blood ran from my eyes, blood ran from the tears in my vagina and my rectum, blood ran from the internal wounds in my uterus, blood ran from the child, from his mouth, from his anus, and everything was blood and nothing was happiness. This heavy smell from inside my body. And the man stood there, outside the blood. I bled away, I disappeared. I named this disappearance Anna.

21.

Is telling a mother-to-be the story that upon the birth of her child she will feel indescribable happiness a way of giving shape to the shapeless? To put the formless event of birth into a form? And to call that happiness?

Should we give the mother-to-be a copy of *Frankenstein* instead?

22.

I know there are women whose experience of the child leaving their body is very different from mine.

Women who may very well have experienced this fabled happiness during childbirth.

To these mothers I want to say: you belong here too.

No two hearts are alike.

Forgive me, I'm not trying to take your happiness away from you. I am trying to give happiness to myself. I found no happiness in the room where I was told to seek it. There was only a pile of ash in the middle of the room. And the ash dried out my mouth. And each child comes into the world as themselves, through their own channel. And I became, I was, sheer channel, nothing but a channel of flesh for the child. And all my walls screamed with pain when he was born. And what was I then, after his arrival, but a used channel? A husk, a slough, discarded by a baby. The eyes moved away from me, they turned to the child. They took him into their arms. I'm still lying on the delivery table. I can't get out. Many years have gone by since then, but no one has noticed that the night they welcomed the child, I died, and what now walks around among them is not a human, but the discarded channel for the child's arrival.

23.

But you can't know.

But I want to know.

But you can't know.

But I want to know.

24.

Today I glimpsed an ending to this book and felt relief.

25.

The ending I suddenly thought I could see was not tangible, more like a feeling of being able to leave the book behind, to step out of it.

Perhaps before the year is over I can make it to the edge of the book.

26.
I shouldn't lie to myself, I have seen such an ending many times. And each time it has been false, no more than an attempt to control writing.

DAY EIGHT

27.

The notion that one must sacrifice everything for the sake of art—that only in this way can it become sublime—implies that anyone who is forced to take care of others, to perform manual labor, cannot become an artist.

If you have family members who are sick, children to raise, expenses to pay for work that's unrelated to art, you cannot be an artist.

To live for the sake of art requires a very particular set of life circumstances. It requires that there be someone other than the artist to keep the house warm. Someone else to put food on the table. Someone else to shop, to change diapers in the morning. Therefore, becoming a mother is unthinkable if one is also to become an artist, and the very concept of pregnancy incompatible with sacrificing everything for the sake of art. This old, entrenched idea that a woman must choose between child and book. This old, entrenched idea that the child obliterates the book and vice versa. I need to get away.

This old, entrenched idea that everything must be sacrificed at the altar of art prevents a mother from writing, since she does not wish to sacrifice her children; I need to get away.

It's nothing but an idea. It's not real, not fact. It's closer to an ideology. An inviolable art. An elevated artwork. Is that why I love *Frankenstein*? Because the creation—the monster—the living patchwork of dead body parts—returns to exact gruesome revenge on its creator?

Often the creation wishes to destroy its creator, but that doesn't mean we must sacrifice everything in the struggle with the unfinished creation.

When the child was born, there was no time to recover. There was no time to recover from the child. You bleed from gaping wounds and must care for an animal that's screaming. The stitches tug at your skin while you pace around at night. There is no moment of calm in which to recover. Life simply presses on at a faster pace. The child's arrival was devastating, and ever since there has not been a moment to gather strength. Out of this lack arose Anna.

28.
Frankenstein:
It was with these feelings that I began the creation of a human being. As the minuteness of the parts formed a great hindrance to my speed, I resolved, contrary to my first intention, to make the being of a gigantic stature, that is to say, about eight feet in height, and proportionally large. After having formed this determination and having spent some months successfully collecting and arranging my materials, I began.

29.
But I, the true murderer, felt the never-dying worm alive in my bosom.

30.
I bore a hell within me which nothing could extinguish.

DAY NINE

31.

Today I worked in the kitchen to keep the child within ear-shot. The blustering wind warps all sounds, so I have to stay close to the boy to hear him.

This will be the last day of my writing hours because tomorrow, on the tenth day, we will leave the house and move to the mountains, driving all day long. Today, the final day of writing in the big man's house, I didn't make it all the way upstairs to his study.

And I think that if I listen carefully, I can hear my husband walking up the stairs, he's going inside, into the study. The child is sleeping. The wind is howling. The palm tree outside the front door thrashes against the metal chimney. Last night, such a peculiar light across the valley. The moon was full and yellow. The wind tore through the olive trees, the leaves coated silver in the night's light. In the afternoon and evening, not a cloud in the sky, just this violent, temperamental wind that rose and fell, wailing around the house and across the landscape. We saw a shrill, sulfurous light sweep across the entire valley. In the distance, on a road bend, we saw the flashing of an ambulance. The dogs were quiet in all the houses. Not a bird has sounded for days. The child is asleep. My husband is now upstairs in the big man's study. Inconspicuously, on this final day as the wind picks up, we have switched places.

Twenty-Eighth Continuation

Dear Anna,

I'm now five months along, my belly is much bigger this time. At first I thought it would be much easier than the last time, but now I'm furious after all. I want time to sink into the pregnancy, to appreciate and enjoy it, but the physical pain that accompanies my belly growing constantly makes me want to get away. I end up in a hopeless in-between state where I can neither enjoy nor escape being pregnant.

How to understand this future human besides through the objects that will surround it? It's like you wrote, Anna. I think of the day at the hospital when I had given birth and you came and sat at my bedside, and I must admit, although you might not want to hear it, I'm very sorry not to have you as a witness this time around. I saw a completely blackened painting from 1884, painted by a woman. A pale figure in a black dress sat by a bush with her hands in the grass, she looked sickly, sullen, half-dead. I looked for the painting's title and read: "In the Garden," and I inadvertently burst out laughing in the silent museum; she had your face.

I really don't know what to do with this last box of your papers. I'm in the final stage, I can't make it fall into place. I tell everyone that things are going really well. Why do I do that, Anna?

YOURS

First Ending

24 hours in Anna's life

2 years, 4 months, and 15 days after the birth

6:00–9:00
It's Saturday, September 22, 2018, and I have precisely one hour and 38 minutes in which to write before I must return to my child, who is currently being looked after by a group of state-employed pedagogues and childcare workers.

"Up here, Mom!" a boy keeps yelling from the top of the stairs at the café where I'm sitting.

The month has been warm, maybe too warm, but the temperature fell by 10 degrees overnight, and today is cold and clear and ablaze.

The night before last, the child slept worse than he had for weeks. He woke up several times screaming, demanded to be carried from room to room, wanted water, was inconsolable. When he woke up, once again, in the middle of the night, I took him into the living room and we sat by the window looking out at the railway tracks. The overnight trains drove by, the headlights of the cars and all the lit windows of the empty office buildings on the other side of the tracks, and the lamps, several hundred of them hanging above the tracks, swung slowly back and forth in the night wind. "Everyone is sleeping," I said.

He lay down in the chair and I carried him into our bed.

Next morning he woke up at six o'clock and got up with his father, he sobbed because he wasn't allowed to disturb me. His sobs were heartbreaking. It was impossible to sleep when he was crying that way. I got up.

"Do you think he has a fever?" his father asked.

"Have you taken his temperature?"

"No."

"So do it."

"My train is leaving soon."

He had to leave for work, but took the boy's temperature anyway.

"38.3"

"Is that a fever?"

"I think so."

"Then I'll have to cancel my chiropractor appointment."

"Do you want to call the nursery or should I?"

"I'll do it."

The child was on the sofa watching television, bleary-eyed. Anna touched his skin, he was hot but not burning. It was hard to tell. The man left.

"See you Sunday!" he said.

"Bye-bye," said the child.

Anna took his temperature again. 38.1.

She googled "2 year old when is it fever" and read that "It's a fever when a child's rectal temperature is above 38°C."

It was 7:45, and drop-off at the nursery was no later than nine o'clock, the chiropractor was in Valby, and her appointment was at 9:30.

I'll just have to take him with me, Anna thought, and she packed a diaper and their iPad and stuck a box of raisins into the top of the bag. The boy didn't really want to eat, he nibbled at a slice of apple. Anna couldn't tell what the right thing to do was. Maybe he was just hot after a bad night. She stared at the boy as though she would be able to tell whether or not he was ill if only she looked at him hard enough.

She texted her colleague at the office, "unfortunately I have to take dependents' leave." She texted a friend she was supposed to see that afternoon, "I'm going to have to cancel today, the boy might be sick and I didn't get any sleep last night, will have to sleep when he sleeps if I'm going to manage being alone with him while the husband is away and because of the anxiety and all that."

Both colleague and friend replied that it was perfectly fine and to get well soon. So at least Anna wouldn't be going to work or out for coffee today.

She looked at the boy again. Was he sick? She couldn't tell. It was eight o'clock, she took his temperature again. 38.2.

Anna went to the bathroom to apply an antifungal cream, she suspected she had thrush but it was hard to tell. She knew that when stressed, she often felt she could sense a sickness flare in her vagina. She couldn't tell whether the pain was real or invented out of shame.

As she ran her fingers over her labia, a thin fluid began to drip from her vagina. It was too thin to be discharge. Anna panicked. She changed underwear.

Without knowing exactly what her plan was, she dressed the boy, gave him his asthma medication, washed his face and brushed his teeth. She put on her own shoes and jacket, went back to the boy who was still watching TV, put on his shoes and sweater, then a thin jacket on top of the sweater so she could more easily regulate his temperature by adding or removing layers.

He was fussy and demanded to be carried down the stairs even though the chiropractor had told her not to.

He cried when she put him in the stroller, but when they got down onto the street, he began to babble at the cars. In the bus, he didn't feel as warm anymore, maybe the wind had cooled him down. He talked about the nursery and about playing on the playground. Anna began to relax. When the bus stopped at the nursery, they got off.

There came a moment on the winding path leading to the nursery when Anna, among the trees shaking in the wind, was struck by a deep uncertainty as to whether she was doing the right thing.

She didn't share her suspicions with the nursery staff. She gave the boy his pacifier. He climbed onto a woman's lap; Anna could tell he was tired but that could just as well be because of last night. He waved to her, happy to be at the nursery. Anna felt relieved. She left.

At the pharmacy by the train station, they were out of over-the-counter antifungal medication and the woman behind the counter told her that yeast infection suppositories and creams were on back order.

"I can check whether they have any at another pharmacy."

Anna suggested two other nearby pharmacies but both were sold out.

"You could call your GP and ask for a prescription."

The prospect of Anna calling her doctor was not good. All healthcare workers scared her. She suspected they knew things about her she was oblivious to. The doctor's was where real pain met pain that was invented out of shame. Where illness and invented illness overlapped. The place where Anna expected to be diagnosed with a grave chronic illness and simultaneously thrown out for suffering from nothing but a weakness of the soul.

"I have an opening today at eleven o'clock," said the doctor's secretary on the phone.

Anna knew she needed to sleep in order to ease her anxiety. "No, I can't make that."

Anna didn't want to. She didn't want to go to the doctor's. She didn't want to get into the gynecologist's chair. She didn't want to get anywhere near the fear that awaited her there, not the hands and the gloves and the frosted windows. Not the swabs and tissue samples and the scans, the pain in places one didn't mention.

"You can call and make an appointment on Monday."

"Okay," said Anna.

It was a misty and damp morning when I stepped out into the meadow on the other side of the road. It was late September. As summer ended, grass and other plants had grown tall and now lay across the earth like long-haired, dewy-brown pillows. Bright drops clung to the bristly straws. Carefully, I took a few steps forward, there was something I needed to find. Immediately my feet sank into the sodden late-summer grass, the yellow. Wherever I went, countless animals had built nests, so I was constantly startled, always just about to tread in their burrows. Larks and other small birds had just hatched their chicks. I saw tiny hedgehogs lumped together, pink, gray, and vulnerable. In a larger hollow lay four glistening, blackened-blue bodies piled like snails, and above them two vigilant black adult peacocks. Blind mice pups squeaked. The grass was teeming with young. A trickling and wriggling among the stalks, slow slimy slitherings, but hardly a sound, except the occasional quiet coo of a bird. Some of the offspring had green human heads with scrunched-up eyes like angry babies. The meadow was filled with their sticky newborns and newly hatched bodies. The insects too had laid their eggs, which now opened, letting out the swarm. Stretched across the landscape was a tenderness radiating from the animals, a restlessness and anxiety, an enormous concentration. All the young had come too early. Everyone bowed protectively over them, wary of my destructive steps. The surrounding mist was white. All the animals in the world had, upon its ending, decided to create as much life as possible before it was too late.

9:00–11:00

"It's much better," said the chiropractor.

"I can tell," said Anna.

But the chiropractor still applied two thrusts to her back and lumbar, and it was very painful.

"Why doesn't my back get better? Why does it keep hurting?"

"Sometimes the joints won't move, they keep locking."

They talked about the aquarium and their distaste for the zoo. The chiropractor had a one-and-a-half-year-old daughter.

Anna was very sore. The day was warm. Outside on the street, she put on her jacket and spotted a pharmacy.

"We don't have suppositories, they're on back order, but I can give you a vaginal cream."

The pharmacist showed Anna how to insert the cream twice a day for eight days using sixteen disposable cardboard applicators. It seemed primitive.

Anna moved among all these workers; women whose job it was to provide care but who had to wear the state in their faces, the instructions, the good.

Anna stopped at a café and ate a soft-boiled egg (12 kroner) and drank a small latte (28 kroner) and read an essay by Susan Griffin (1978).

Last night Anna had had a dream where she was sent on a quest, half computer game, half mythological journey. After much effort, she had managed to track down a central character, a wise man, one of the oracles, and he had informed her that he wanted to bequeath her the first truth of creation, whatever that meant. He leaned in, supporting himself on his staff, "the spirit is flesh" he said, smiling, and Anna nodded and left. Later in the dream, she saw from above how to position four walls in order to build a house, and in the dream she understood that the next step in creation was *the home*.

Anna thought of the friend she was supposed to see today, and how at her friend's son's kindergarten there was an "iPad day," and the children whose parents couldn't afford an iPad would wince. She thought of winter boots and diapers and strollers, of the 3,500 kroner they paid every month for the child's nursery, and she thought of the recently published study showing that on average, Danish women's wages were halved after the birth of their first child, and few women returned to the same income level as before they had children, while men's earnings increased steadily throughout life, whether or not they had children.

Anna took a bite of her egg and continued reading Susan Griffin's essay.

"The experience of mothering changes one; that it is learned."

She read on.

"That a mother is asked to give up her life for her children; that mothers are hated; that children are unhappy [...] that women go mad; that the order of life as we live it now is dangerous."

Had Aksel learned it; had he learned *to mother*? Had it changed him the same way it had changed Anna?

Bridget of Sweden (1303–1373) or Saint Birgitta is considered by historians to be the first female author in Nordic literary history. From her early childhood, she had religious revelations. After her husband died (Bridget was 41), she suddenly received a message in a vision from Christ to immediately travel to Rome and remain there until the pope returned from his exile in Avignon. Besides that, Jesus also told her to write the rules for a new religious order, which she was to establish in Vadstena, Sweden. She recorded her revelations in Latin together with a number of so-called confessors, but not until 1957, nearly 600 years later, were her revelations translated and published in her mother tongue, Swedish. Among her most renowned works are a series of prayers, known as the Fifteen O's, *structured around the last seven words Jesus spoke on the cross. Eight children, one husband, one sainthood.*

11:00–15:00

Were they not all of them weak women? wearing crinolines the better to conceal the fact; the great fact; the only fact; but nevertheless, the deplorable fact; which every modest woman did her best to deny until denial was impossible; the fact that she was about to bear a child? to bear fifteen or twenty children indeed, so the most of a modest woman's life was spent, after all, in denying what, on one day at least every year, was made obvious.

Anna tried to read Virginia Woolf but was too tired to concentrate. She needed to sleep if she was to make it through the day. She packed up her books and left the café. She took the train. She was very tired. She needed to go home and sleep. She ate the homemade pizza from yesterday in bed. It was hard to fall asleep, she listened to the radio to quiet her thoughts but it didn't help, she put her phone on silent, a telemarketing number kept calling, she dozed but couldn't quite fall asleep, she lay there for a long time, then she put on a meditation exercise they had listened to at the Psychotherapy Clinic. None of the others in the group knew, but Anna could tell that the woman in the recording was Minna, the psychologist Anna had seen while she was pregnant. It was Minna who had kept Anna's patient records then.

Anna had liked her, even though she was ultimately wrong about Anna on several counts. Many of these female psychologists and therapists had this extraordinary way of dressing, not exactly stylish but striving to be by elevating their average wardrobes with a single outrageously fashionable accent; crinkly vinyl pants or platform boots or one of those floor-length, flowery chiffon dresses with puffy sleeves and ruffles and checks, *Little House on the Prairie*–style, which was presumably not a trend developed with the psychotherapy clinic in mind, and Anna gaped at these failed attempts at chicness, and it was perhaps, above all, these fashion faux pas that made Anna fond of so many of these women she encountered through the system. The clothes exposed them, and Anna saw that they were people struggling, just like her, to find their place in life.

She knew the tired boy would have to be picked up early. She had set her alarm to 2:30 p.m. so she could pick him up at 3:00. Anna slept lightly for twenty minutes and woke up again just before 2:00. She checked her phone. The nursery had called while she was asleep and left a message; they thought the boy had a fever. She called them back to say she was on her way.

At the nursery he sat on the sofa with a blank expression on his face, watching the others play. He felt warm, but not hot. She conferred with the nursery teacher. She put his shoes and jacket on him. He raced down the corridor and hid like he usually did, grinning widely up at her. He can't be that sick, Anna thought. In the elevator he began talking about cake.

"Are you saying we should go get some cake for you at the bakery?"

"Mommy cake too?"

"Should we eat the cake there, what do you think?"

"Yes, chairs."

"That's a good idea. Let's fika."

It was one of his favorite words, *fika*, Swedish for coffee and cake.

"Yeah, fika!" shouted the boy, pale-faced and delighted.

337

"Should we have chocolate cake?" He squinted. Outside the nursery, he played with some rocks in the grass.

"Come on, sweetheart." She lifted him into the stroller, could feel the chiropractor's adjustments. They headed for the bakery, it was very windy. While half-asleep, Anna had heard something on the radio about a storm later today. She drew up the stroller's hood to shelter the boy from the wind. He leaned back in his seat, unusually quiet.

At the bakery he didn't want to get out of the stroller, and he didn't touch his muffin. Fika had been his idea, but now his fever was climbing so quickly he couldn't see it through. Outside it had started to rain. They still needed to stop by the supermarket. Mainly because they had run out of diapers. Anna wrapped up the muffin in a paper bag, left behind her expensive coffee (38 kroner), and kissed the child who sat in the stroller, subdued and colorless. Anna was no longer in doubt that he was sick. His rejection of cake made her certain. The doubt about his illness dissipating, this certainty at last, felt like a migraine lifting. Tenderness and strength rushed through her.

"Listen, sweetheart. We're going to stop by the supermarket and buy diapers and milk, and then we'll take the train home and watch a film."

"Train?" said the boy.

She made the trip through the supermarket as quickly as she could, even though grocery shopping always made her anxious. The whole time, the boy sat silently in the stroller sucking on his pacifier, following everything with his eyes.

By the time they had made it through the checkout, and Anna had bought children's paracetamol at the pharmacy in front, it had started to pour outside. The storm was building. There was an umbrella in the bottom compartment of the stroller. Anna stroked the boy's cheek. He felt hot now.

"Look at the rain." He looked. Inside the supermarket she put the rain cover over the stroller and opened the umbrella.

There was a long line for the station elevator, many cyclists had decided to take the train. The wind tore at the umbrella and broke one of its ribs. The child was so quiet. But Anna wasn't worried. It may have been storming, and it may have been a hassle to take the train, and they may have been standing here alone in the rain, and Aksel may have been working somewhere far away in Sweden, and the child, he may have had a high fever, but Anna knew all these facts, and she didn't doubt them. It wasn't like pain in her body, which she always doubted. It was this certainty that gave her strength. I would go so far as to say her spirits were high. The fact that she could protect the child against the elements, could get him home safely, could read him and understand his symptoms and carry him; all that filled her with joy. She was the child's mother, she was Anna in the rain in the line for the elevator, full of light, a lamp.

Thomasine Gyllembourg (1773–1856) had one child at the age of 18. After a horrible public divorce, she was forced to leave the boy when he was 10. Debuted at age 54 in her son's literary journal with a serial novel. 25 books published at the time of her death 29 years later, 83 years old.

15:00–17:00

It was half past three by the time they got home. Anna carried the child all the way up to the fifth floor even though the chiropractor had given her strict orders not to, but he was so pale and weak and glossy-eyed that it had been difficult to get him to walk on his own. She carried him with one arm and held the grocery bag and diapers in the other, she could tell it was no good.

In the apartment she carefully took off the boy's clothes, his shoes and jacket, socks and sweater, so he was only wearing an undershirt and leggings. She sat down with him on the sofa, talked to him, he leaned his head against her chest and touched her hair. His forehead was hotter now, not alarmingly so, but he definitely had a fever. He fell asleep in her lap. He was heavy in her arms. She was cradling him with her bad arm. The arm she always carried him with, the arm he rested on when she breast-fed him, the arm by the good breast, the arm whose shoulder was now so sore and locked that she had to have it treated once a week. Carefully she moved him onto the sofa, he rolled onto his stomach in his sleep and pulled his legs up beneath him so his bottom jutted up into the air. She fetched a blanket to cover him with. He woke up and whimpered, stretched his arms up toward her, and when she lay down beside him, he immediately took hold of her hair and closed his eyes. Anna lay with the child's hands in her hair until he was fast asleep. She felt his hands and feet; they weren't cold, which meant the fever wasn't increasing. His nose was runny and he was coughing in

341

his sleep. She was fairly certain it was only a cold. But to tell the truth, it did cross her mind that she was in the middle of a storm with a child who was falling fatally ill. She pushed the thought aside. She did a load of laundry. Silk and wool, 38 minutes. The boy slept. She tidied up. Checked on him regularly. Hung up the laundry and started another load, also wool and silk, delicate wash, mostly Aksel's work shirts and things. Outside, the wind whipped through the trees along the train tracks. It felt nice to be inside with the sleeping child and the laundry while it rained outside. Despite the storm, the sky was bright, and it sent its watery glow into the apartment. It reminded Anna of being a child, when her mother would light two candles on the windowsill and Anna would sit in the armchair looking at autumn outside. Anna loved being here with the child. The laundry was done, she did another load, 40 degrees, quick wash, 60 minutes, and hung up the wet clothes.

They had two drying racks. She set one up in the bedroom and the other in the living room where the child was sleeping so she could keep an eye on him while she hung up the clothes. Most of the delicates had to dry on hangers, which she hung up around the apartment on door handles and closet doors. That way, she saved space and could do more loads, since there was still room on the racks. The child slept. The rain beat against the windows. It was a Friday afternoon in September, soon the darkness crept in from the sea beyond the train tracks and the office buildings and gas station, from the canal and the shopping center and the harbor bath; the darkness which, in this apartment with its view of so much sky, often announced its arrival by setting the clouds alight in a wash of yellow and pink, a single spot of gold setting behind the church spire in Sydhavnen. Anna sat down with her phone and read the news online.

Leonora Christina Ulfeldt (1621–1698) had 15 children, the first when she was 16. One book, published 171 years after her death. Began the book by saying she had written it so her children could read her story. Following an international political scandal, she was accused of treason and imprisoned in a tower for 22 years. Wrote her book in this room. When she was released in 1685, only 5 of her children were still alive. A writer because of, not in spite of, her children.

17:00–21:00

The boy had been sleeping for two hours now. They had said at the nursery that he had hardly eaten anything, and at breakfast he had only picked at his food. It was less than six months since he had been hospitalized with dehydration, and dinnertime was approaching. Anna wasn't worried, but she was taking precautions. She fetched a diaper, a thermometer, a tube of lotion, and a paracetamol suppository. It was important to get the fever down so he could drink and maybe eat something. Carefully she turned the boy over so he was lying on his back, pulled his leggings off, undid his diaper, saw it was wet, a good sign, applied lotion to the thermometer, took hold of his warm ankles with one hand, and lifted his legs up over his stomach so she could more easily insert the thermometer into his rectum. He blinked and began to stir.

"Hi, sweetheart. I'm just taking your temperature."

He didn't say anything, just lay there looking at her while he woke up. 39.1.

"I'm going to give you your medicine now, then you'll feel much better."

She took the pill out of its plastic packaging, dabbed lotion on it, and inserted it into his bottom with the pointy end toward her. He squirmed a little. The pill slipped easily into place.

"There."

She lifted his legs again and laid the new diaper out beneath him, folded the opposite side of it over his genitals, and attached the front and back side over his stomach with two adhesive tabs. He was more awake now.

"I'm just going to wash my hands."

In the bathroom, she cleaned the thermometer so it was ready for later, washed her hands, and threw out the old diaper and the pill packaging.

"Film now?" asked the boy.

"Why don't I make some food? You can sit here with your duvet while I cook."

She helped the boy sit up by propping a few pillows behind his back, he was warm, but less fussy than earlier. She rolled out the TV and scrolled through films on Netflix with the boy for a while before Chromecasting a children's program from her phone instead. The boy followed along, fascinated.

"I'm going to go make us some food, sweetheart." It was just past five.

The frozen meatballs needed 15 minutes at 200 degrees in a fan-assisted oven. She turned on the oven and laid out four of them in an ovenproof dish. Then she took out a pot, measured the rice, and put the pot on the stove to boil. She wanted to cook carrots for the boy, which he loved, but realized there was only one left in the fridge drawer. It would have to do. She peeled the carrot and cut it into sticks which she covered with water in a pot and brought to boil next to the rice. The oven took a long time to heat up. Now the boy came out to the kitchen, pushed a chair over to the counter and climbed up.

"Look, we're having meatballs," she said.

"Meatballs!" he exclaimed and reached for them. His interest in food made her shoulders relax.

"We can't eat them yet, they need to be heated."

He touched one and looked at the frozen meatball with confusion.

"They're still cold," she said.

"Oh."

"We have to wait for a bit. Come on, I'll watch TV with you."

She helped him climb down from the chair and they walked hand in hand back to the sofa. She sat with him and watched the program. It was actually quite good. Emil and Ida were searching for a hen.

Anna took out her phone and checked the news. She clicked on a headline: OVERLOOKED DISEASE RUINS WOMEN'S SEX LIVES: OFTEN MISTAKEN FOR YEAST INFECTION.

She read on:

An increasing number of women are afflicted by a disease which causes narrowing of the vagina.

When Anita Alvarez went to her GP to have her hormonal IUD removed, her physician asked a question which would ultimately explain the mysterious pains she had been suffering from for years.

"She asked whether I was aware I had quite a lot of scarring in the genital area, and whether I had suffered any discomfort as a result," Alvarez remembers.

The 25-year-old woman had indeed suffered from considerable pain. Her physician confirmed that Alvarez suffers from lichen sclerosus (LS), a disease which, if left untreated, can cause pain during sex or when going to the bathroom, or even make the labia shrink and almost disappear.

Lichen sclerosus et atrophicus is considered an autoimmune skin disease which initially manifests as whitish and patchy skin around the genitals and anus. It causes itching and increased sensitivity, and over time the skin can become thin, white, and wrinkled. Pain may occur during intercourse. The condition most commonly affects postmenopausal women but can also occur in children (particularly girls) before puberty as well as men. Among women, the affected tissue may shrink and the vaginal opening may narrow. The condition is often treated with potent steroid creams, which are prescribed for approximately two months and eventually phased out. The disease cannot be prevented, but early treatment can relieve symptoms and possibly prevent the disease from further progressing. It cannot be cured.

Anna continued reading about Anita and the many years of improper treatment. Anna felt uneasy. Maybe this was the disease she was suffering from? And not a normal yeast infection? Anna knew it would be very hard to go to the doctor; would she then have to live with this narrowing of her vagina?

She couldn't wait for the oven any longer and put in the meatballs even though it still wasn't quite hot enough, she'd just have to give them 20 minutes instead. She took out the boy's divided plate and a deep plate for herself, placed both on a tray, cut a few slices of cucumber for the two of them, checked Instagram. Nothing much was going on. The kitchen had grown dark. Outside the window, the courtyard was gray and empty and the flagstones dark and soaked with rain. She turned on the lights. She put some slices of pickled beets on their plates. Time passed. The rice boiled. Anna waited, pleased with the prospect of a simple, hearty meal. She poured frozen peas into the pot with the carrot. Switched off the rice. Took out the meatballs so they could cool down for the boy. She turned off the oven. Ladled rice onto the two plates and topped both portions with a pat of butter. The boy preferred to eat the same thing as the grown-ups, so Anna would also eat frozen meatballs. She needed to get food into him. And frankly, she had nothing against it, Anna preferred children's food. She drained and divided the vegetables between them, he got all the carrot. She filled a cup of water and took a beer for herself. Got out cutlery. He liked the spoon with the green handle and the fork with the lavender handle best, so she picked them. Then she carried the tray over to him on the sofa. The medicine had started to work, he bounced around a little.

"Look, dinnertime."

It was risky to give him food in front of the TV, because he would demand to eat there again in the future, but Anna didn't know how sick he was getting, and she knew she had to get him to eat by whatever means. She didn't want to have to take him back to the hospital, and especially not while Aksel was away. They ate. He ate well. Started with the meatball, which he ate with his fingers. Ate the rice at the very end. "Eeee-miiiil!" he shouted, like the father on TV. "Uh-oh!" he yelled each time someone got hurt, got their foot caught in a mouse-trap or had blood-dumpling dough poured on them. "Hurry! Close the door," he said when Emil fled to the woodshed.

When they had finished eating, Anna carried out the tray, rinsed the plates and put them in the dishwasher, washed the pots and wooden utensils. He continued watching television in the next room, noticeably less warm.

She turned on the dishwasher. The laundry was done. She started another load (40 degrees, quick wash), hung up the wet clothes. The boy came in and helped her with the socks, but he was still too tired and plodded back to the sofa. She fetched the thermometer, lotion, diaper, wet wipes, changed him, and took his temperature on the sofa while he watched TV. 37.7 degrees. Went back out and washed the thermometer, her hands, threw out the diaper. The program was over. It was eight o'clock. Anna thought she'd better hold off on putting him to bed since he had napped at the nursery and on the sofa this afternoon.

"Come on, let's go make ourselves a dessert platter."

This was a concept she would never have introduced had

Aksel been home. She would be far too self-conscious and start to question the healthiness of her relationship with food. Even though Aksel probably wouldn't object, she caught herself keeping it a secret whenever she gave the child sweets.

They got out the chocolate muffin from the bakery. Anna divided it into bite-size pieces and arranged them on a plate with two TUC crackers (good in case of fever, a doctor once told her, they make children thirsty) and two jumbo marshmallows. The boy proudly carried the plate to the sofa. Some cute children's program was playing, and she cradled him in her lap, a blanket over them while they ate. "Mommy crackers," said the boy, giving her one and taking the other. "Cheers!" he said and they knocked the two crackers against each other and ate. "I love you," he said and fiddled with her hair.

Dea Trier Mørch (1941–2001). Visual artist. Stated that after the birth of her first child, she understood that the typewriter was the artistic tool best suited to a life with small children. The typewriter didn't take up much space and could be used anywhere. She didn't need to go to a studio but could write over the course of the day at intervals adapted to the children's rhythm. Helped found the left-wing artist group Red Mother. Her first novel, Winter's Child, *about a group of women at the maternity ward at Rigshospitalet, brought her nationwide acclaim. 27 books, 3 children.*

21:00–22:00
It was approaching nine o'clock and the laundry was done. Anna hung it up and started yet another load, quick wash, 60 degrees. There was almost no more room left on the racks, so she would have to come up with something else. Anna fetched a diaper, thermometer, lotion, and another lotion for the mild eczema on the boy's face, which he got because of his pacifier, as well as the spacer they used for giving him his asthma medication, and laid it all on the sofa. Then she fetched a washcloth, wet half of it with warm water and also poured a cup of cold water, put children's toothpaste on his toothbrush, and carried these to the living room.

She gave him his asthma medication while he watched TV. Then she brushed his teeth under a great deal of protest and he drank a few sips of water. She washed his face, dabbed it with the dry end of the cloth, and applied the face lotion. Next, she removed all his clothes and took off his diaper and had him stand up on the sofa. She washed his hands and feet and then his penis, scrotum, and bottom. Afterward, she took his temperature again, still 37.7, and put on a clean diaper. He smiled up at her. She took the cloth and his clothing and put them in the laundry basket, cleaned the thermometer and her hands, threw out the diaper, rinsed the toothbrush, and put it away, carried the cup to the kitchen, put the spacer and lotion back in the boy's room, and then returned to him.

She sat with him in her lap and talked a bit about what was happening on the TV and told him it was time to turn it off.

Reluctantly, he accepted. They walked hand in hand to his room, he found a tractor and pushed it around. Anna drew the curtains and turned on lamps, shook out his duvet and fetched his teddy bear from her bed.

They discussed which book to read, and because it was just the two of them, and because the boy was sick—or had been, at any rate, seeing as he no longer had a fever, but maybe that was just because the pill had taken effect—they read three books together in the boy's bed. Then Anna got up, put the books away (because the boy was very concerned about them being put away), and turned off all the lights except the boy's night-light. He was sitting up in bed, and she helped him lie down. She had already given him his pacifier.

"Mommy lie down," he said.

"I'll sit with you, sweetheart."

She sat on a stool by the bed, leaned over to kiss him good night, and he grabbed her hair. So she sat like that, awkwardly bent over him, singing lullabies. She tried to straighten up, the small of her back hurt, but he protested at not being able to touch her hair. She stroked his forehead. He wasn't warm. He quieted, and she sat with her back to him and looked at her phone until she could tell by his breathing that he was asleep.

Then she tiptoed out and fetched the thermometer, went back into his room and laid out a diaper, thermometer, lotion and pill next to his bed in case she needed to give him a pill later in the night.

The laundry was done and she hung the towels, dishcloths ,and cloth diapers on the dining room chairs, there was still room for a few items on the racks if she rearranged things. Outside the rain had stopped, it was dark, and Anna couldn't tell whether the wind had died down too. It was nearly ten o'clock.

Thit Jensen (1876–1957). No children. Many books. Feminist pioneer who advocated for free abortion and women's right to vote. Believed that the common good, including women's rights, was inextricably linked to eugenics through forced sterilization. Adamant critic of homosexuality. Wrote in 1929: "Society too harbors the childish belief that when the child is removed from the swamp, the result will be a human being; they do not believe the semen of the thief in the loins of the unchastely girl is supernegatively formed before it is born." When her husband left her for a younger woman, she allegedly drew a trapdoor with a latch on her floor in chalk and told herself her husband was trapped beneath it. When in despair, she would go stand on the trapdoor and shout "the latch is ON."

22:00–1:00

Anna was tired. She ate another jumbo marshmallow. Made tea and turned off the lights. The part of the apartment facing the street lay in darkness, and only the bedroom glowed with the warm light of a single lamp, like a secret refuge. She got into bed and watched *Maniac*, a new series in which *two struggling strangers connect during a mind-bending pharmaceutical trial*. She watched episode after episode until she could no longer keep her eyes open. Then she got up and brushed her teeth, washed her face with water, changed into pajamas. She checked on the boy, who was asleep, tucked the duvet around him, and got back into bed. While the next episode of *Maniac* played, she attached the cardboard applicator to the tube of vaginal cream like the pharmacist had shown her. She squeezed the tube so cream filled the applicator, pushing the plunger up and out of the barrel, like a tampon. Anna pressed until a triangle with the word STOP appeared on the plunger. She carefully removed the applicator from the tube, lay down on her back, drew her knees to her chest, pulled her underpants aside, and inserted the applicator into her vagina. Slowly she pressed the plunger into the barrel so the cream was pushed into her. "Insert the applicator as deep into the vagina as possible." Anna didn't know what *deep* meant in this context, and she had never known. Since giving birth she had never had quite the same relationship to her vagina and labia. Her clitoris was the same as before, but her vagina and labia remembered the pain, and now, two and a half years later, her genitals still made her queasy, remembering the nightmares her vagina and vulva had wrought upon her, the catastrophe her genitalia had caused.

Anna still hadn't "looked down there" since giving birth, as the midwife from the childbirth class had recommended they do, always with this *pocket mirror* that all healthcare professionals and STI pamphlets and sex-positive columns Anna had ever come across in her life referred to, this infamous pocket mirror no one owned, the pocket mirror with which to look at one's pussy.

Anna's doctor had said at the postnatal checkup when the child was eight weeks old that there was a *split*, but she also said it was purely cosmetic and that Anna wouldn't be able to feel the difference. It was true; Anna could not physically, when having sex, feel any difference, but she could feel the nervousness in her flesh, a stress down below, a trauma.

Anna got out of bed and rummaged around her makeup shelf, the plastic cases rattling against strings of beads. She took out a powder compact and opened it with a click, the mirror was dusty with pink powder which she wiped away.

What she saw in the mirror was the two inner labia cleaved horizontally across the middle, such that she no longer had two intact inner labia, but four small, floppy ones. Blood rushed to the surface of her skin. Her entire body seethed. She wanted to cry, but couldn't. I hate it, Anna thought, I hate it, I hate it, I hate it. She snapped the compact shut and threw it aside. It was these four inner labia that made it difficult for her to imagine ever having any more children. And it was these four inner labia that made it difficult for Anna to allow any body part or human to approach them.

Anna was tired, it was just past midnight, she reached for Aksel's duvet and rolled it up into a sausage on the opposite side of the bed so if the boy came to her during the night, he wouldn't fall out. She turned off the lights, let *Maniac* play, slept.

355

Anna-Maija Ylimaula (1950–). Five children. Nine books so far. Grew up in a religious community in Finland where birth control was forbidden. Alongside her career as a writer, works as an architect and professor. Debuted at age 26 with the novel The Clergyman's Daughter. *Has said that "a breastfeeding mother is left alone in life like a queen bee. Life beyond maternity leave ends like a wall." I have Google Translated the quote and haven't been able to read any of her books because I can't understand Finnish, but I understand that her novel* Idyll *from 1984 is about the researcher Ansa who, juggling both children and career, cannot achieve the so-called happy family, and so, upon realizing she is pregnant again, drowns herself and her children in a swimming pool.*

Bodil Bech (1889–1942). No children. Debuted at age 45. In the following 8 years, she published 6 poetry collections and one young adult novel before her death at 53 of a stroke. I have heard that toward the end of her life, Bodil Bech lived mostly off the fish that fishermen dropped on the ground, and that she wrote occasionally for women's magazines. Painter Oluf Høst wrote of her funeral in his journal: "Bodil Bech cremated in Rønne. The family was in a rush and rather disinterested, the police handled the matter. However, the family did take an interest in B.B.'s golden bracelet and bicycle. Call from the Danish Authors' Society: When and where would the funeral take place, and if it was taking place here, would I order a wreath with ribbons in the national colors inscribed with "Danish Authors' Society." Price 15 kroner. Our maid, Bodil Ipsen, was waiting for me in the garden, said: B.B. died here. I asked: Where is she? Bodil I.: She is lying on your bed. According to Håkø, Bodil Bech's family found it acceptable to burn the body in her nightgown. The police objected."

On that misty morning I forced myself away, down into the laundry room. The light stood through the thin, wet windowpanes like gold. I transferred white items into white containers. I saw brutality, tall glittering reeds, lyme grass, the sea and the news, this incredible faith in my own significance, partially washed away by the sun's return. To do everything right would be a form of death. When we looked upon his dead aunt in the coffin I saw her culmination, her hair like a veil around her face, the rings on her fingers, a gruesome sight. Outside, the pale girls on their way to school. The laundry room opens its smell to the earth behind the walls, I'm in the basement, the child is calling, why are those girls so quiet in the light, along the hills, they are only half as big as they once were, I am one-eyed, doused in chlorine, my hands. These girls are searching for something that is not flowers. Children fill the small paddock. I must take into my hands what wishes to kill and die inside me and carry on. The girls' crowns gleam like teeth in the glare of the sea. Tell me, beloved who makes my bed, should I thank you for your efforts, for loving me? Am I capable of lifting up these children with their jingling, their disguises, and their lanterns of fruit? Their inbuilt evil, their games, their violence? How superior you are to me, with everything systematized, reasonable, surgical. This way in which you work together without seeing, in ancient Greek forms. And I am merely one of these columns, replicated, ornamented, a yoga mat. I will never let you do our laundry. I am one-eyed, one-eyed. The wet sheets hung on lines beneath the ceiling like corpses. Soap-colored stones, polished by the

*sea, collected by children. The sun heals the coagulated blood. He
gave me a ring. I become a guardian of the children's violence. I
must carry on washing.*

1:00–8:00

At 1:37 the boy woke up and called for her. She went to his room and gave him his pacifier, tucked him in, he slept.

At 3:01 the boy woke up and called for her. She went to him, tucked him in, gave him his pacifier.

At 5:14 the boy woke up and called for her. She went to him, he was sitting up in bed, reaching out his arms toward her. Drowsily she picked him up, gathered his duvet and his stuffed animal and carried him to her bed.

She laid him in the middle of the bed, gave him his teddy bear and tucked the duvet around him, lay down beside him and swept her hair across the back of her neck to the child's side, he grabbed hold and played with it in the dark. "Time to sleep," she said, and they slept.

They woke up at 7:30. The boy snuggled under the duvet, she felt his forehead, he no longer had a fever. Curiosity drove me, Anna thought, I wanted to test the boundaries of my own being. It was a private examination that ultimately transformed me into public property. The child turned in bed the way he once turned in her belly. Outside the window stood the elder, heavy with fruit, its purple-black berries glinting with the morning's newly quieted rain.

Second Ending

When the child was a few weeks old and they still lived in Copenhagen, Anna wanted nothing more than a latte to go and two organic mini-muffins from Emmery's. Aksel would be sent off and they would share the meal in bed.

She knew that she still had this softness about her, like Aksel when he had just awoken; as if in these first weeks after giving birth she was slowly waking up. Her body was blank and yielding, her skin supernaturally smooth, and she loved Aksel in these weeks with an unprecedented fierceness. Her breasts filled with milk, grew enormous and taut, the park outside the window blossomed, and Anna cried with happiness the day they left the hospital, relieved that they all had survived.

While at the hospital, spring had come, winter coats were at once hot and shapeless. The child sweat in the knitted onesie and navy hat trimmed with white purchased for this very day when she sat with him in the bassinet on her lap in the taxi, dizzy to be back out in a world where she had previously existed, and neither of them could understand that the child was real. When they gently pulled off his clothes at home and swaddled him in a white blanket, he still smelled of her womb, of blood and body.

"When do you think I can go outside?" Anna asked as they ate their muffins. "What do people on the streets look like?"

"We could go now?" Aksel suggested.

Anna lifted the child gently into the black bassinet. There he lay looking up into nothingness. He waved his clenched fists.

Anna leaned her weight against the stroller and staggered through the park, where everything had opened up in her absence. The lake shone, the sun flickered through the leaves of the trees. She could faintly feel the stitches in her left side, they tugged at her as she walked, she was sweating, the wind slid across her.

As if by a miracle, the child napped in the stroller where he previously refused to sleep, he lay with his arms stretched over his head.

"It will be strange to have to leave you," Aksel said. He had a four-month contract at a theater in Malmö and started work on Monday.

"I don't understand it either," said Anna. "How does any of this make sense?"

Third Ending

What a horrible thing, to become a mother. Like waking from a sweet dream in which men and women are equal.

Writing about my pregnancy did not feel like writing, but like conjuring a spirit. The spirit of pregnancy. A thistle of smoke, a madness.

Because I had lived solely in relation to others for so long, I became estranged from the resources of my own nature. I must unteach myself the shame of writing a woman's life, a mother's life. I must stop writing very soon.

Fourth Ending

I stepped out into the bright night and walked along the railway tracks to the forest and the clearing with the cherry tree.

In the cherry tree grew a flying rowan and I recognized these two intertwined trees from my childhood. I broke off a branch from the rowan to harvest it and its midsummer power. The night air was filled with fertile smells. But on the way home, I left the branch on a bench. I didn't want to believe that the branch was magic; it was the act of taking it into my hand that transformed me, and I realized I no longer needed it.

Fifth Ending

Dear Anna,

The child lies sideways and kicks furiously at night, keeping me awake with its movements in our small room. This is, so far, the child's only language, all that it has said to me. It jostles my organs. Swims in our fluid. Far away, like a green sun hovering over the horizon, permeable like a membrane or a grape. It's snowing now at the end of November, and the boy loves it. Inside me glows a plush, pink night where the child wakes up, and this space expands infinitely, is my stomach's interior, our bedroom, a secret, my thoughts and feelings all at once.

I'm very, very tired of being pregnant, and at the same time I long for it never to end.

I have been sick and distressed and unable to finish writing your book. It began to scare me again because it became so far removed from me. I was hospitalized for a single night. I saw my husband's eyes disappear, his beauty when he boarded the train, and my love threw itself against him. I can no longer bear what I once wished for. The child in my body is too heavy. But my hope and my suspicion converge: completing your work is not about maintaining a certain standard, is not about any kind of artistic triumph, but simply about finishing the laundry, hanging it up, taking it down, putting it in its place. Getting up, moving on, holding the child's hand.

I'm seven months along.

Your devoted

Sixth Ending

When the boy won't stop crying, I tell myself that he is not my child, just a boy in my custody. Otherwise I go into a kind of trance; sweat pricks at my skin and while I alternate between comforting and scolding him, all I can think is what have I done wrong as a mother, what is he trying to tell me with his outburst, and these thoughts lead me directly to a feeling of narcissism in which everything the child does is a reflection of me. So I say to myself that he is not my son at all but some other boy, that I'm not responsible for his damn meltdown. Then I can suddenly see him for the person he is, console him, and I'm realizing that my work as his mother also consists in pulling away so that he can become clear to the both of us. It is, although there is shame in saying so, a relief to not always be his reason.

Seventh Ending

3 years after the birth

*

something new

a moment in the sun

a swallow

dived past my shoulder

its wing

grazed my cheek

like my child's hand

I became both swallow and child

and the stairwell from which

I had just stepped

I became only cheek

and its fine mesh of blood

the hollow heart of the swallow

my boy's name

as it will be said

by him

one day

when I no longer

exist

*

pollen and little leaves
blow through
our open window

you whisper
oh Rapunzel
I'm so sad
to your doll
you're inside a happy game
and throw a toy frying pan
into a tower
of blocks
you say
bye-bye Mama
have a nice day

I tidy our mess
put each thing in its place
even the things
without a place
must be given
a temporary one
certain insects
have no nest
unlike the moths

whose origin
we cannot
locate
not behind the cabinets
not behind the drawers
not in the flour or cereal or oats
and yet
day after day
a moth
flutters through the living room
where we are slowly
filled by sun
day by day
spring

*
finally
        I might say
                alone
            sparse
                        superfluous
                    submerged
                        in a luxury of
                        time and nourishment

that I seek
        the thing itself
          and not its myth
          and not the root of the myth

          my beloved
                far away
        I celebrate my
                exploits
                        myself
          I am no one
                an upbringing
        yet here
          terrified
          but in the terror upright

there are
　　only a few places left
　　to be inserted

　　　sideways
a woman
　　　　in the third
　　　　　　　　　person
　　to create her
　　　　and later
　　　　　like a time
　　　　abandon it
I am my own proof

*

the day lies down on me
the child

the easy green in the air across
the boulevard

I let the bathwater drain
after his body glistening wet
he runs
off
into
the living room

here in the shadow of my age
grant me a daisy I know how to
hold it in my hand

the poem heals
the wound inflicted by reason

the eyelets of the ruffles
along the neckline of his sweater

the sewing machine given to me
the threads inside the eye

and
the second child
I carry still

arose with him
like a shadow still
alive in my body
infant but also

his age
three years

the second child
his double
who stayed behind
among the organs
that day
in the delivery room
the child
who looks like the both of us
and now

is mirrored in the day's light
like nourishment
a sound reaching across
the boulevard

where we walk
the boy and I
hand in hand
toward the flowers
newly burst

in the too-hot spring
in the worldwide war
a daisy

my boy picks
I cry
hopeless
I am just a poet
to the world
a mother

*

to become your mother
not by adapting to your rhythm
but surrendering to your breath

Eighth Ending

Aksel and Anna were out walking. In the stroller in front of them, the boy had fallen asleep even though he was really too old for naps. Suddenly they were back in the old days when the child was little, when they would take these long walks to get him to sleep. They shivered in the blustery weather. In the trees' crowns along the boulevard, a veil of buds.

"I think I might be pregnant," said Anna.

"Are you sure?" said Aksel.

"It's just a hunch."

"How long has he been sleeping?"

"Forty-five minutes."

"Last time I could tell you weren't feeling well."

"I know."

"I didn't realize we would be parents forever."

"Maybe it was all a misunderstanding."

"Do you think we'll get divorced if we have another?" asked Aksel.

"The statistics say so." Anna took his hand.

They turned left at the crossing toward the cemetery. We see Aksel rub his face with one hand, as if to protect it from the surroundings. He starts telling Anna about the time he worked as a porter at the maternity ward at Karolinska University Hospital in Stockholm; he was nineteen, he worked nights.

One of his responsibilities was to transport women to their rooms after they had given birth. The new mother was put in a wheelchair with the child in her arms, and then Aksel rolled them from the delivery ward into an elevator that took them to the basement, where they would walk down a long underground corridor to get up to the postnatal ward in an adjacent building. Night after night he led these women through the underground corridors and up to their new rooms.

"It was a very vulnerable moment to be privy to," Aksel explained. "It was the first time the mother and child were alone together. Most of them were so engrossed in their child they hardly noticed me."

In the taxi to the hospital, back when Anna was so pregnant she could hardly walk, this period when Aksel had worked at the maternity ward at one of Stockholm's biggest hospitals had led Anna to believe that although she was the one about to give birth, Aksel knew far more about it than she.

At the time, he had told her almost nothing about that period other than it was a job he'd had, yet it still inspired an odd sense of security.

"Do you think I'm capable of giving birth?" Anna asked in the taxi. "Maybe I'm not strong enough."

"Everyone can give birth. We're here," said Aksel and paid the driver. "I've seen very overweight women give birth and I've seen sick women give birth. The body is strong. Trust in that."

But later, perhaps now, walking with the stroller—all these walks with the stroller combined into one single walk, a swish through space, a trundle across the rotating planet—Aksel told her that not all women could give birth, that some simply gave up and had to be whisked away for a C-section, that they said "no, I can't do it," and Anna believed him, and because Anna had been able to give birth, she sighed with relief.

"Tell me about the day I gave birth," she asked, as she had

so many times before. And he began to tell their shared story.

But later on that walk, after Aksel had headed home and Anna continued on her own with the boy in the stroller, she sat down on a bench by the canal to write, elated at the writing and fearful of the child waking up and bringing the writing time to an end, and thought back to what Aksel had said about the women who couldn't give birth.

"What does he know about it?" Anna wrote. She ran her tongue across the glue on a chipped tooth. "What a horrible thing to say. As though a C-section isn't a birth, as though these women's children never *came out*, but live, still, as overgrown or shriveled-up geriatric, nubby scraps inside the sad, fat, shameful women bodies," wrote Anna.

Aksel still lived under the illusion that there was no bodily experience the will could not conquer and mold. He subscribed to the mind-body divide. Anna shook her head. She touched her breasts, they were heavy and sore, perhaps at this very moment she was again carrying this man's child. "He knows nothing about giving birth," Anna wrote. "Any human who has ever been alive was given birth to by someone who surrendered their will to the body," Anna wrote. "Suck on that, bitches." She stood up and continued along the canal with the stroller. The child slept. After some time, he opened his eyes and looked at her.

Ninth Ending

On the square, the wind sweeps the winter leaves against my bicycle and they whirl up around me. The rain, nearly imperceptible; a wet film that clings to us.

"Now we just need to settle one last thing," says the publisher, slapping the manuscript on the table in front of him. "Who wrote it?"

"I did, of course," I say and leave his office. I need to hurry if I'm to pick up the boy from kindergarten on time.

Something we rarely mentioned but which flowed beneath our conversations like a nightly stream was that we were afraid of being alone with our children. My belly makes walking nearly impossible, so I cycle instead.

Having a child is like getting lost in a forest. Or, to use a different image: black birds circled above me at every moment. Or another: style had to submit to emotion.

Instead of a form, you were more like time. January this year, suspiciously warm. In my bag I have the pages, arranged and proofread. In front of the supermarket are potted lilies on offer and on the news, news about the unstoppable. I turn down the street toward the kindergarten, I can only cycle in the lowest gear, I am a woman of childbearing age, nine months pregnant with disheveled hair. The fetus has positioned itself with its head in my pelvis as it's meant to. This unknown person who will walk beneath these wet trees one day in twenty or thirty years, supply their mouth with an apple without giving me a second thought and look up at the sky, consumed by their own life.

The closer I get to the birth, the more I forget everything I have spent the past many years trying to understand, everything I've learned about giving birth to a child. I'm facing the great transformation, it feels like a drowse.

With each day it grows the fetus feels older than me, more capable of life, like a wise, ancient god guiding me. When it's born, I know this age will fall away day by day like a skin. The due date is three weeks away. I'm on my way back into the room, I'm already in the corridor. Soon it will gather speed again, the separation, the long, slow severing when the water breaks, the contractions grow stronger, and my work begins.

Acknowledgments

The Danish text embeds short quotes from other texts, and the English translation follows this convention. Every effort has been made to acknowledge other sources.

p. 3—Let's call her Anna
My protagonist Anna is named after the main character Anna Wulf in Doris Lessing's *The Golden Notebook* (Simon & Schuster, 1962), which I was very inspired by. The book is made up of Anna Wulf's various notebooks, and I've simply borrowed this device. I recognized myself in it.

p. 40—Bodil Bech
The poems referenced are from Bodil Bech's collection *Ildtunger danser* (Gyldendal, 1935). A special thank you to Dennis Gade Kofod for encouraging me to write poems inspired by Bech's suite "Gudhjem," from the same book. An earlier version of this suite of poems was published in the catalog for the 2016 Jakob Hansen Literature Festival and the anthology *Nordisk nu 2017* (Flamme forlag, 2017).

p. 63—birth was an assassination of the child ...
Anna misremembers the quote. What Duras actually says is: "L'accouchement, je le vois comme une culpabilité. Comme si on lâchait l'enfant, qu'on l'abandonne. Ce que j'ai vu de plus proche de l'assassinat, ce sont des accouchements." [Childbirth, I see it as guilt. As though one were letting go of the child, abandoning it. The closest

thing I've seen to assassination is birth.] The quote is from *Les Lieux de Marguerite Duras* by Marguerite Duras and Michelle Porte (Les Éditions de Minuit, 2012). Translated by Sophia Hersi Smith.

p. 68—The child was her flesh and blood, literally ...
Reference to Dea Trier Mørch, *Vinterbørn* (Gyldendal, 1976), p. 206. Translated by Sophia Hersi Smith and Jennifer Russell.

p. 77—When a mother gives birth to her child, something radical happens to her ...
This section paraphrases a passage in Rachel Cusk, *A Life's Work* (Picador, 2021), p. 7: "Another person has existed in her, and after their birth they live within the jurisdiction of her consciousness. When she is with them she is not herself; when she is without them she is not herself; and so it is as difficult to leave your children as it is to stay with them. To discover this is to feel that your life has become irretrievably mired in conflict, or caught in some mythic snare in which you will perpetually vainly struggle."

p. 115—I hope / a poem can be bad ...
These lines were written by Isabella Siegel, in Swedish: *jag hoppas att / en dikt kan vara dålig / och fortfarande / vara del av någonting / bra.* Published here with her permission. Translated by Sophia Hersi Smith and Jennifer Russell.

p. 118—Defeated and exhausted, I will perhaps go a little further
Reference to Agnes Martin, *Writings* (Hatje Cantz, 1998), p. 70.

p. 120—I'm not writing a poem about the bedspread from Hay ...
This section is inspired by Anne Boyer's prose poem "Not Writing" from *Garments Against Women* (Penguin Books, 2019), p. 57.

p. 140—I burn the way money burns
This quote comes from "The Breast" by Anne Sexton, *The Complete Poems* (Houghton Mifflin Company, 1981), pp. 175–76.

p. 164—When 2 become 3—sex after birth
This section cites a pamphlet by the same name written and published by Sex & Samfund [Sex & Society], first published in 1998 and revised in 2004. An updated version has since been published. Translated by Sophia Hersi Smith and Jennifer Russell.

p. 168—Precautions during pregnancy: dos and don'ts
This section cites the pamphlet "Ren information om—Kemiske stoffer i produkter til gravide og små børn" (Informationscenter Miljø & Sundhed, 2011). Translated by Sophia Hersi Smith and Jennifer Russell.

p. 188—I thought I could maintain modesty by writing prose
The quote comes from the prose poem "*Ma Vie en Bling*: A Memoir," Anne Boyer, *Garments Against Women* (Penguin Books, 2019), p. 67.

p. 225–30—The Earth Almanac
The quotes are from *Naturlommekalenderen 2019*, written by Bent Lauge Madsen, Henrik Carl, Peter Rask Møller, Lene Bech Sanderhoff, Tommy Dybbro, Jesper Johannes Madsen, Lykke Pedersen, and Anders P. Tøttrup (Forlaget Rhodos, 2018). Translated by Sophia Hersi Smith and Jennifer Russell.

p. 237—All she can see from the window is a building …
The quote is from Margaret Atwood's short story "Giving Birth," from *Dancing Girls* (Anchor Books / Random House, 1998), p. 242.

p. 241—A woman when she is in travail hath sorrow …
John 16:21, King James Version.

p. 241—Unto the woman he said …
Genesis 3:16, King James Version.

p. 247—Welcome to Mixed Anxiety …
The section cites material given to patients at the Psychotherapy

Clinic, Psychiatric Center Copenhagen, 2017. Translated by Sophia Hersi Smith and Jennifer Russell.

p. 293—If a physician of high standing, and one's own husband ...
Charlotte Perkins Gilman, *The Yellow Wallpaper* (Virago Press, 2009), p. 4.

p. 297—Kumiko-san / Congratulations on your abortion ...
Killing Kanoko: Selected Poems by Itō Hiromi, translated by Jeffrey Angles (Action Books, 2009), pp. 38–39. We thank Tilted Axis for their permission to cite this work.

p. 298—Itō and Schunnesson interview
Tone Schunnesson's interview with Itō Hiromi was published in the Swedish journal *Bon*, November 1, 2016 (https://bon.se/article/poesi-for-trasiga-kvinnor/). Translated by Sophia Hersi Smith and Jennifer Russell.

p. 299—A woman and her book are identical ...
Edgar Allan Poe's 1844 review of Elizabeth Barrett Browning's *A Drama of Exile and Other Poems* is found in *The Works of the Late Edgar Allan Poe* (Griswold edition, 1850–1856).

p. 301—Now it's time
Unica Zürn, *The Trumpets of Jericho* (Wakefield Press, 2015), translated by Christina Svendsen, p. 6. We thank Wakefield Press for their permission to cite this work.

p. 301—A general note on Mary Shelley's journals and letters
Suzanne Burdon's work first brought my attention to Mary Shelley's relationship with her children as expressed in her journals and letters. More can be read here: http://www.suzanneburdon.com/blog/2017/5/13/mary-shelley-and-motherhood.

p. 302—find my baby dead
The *Journals of Mary Shelley 1814–1844*, vol. 2, Paula R. Feldman and Diana Scott-Kilvert (eds.) (Clarendon, 1987), p. 68.

p. 302—dream that my little baby came to life again …
The *Journals of Mary Shelley 1814–1844*, vol. 2, Paula R. Feldman and Diana Scott-Kilvert (eds.) (Clarendon, 1987), p. 70.

p. 302—Blue eyes—gets dearer and sweeter every day …
Letter to Percy Shelley, January 17, 1817, *The Letters of Mary Wollstonecraft Shelley*, vol. 1, "A part of the Elect," Betty T. Bennett (ed.) (John Hopkins University Press, 1980), p. 28.

p. 302—The blue eyes of your sweet boy …
Letter to Percy Shelley, December 5, 1816, *The Letters of Mary Wollstonecraft Shelley*, vol. 1, "A part of the Elect," Betty T. Bennett (ed.) (John Hopkins University Press, 1980), pp. 22–23.

p. 303—The misery of these hours is beyond calculation …
Letter to Maria Gisborne, June 5, 1819, *The Letters of Mary Wollstonecraft Shelley*, vol. 1, "A part of the Elect," Betty T. Bennett (ed.) (John Hopkins University Press, 1980), p. 99.

p. 303—The last journal entries from June 3 and 4, 1819
The *Journals of Mary Shelley 1814–1844*, vol. 2, Paula R. Feldman and Diana Scott-Kilvert (eds.) (Clarendon, 1987), p. 265.

p. 303—The journal ends here—P.B.S.
I was not able to find Percy Shelley's note in the journal, but read about it in *The Life and Letters of Mary Wollstonecraft Shelley*, vol. 1, Florence A. Thomas Marshall (ed.) (Richard Bentley & Son, 1889), p. 243.

p. 303—It is a bitter thought that all should be risked on one …
Letter to Marianne Hunt, November 24 (25), 1819, *The Letters of Mary*

Wollstonecraft Shelley, vol. 1, "A part of the Elect," Betty T. Bennett (ed.) (John Hopkins University Press, 1980), p. 114.

p. 303—a table spoonful of the spirit of aniseed ...
The Journals of Mary Shelley 1814–1844, vol. 2, Paula R. Feldman and Diana Scott-Kilvert (eds.) (Clarendon, 1987), p. 80.

p. 303—Bless her little soul! [...] she shall be as sick as she pleases!
Charlotte Perkins Gilman, *The Yellow Wallpaper* (Virago Press, 2009), p. 14.

p. 324—It was with these feelings ...
Mary Shelley, *Frankenstein; or, The Modern Prometheus* (Penguin Popular Classics, 1994), p. 51.

p. 324—But I, the true murderer, felt the never-dying worm alive in my bosom.
Mary Shelley, *Frankenstein; or, The Modern Prometheus* (Penguin Popular Classics, 1994), p. 84.

p. 324—I bore a hell within me ...
Mary Shelley, *Frankenstein; or, The Modern Prometheus* (Penguin Popular Classics, 1994), p. 84.

p. 326—In the Garden
Painting by Anna Ancher, 1884, Skagens Museum.

p. 334—she thought of the recently published study showing that on average, Danish women's wages ...
The study in question is "Children and Gender Inequality: Evidence from Denmark," Henrik Kleven, Camille Landais, Jakob Egholt Søgaard (University of Copenhagen, 2019).

p. 334—The experience of mothering changes one ...
Susan Griffin, "Feminism and Motherhood" (Alta, 1973). I read Susan
Griffin's essay in the anthology *Mother Reader*, edited by Moyra Davey
(Seven Stories Press, 2001)—an anthology which was a great source
of inspiration during my work with this book. The sentence "The
experience of mothering changes one; that it is learned" is on p. 44.

p. 336—Were they not all of them weak women? ...
Virginia Woolf, *Orlando*, (Wordsworth Classics, 2003), pp. 115–16.

p. 343—A writer because of, not in spite of, her children
Reference to Alice Walker, "A Writer Because of, Not in Spite of, Her
Children," *Mother Reader*, Moyra Davey (ed.) (Seven Stories Press,
2001), p. 99.

*p. 346—OVERLOOKED DISEASE RUINS WOMEN'S SEX LIVES: OFTEN
MISTAKEN FOR YEAST INFECTION*
The quoted article is written by Michael Strandfeldt and Amal
Guerdali, published on dr.dk on September 20, 2018 (https://www.
dr.dk/nyheder/regionale/nordjylland/overset-sygdom-oedelaeg-
ger-kvinders-sexliv-forveksles-ofte-med-svamp). I have changed the
name of the woman in the article. Translated by Sophia Hersi Smith
and Jennifer Russell.

p. 353—Society too harbors the childish belief ...
Thit Jensen, *Storken* (unpublished play, c. 1928). I found the quote
in Lene Koch's *Racehygieine* (Informations Forlag, 2014). The play
was adapted to film in 1943 under the title *Det brændende spørgsmaal.*
Translated by Sophia Hersi Smith and Jennifer Russell.

p. 356—Anna-Maija Ylimaula
In this section, I'm indirectly quoting the article "Bagsiden af fami-
lieidyllen" by Elisabeth Nordgren, nordicwomensliterature.net, 2011.

The Finnish quote about the queen bee was found here: https://www.ouka.fi/oulu/pohjoista-kirjallisuutta/ylimaula-elama. Translated by Sophia Hersi Smith and Jennifer Russell.

p. 357—Bodil Bech cremated in Rønne
I found the quote from Oluf Høst's journal in the catalog for the 2016 Jakob Hansen Literature Festival. Translated by Sophia Hersi Smith and Jennifer Russell.

p. 373—the poem heals / the wounds inflicted by reason
Reference to Novalis, "Poetry heals the wounds inflicted by reason."

Thank You

Thank you to Tom Silkeberg, Johanne Lykke Holm, Morten Chemnitz, Line Knutzon, Julie Paludan-Müller, Mette Mortensen, Simon Pasternak and Line Miller for readings, advice and guidance.

The translators would like to thank the midwife Sam Rosamund for consulting on the translation of the Fifth Beginning.